STONE SOCIETY

STONE SOCIETY BOOK 15

BY FAITH GIBSON

This book is a work of fiction. Names, characters, places, and incidents are the product of the author's imagination or are used fictitiously. Any resemblance to actual events, locations, or persons, living or dead, is coincidental.

The author acknowledges the copyrighted or trademarked status and trademark owners of the wordmarks mentioned in this work of fiction.

Copyright © 2022 by Faith Gibson

Published by: Bramblerose Press LLC

Editor: Candice Royer, KDL Editing

First edition: February 2022

Cover design: Jay Aheer, ©Simply Defined Art

Cover photography: ©FuriousFotog®

Cover model: Zach Fox

ISBN: 978-1736890035

Dedication

This one's for Katie. Thank you for making me smile every single day.

Prologue

March 1946

THIS WAS NOT the future Jordana envisioned for herself. As she stood next to one of the ornate stained-glass windows of the *Theatro Municipal de São Paulo*, the photographer told her to smile. Jordana did her best, but how could she smile when her heart was breaking? The building she was in was a breathtaking structure. Jordana had roamed its many halls and rooms with her mama, a famous opera singer. Jordana had once loved the architecture. The ambiance. It was cruel, in her opinion, her parents choosing this place out of all the buildings in São Paulo for this occasion. What was even more cruel was the reason for her being there today.

"Jordana," the photographer chastised. Again. "This is supposed to be the happiest day of your life."

"Supposed to be, yes." But it wasn't. The man behind the camera didn't know the truth. Didn't know she was getting married to the wrong brother. She shouldn't be getting married at all. She didn't need the ceremony to make a commitment. She was a Gargoyle after all, and as such, an extravagant ceremony was nothing more than a human construct. If she were marrying the one the fates had chosen for her, Jordana would be beaming. The photographer would probably tell her to tone down her smile. But her papa didn't care about the fates. Didn't care that the one they chose for Jordana had only transitioned a few years before. Jordana was willing to wait on her mate to age. To come into his own Gargoyle.

1

It wasn't to be.

When she found out what her father had done – made a bargain with the King to give Jordana to his oldest son – she had yelled. Cried. Rebelled. She even tried to run away. But both the King and her papa were powerful males with eyes all around the city. When returned to her home, her papa let her know what would happen to her mate should she refuse to go through with the marriage. Neither he nor the King cared that she was fated to be with Lorenzo. They only cared that she was the last of her kind in all of South America – an unmated female Gargoyle. Her marriage to Leonardo was to ensure the Santos bloodline continued. Jordana argued that would happen if she mated with Lorenzo, but he wasn't the eldest brother. He wasn't the one destined to be King.

Heavy footsteps had Jordana turning away from the camera.

"It is time, *minha filha*." The male's voice grated where it once had filled her with love. She would never forgive the one she once called papa. Pedro Callas was an imposing male as were most Gargoyles. He gripped her elbow and led her away from the photographer. Led her to the front of the building where he would escort her to the stage for hundreds to witness the union of Jordana Callas to Leonardo Santos. Jordana's claws ached to extend from her fingertips. Threatened to shred the expensive dress. Or Pedro's face. Not that it would do any good. He would heal almost immediately. No, lashing out at the male would only result in something bad happening to Lorenzo.

In that moment, Jordana remembered bright, blue eyes filled with tears as she told Lorenzo she was to marry his brother. Lorenzo's heartbreak at the news ached in her own chest. By Gargoyle standards, he was still a boy, but to her, Lorenzo was everything. The one she was supposed to be with. To grow old with. To see the world as it changed over the many years they would be together. The anguish and

2

betrayal on his beautiful face had gutted her, and Jordana hadn't smiled since. She had no reason to. Knowing she would live as his brother's wife in the same house was the cruelest of jokes.

Jordana's beast reached out, searching for the one heartbeat she knew as well as her own, but it wasn't to be felt. Lorenzo wasn't in the building. She couldn't blame him. She would have escaped this charade, too, if it were possible. The wedding went by in a blur. The reception was a spectacle. One in which she was an unwilling participant. She didn't eat the exquisite meal set before her. She only danced with Leonardo when her father made threats against her mate in her ear. Jordana wordlessly, with a fake smile, went through the motions until she and Leonardo were escorted to the car that would drive them to the coast for their honeymoon.

Once inside their hotel room, Leonardo closed the door after thanking the bellhop and began removing his tuxedo. He had tried engaging her in conversation during the ride, but Jordana sat as far away as possible in the enclosed vehicle, staring out the window.

"Jordana, it is done. I know I'm not your choice, but what were we to do? I am the King's son. His heir. His word is law," Leo pled in Portuguese. "Give me a son, then I will release you from our vows to be with Lorenzo."

Jordana rounded on the male, pointing a sharp claw at the face that looked so much like her mate's. "You try that, and I'll cut your dick off."

Leo sighed, scrubbing a hand down his face. He could overpower her. She knew that. He knew that. Thankfully, Leonardo was a somewhat honorable male, unwanted marriage notwithstanding. He had tried reasoning with her when their fathers first told them they were to be married. Both males knew Leo wasn't Jordana's mate, but neither one cared. Jordana didn't know what it was like to be the heir to the throne. Leo tried to explain how it was his responsibility

3

to the Santos family to continue the bloodline. He apologized, begged, promised she would have a good life as future Queen.

Leonardo wasn't a bad male. If the fates had chosen him as her mate, she would gladly have accepted the bond. But he wasn't. Lorenzo was, and as long as Jordana and Lor were apart, she would never be whole. Happy.

"Jordana, please—"

"No. I will kill myself before I let someone other than my mate touch me. I'm going to get out of this stupid dress and order room service. You should go down to the bar and find a pretty human if you feel the need to..." Jordana waved her hand in the air. "I'm not joking. You will never touch me."

Leo sighed again and nodded. He opened his suitcase and pulled out a change of clothes, taking them into the bathroom. When he emerged, he grabbed the room key and left her alone. Jordana didn't waste any time shredding her wedding gown instead of attempting to unbutton the dozens of tiny pearl dots on the back of the dress. She retrieved her own clothes from her suitcase and changed into something comfortable before ordering several items from room service. Since she'd refused to eat at the reception, she was starving.

The week went by at a snail's pace. Jordana refused to leave the room, and Leo gave her space. He tried more than once to talk her into being civil. He begged her to at least leave the room and go with him to the beach. Jordana loved the beach. Always had. But she wasn't about to enjoy the surf with the wrong brother.

When their honeymoon was over, they drove back to the grand house she was to share with her new husband, his parents, and the mate she couldn't have. Jordana's heart was caught in her throat as Leonardo escorted her inside. She reached out with her senses to find her mate, but he wasn't there. The mood in the house was tense, and it didn't take

4

long to find out the reason.

Lorenzo was gone.

CHAPTER ONE

MARCH 2049

RAFAEL TOOK SEBASTIAN'S diaper bag out to their new crossover SUV. He had left it parked in front of the garage after taking Priscilla to Frey's earlier so she could help set up Amelia's birthday party. Their Clan was doing its best to lead normal lives while constantly looking over their shoulders. It was a shitty way to go about their days, but they had no choice. He loathed leaving Kaya and Bas home without him, but Mason and Willow came by to stay with them in his short absence. He shut the back car door just as birds scattered in the trees. Rafe opened his senses, and his beast bristled.

There's someone out there.

Rafael turned toward the woods to the east when the sound of a rifle slide met his ears. Rafael ran that direction, and a shot rang out, the bullet hitting him square in the chest. It was powerful enough to rock him backward a step but not enough to stop him. He continued on, catching sight of the human who was now scrambling to get away. *Not happening, you fucker.* Rafe easily caught the man and slammed him to the ground. Rafael turned him to his back and punched him in the side of the head, rendering him unconscious. As mad as he was, Rafe needed answers, and dead men could tell no tales as the saying went. Not only that, Kaya was yelling for him from the house.

He called out to Mason so the male could tell Kaya he was fine while dragging the shooter closer to the manor.

6

Rafael rushed to the garage and found a long drop cord, which he used to tie the man to a tree for retrieval later. All the while, he kept his senses open to any other threats, but there was no one else around to attack him or his family. Not taking any chances, Rafael grabbed the man's rifle and used his shifter strength to destroy it. He tossed the pieces into a box in the garage before going into the house. Once inside, he dragged Kaya and Bas into his arms, thanking the gods they both were safe.

"Was that a gunshot?" Kaya asked against his chest.

"Yes." Rafael released them, then pressed his palms to Kaya's face and kissed her forehead.

"Is it ever going to stop?" Kaya whispered.

"Gods, I hope so. Whoever that is, whoever sent him, obviously doesn't know I'm a Goyle, or they'd know a bullet wouldn't stop me. That gives us an advantage. But it does mean we need to be extra vigilant. Bullets won't hurt me, but you and Bas are a different story, and I won't let anything happen to either of you. After Amelia's party, I think we should all go away for a while. Somewhere nobody knows who we are."

Kaya took a step back, bouncing their whimpering son on her hip. Sebastian was in tune with their moods, and the child could no doubt feel the distress coming from both parents. "Rafe, we just got back home." Rafael hated the tremor in Kaya's voice. His mate had been through so much. Too much. She was the strongest female he knew, and he loved her more than life itself.

"What would you have me do?"

Mason took Willow's hand. "We'll meet up with you at Frey's."

"Thank you, Mason."

When the couple was gone, Kaya answered Rafe's question. "Trust the Clan to guard us. I love you; you know that. And I trust you to make the right decision for us, but please think about it."

7

Rafael wrapped his arms around his little family and pressed a kiss to Kaya's temple. Just then, Sebastian grunted, and the smell of a messy diaper met Rafe's nose. He couldn't help but groan. "I guess that's our little man's way of letting me know how he feels. Give him here, and I'll change him."

"I think you need to change us both." Kaya laughed, and when Rafael took a step back, he had to laugh too. Kaya's hand that had been holding Sebastian's bottom was brownish green. The runny poop had leaked out of the diaper.

"No more peas for you," Rafael told his son as he took him to the bathroom. They had introduced the baby to puréed food and were finding what he could and couldn't tolerate. Rafael loved bath time, but they were already running late for Amelia's birthday party, so Rafe quickly cleaned his son up and got him into a fresh diaper and clothes. His worry about the shooter hovered at the back of his mind, but he wouldn't make a rash decision about whisking his family away until he spoke to Frey. He didn't want to leave so soon after returning from Italy, nor did he want to ask Frey to once again step in to lead the Clan, but if that's what it took to keep his family safe, he would.

GREGOR PLACED AMELIA'S presents in the back of the Hummer and closed the door. Tessa had gone overboard with gifts for their niece, but Gregor didn't say anything. He enjoyed watching his mate with the kids and knew she was going to make a wonderful mother someday. He also knew she was worried she hadn't gotten pregnant yet, but he kept telling her it would happen when it was supposed to. Until then, they would keep practicing. And practice they did. Tessa was a feisty female, and that translated into the best sex of his life. His fiery redhead had a kinky side, and Gregor was one lucky male.

Once seated in the vehicle, Gregor rolled down the driveway while Tessa found a song she wanted to listen to. His mate preferred classic rock, but she had branched out lately and was flipping through the satellite channels until she landed on one of the newer, hard rock stations. He slowed as he reached the gate, waiting on the iron barrier to open. Tessa leaned over and kissed him. Just as she returned to her side of the vehicle, the windshield shattered.

"Mother fucker!" she yelled, punching the dash.

Gregor threw the vehicle in park. "Tessa!" He pushed his mate's head down as far as it would go with the seatbelt holding her in place.

"I'm okay. What the fuck, Stone?"

"Wait here, and stay down." Gregor didn't wait to see if she followed his order. He pushed open the door and opened his senses. As soon as he got a lock on the shooter, Gregor took off through the trees. A large man wearing camouflage with a rifle strapped to his back was running through the woods toward the road. Being a Gargoyle, Gregor easily caught him. He didn't bother asking questions. Gregor twisted the man's head, snapping his neck. His beast fought to get loose, wanting to rip the human to shreds. Gregor felt the same way. The shot had been too fucking close. Gregor took a deep breath, and his beast retreated somewhat. Tessa was safe. For now. He jogged back to the Hummer, reaching out to make sure the human was alone. He didn't sense anyone else out there.

He slowed his steps as he neared his Hummer. When he saw where the bullet entered, Gregor threw his head back and roared. One second sooner and... Tessa's head popped up, and she scrambled to undo the restraint so she could get out of the vehicle. She threw herself into his arms, and he held his mate tight.

"I hope you ripped their fucking head off," she

muttered against his neck.

"Close. He won't be shooting at anyone else." Gregor put Tessa on her feet so he could check her injuries. The glass had hit her gorgeous face, but the cuts weren't deep. Thank the gods she was a half-blood.

"I'm fine, Stone, but what the fuck?" she asked again.

"I probably should have questioned him first, but knowing how close... I didn't think. Couldn't think." Gregor placed his hands on her face, softly brushing the scrapes that were already healing.

Tessa grasped both his wrists and held on. Her heart was still beating too quickly from the adrenaline, and her face was fierce. "No judgment here, baby. I can heal from a few cuts, but a high-powered bullet? Yeah, there's no coming back from that. What are you going to do with the body?"

"I'll put him in the garage until after the party. He's not going anywhere."

"We need to take my car. I don't think showing up to a kid's party with a shattered windshield is a good idea."

Gregor agreed, but before he let Tessa back in the car, he kissed her. Hard. She was the most precious thing in the world to him. He poured his love into the kiss, and she met him with equal fervor. When they pulled apart, Tessa winked at him. "Enough of that shit. We're already late, and you know what your mouth does to me." His mate slapped him on the ass before climbing back into the passenger seat. Gods, he adored his female.

While Tessa transferred the presents from the Hummer to her SUV, Gregor retrieved the shooter's body along with his rifle and stored both in the garage. Forty-five minutes later, they were on their way to Frey's.

THE HOUSE WAS too quiet without Connor there. Not that his son was loud, but the boy's presence was larger than life, even if he was in his room drawing or reading. After Connor's last vision, Dante called Julian and had him install motion detectors all around their property. Dante had a feeling the vision would come to pass sooner rather than later, so he had taken Connor to stay with Frey and Abbi. Connor loved spending time with Amelia, but the child was also smart enough to realize why Dante wanted him out of the house. When Dante dropped him off a few days ago, Connor pressed his forehead to Dante's.

Be safe, Da, he said in his mind.

Always, My Son, Dante replied in kind. Frey had arched an eyebrow at the exchange but didn't say anything. Their Clan was used to the silent conversations between father and son.

Their presents were already in the car — a new pair of Converse from Dante and Isabelle and a new tutu from Connor along with the usual drawing Connor gave everyone as a gift. Isabelle had the drawing framed - this one a whimsical rendition of Amelia riding a unicorn while dressed in her pink kicks and a matching tutu. Dante wondered if the girl would ever grow out of her fascination with the fluffy skirts. Then again, she was studying to be a dancer like Abbi, and even adult ballerinas wore tutus when they danced.

"Ready?" Isabelle asked. His mate had never looked more beautiful. Her belly had a slight roundness where she carried his other son, and the sight had Dante ready to strip her bare so he could make love to her. Isabelle reached out her hand to him, but in that moment, Dante's phone beeped.

"Fuck." He pulled the device out and opened the app attached to the motion sensors. "Get in the panic room."

"Stay safe," Isabelle demanded. She grabbed his face and kissed him hard before rushing to the secure room he had installed right after the incident with the jet.

Dante took off out the back door so he could move through the property and come up behind whoever had set off the alarm. What he found made his blood boil and had his beast fight to get out. A man dressed in black military gear was perched against a tree with a rifle aimed at the house. The scene was almost exactly as Connor had drawn it. As badly as Dante wanted to let the beast loose and rip the human apart, he needed answers about who the man was. If he was working alone or if someone had put him up to attacking Dante and his family. Dante eased his way behind the sniper and wrapped an arm around the human's neck. His Goyle fought with Dante to kill the man, but Dante pushed against it as he rendered the would-be shooter unconscious.

After making sure there were no other threats, Dante tossed the male over his shoulder and carried him back to the house. He dropped him on the ground outside the garage, then retrieved zip-ties and duct tape he'd bought just for this occasion. Not willing to take any chances of the man waking before he got him to the Pen, Dante injected the human with a high-dose muscle relaxant, then got his body situated in the back of Isabelle's vehicle. He transferred the presents from his Jaguar before going inside to get his mate.

He punched in the code to the panic room, and as soon as he pushed open the door, Isabelle was in his arms. "Who was that?" she asked after kissing him soundly. There were monitors in the room showing all sides of their home. Isabelle wouldn't have seen what happened in the woods, but she could see him carrying the human toward the house.

"No idea. He's secure for now, but I want to get him to the Pen. We'll leave him there until after the party."

"Something has to give. Haven't we all been through enough?" Isabelle's eyes were shiny with unshed tears.

"I agree. Hopefully, he will be able to give us the answers we need to find out who's behind the threat."

Dante held his mate for long minutes, relishing in the steady beat of her heart. Dante vowed silently to figure out who their latest threat was and put an end to them.

MASON HATED LEAVING the manor when Rafael and Kaya were so upset, but he knew his King would do the right thing. Say the words Kaya needed to hear. When he returned from Italy, Rafael had admitted to Mason all his insecurities. The two spent quality time together while the mates, Willow included, surrounded Kaya with love and support. After Rafe poured his heart out to Mason, Mason admitted to Rafael his own insecurities. Being the youngest of the Clan, Mason often felt left out. Willow had offers to hang out with the other females, but no one reached out to Mason unless they needed him for guard duty. He wasn't invited to just hang out with anyone, so Willow usually turned down her own offers so Mason wouldn't be alone.

"Do you think they'll leave again?" Willow asked once they were on their way to Frey's.

"If it's what is needed to keep Kaya and Bas safe? Yes. Although it will take a toll on them all."

"I wish there was more we could do. I hate feeling so helpless."

Mason grabbed his mate's hand and threaded their fingers. "You aren't helpless. You keep the office running in Rafe's absence." Willow was so much more than an admin. Over the last year, she had taken over Stone, Incorporated. His mate had a sharp mind for business, and with no one else overseeing the office, she made sure all the jobs were completed using the skilled professionals on staff. Travis had stepped into the role of their head architect, and even traveling to Norway with Brynna, the man worked with Willow seamlessly.

If anyone felt helpless, it was Mason. All he did was sit at the office and make sure his mate was safe. When he first came to live with Rafael, Mason had grand ideas of becoming a fierce Gargoyle. He had been young, and his parents were in the last years of their long lives. They pawned him off on Rafe, and soon after, both had crossed over. Mason understood life happened. Rafael had endured one hardship after another and couldn't devote his time to coddling Mason, but he felt adrift. Without Willow, Mason didn't know how he would get through his days.

He was still young in Gargoyle years, barely an adult, and most days he felt like a kid. It was the main reason he asked Willow to wait a few years before they tried for a child of their own. Willow asked him often what he wanted to be when he grew up, a joke between them, but it often made him feel worse. With his parents' money sitting in a bank account gaining interest, Mason didn't have to worry about finances. What he did worry about was what he wanted to do with his life other than sit and watch his mate day in and day out. He didn't begrudge Willow her job or her friendships with the other mates. He just hated feeling so lost.

When he and Rafe had their heart-to-heart, Rafael promised he would spend more time with Mason and help him figure out his future. With this latest threat, and with Rafe probably heading off somewhere to hide his family, Mason knew he was on his own once again.

"Hey." Willow shook their joined hands. "Talk to me."

"Just having another pity party," he admitted.

Willow lifted their hands and kissed his knuckles, but she didn't offer platitudes. They had spent so many nights before falling asleep going over different options for what might interest Mason, and that was the rub. He didn't know what interested him. There wasn't any one subject in school he preferred over the others. He wasn't smart enough to be a doctor. He didn't have artistic skills to use as something

14

like an architect. All he was good at was being a guard. Was that it? Should he offer his services guarding others once things in the Clan calmed down?

"What just went through your mind?" Willow asked.

Mason glanced over at his pretty mate before returning his eyes to the road. "What do you mean?"

"You tensed, but not in a bad way."

"I was thinking..." Could it really be that simple? "What do you think about me being a bodyguard?"

"I think you already are, Sweetie."

"No, I mean as in a business. Not now, obviously, but when things with this latest threat are over and you no longer need a babysitter twenty-four seven."

"I think you would be the best bodyguard anyone had guarding their body. As long as it isn't some pretty actress, because then I'd have to guard *your* body."

Mason chuckled. "You're ridiculous. You know you're the only one for me."

Willow squeezed his hand. "I do know that. But seriously, Mase, if you think it's something you would enjoy, then I say go for it."

Mason's heartbeat sped up. Why hadn't he thought of this before now? "I know there's more to it than putting up a billboard saying, 'Need a bodyguard? I'm your male.' But yeah, I think it's something I would enjoy doing."

Willow removed her hand from his and stroked the back of his head, running her fingers through his black curls. "I'm so proud of you. I knew you'd figure it out."

Warmth spread through Mason's chest. Willow was his biggest champion. Other than Rafe, she was the only one on his side. He knew that wasn't technically true. His other cousins would be there in a heartbeat if he needed them, but they had their own lives and issues. Mason was truly blessed to have this gorgeous female beside him.

"Thank you, Willow. You know I love you more than life itself, but I'm not sure you know how much I appreciate

15

you."

Willow tugged on his hair. "I do know. You show me every single day, but if you want to show me again when we get home from the party, maybe without clothes, I won't object."

Mason grinned over at his pretty female. "Yeah, I can definitely do that."

CHAPTER TWO

LORENZO BLEW OUT a breath and blinked the mist from his eyes. Dwelling on the past did no good, but every year that went by took him further away from her. Further away from the life he always dreamed of. Today was a happy occasion, even if Amelia's birthday coincided with the date that ended his happiness. He needed to keep all his wits about him and his senses open. Lor had one of the most important jobs in the Clan – keeping Amelia and Connor safe. There were several new babies in the Clan, and he would watch over them as well if needed. Banyan and Urijah had adopted two siblings, but they didn't need help. What he wouldn't give for his own children. But since that wouldn't happen anytime soon, he happily watched over his Brothers' kids.

"Uncle Lor! Look at me!" Amelia ran out onto the back deck where he was hiding from the chaos inside Frey's home. With so many of the Clan gathered for Amelia's birthday party, his only duty for the day was to enjoy himself. If only. The child twirling her new dress couldn't help the fact that her birthday was the date that caused him so much pain.

"Wow. You look amazing." Lor was surprised she wasn't wearing a tutu. Amelia had them in every color of the rainbow plus combinations for each holiday. What didn't surprise him was the matching sneakers. Amelia might be a dancer who thought she was a princess, but the girl loved her Converse. She loved them so much she insisted her two best friends needed them as well. Rain, who

17

was rarely far away from the female whirlwind, had on a matching pair. Lor smiled at the pink shoes on the boy's feet. Remy and Isla had brought their son back to New Atlanta for the party. Banyan and Uri's son, Levi, was with them, sans pink shoes.

This Rain was a far cry from the one who had been found beneath a church several months ago. Having been reunited with both his parents had done wonders for the child. When Amelia took Rain's hands, he didn't hesitate to dance in circles with his friend, even though there was no music. Levi grinned as the other two kids twirled and giggled, the sound warming Lor's heart. Children laughing was the best noise in the world.

A large hand clamped down on his shoulder. Having spent so much time around the large Goyle, Lor knew who it was as soon as Frey stepped out the back door. The two males stood together watching the children having fun. Frey squeezed once, then removed his grip.

"I was sent to retrieve the birthday girl." Frey crossed his arms over his massive chest, enjoying his daughter being a little girl. Lor knew why Frey wasn't insisting Amelia head back inside. As proven by events over the last few months, life was precious. It was precarious and fragile. Being Gargoyles didn't protect them from the evil in the world. It was important to grab these small moments and enjoy them, even if they were observing and not participating.

Amelia twirled close to Frey, and she turned loose of Rain so she could take Frey's hand. The large male obliged his daughter with a dance. Rain clapped to a beat only he could hear while he stood alongside Lorenzo, and Levi joined in. When Rain looked up grinning, Lor began clapping to the same beat. One that matched his heart thumping in his chest. When Lor's phone buzzed in his back pocket, he almost ignored it. He couldn't imagine who would be calling since everyone he cared about talking to was there or arriving soon for the party. When he saw his mother's name on the caller ID, Lor did ignore the call. He hadn't spoken to her in almost twenty years. Even if it was an emergency, Lorenzo had washed his hands of his family a long time ago. Those gathered for Amelia's party were his family now. His phone buzzed again, this time with a voice message. Lor ignored that too.

"Are you ready for presents, Little One?" Frey asked Amelia after a few minutes of dancing. Lorenzo caught the strain in Frey's voice.

"Is everyone here?" Amelia asked. For whatever reason, Rafael, Gregor, and Dante were all late to the party.

"Rafael, Kaya, and Bas just got here, but we're not going to make you wait any longer."

"Okay, but we gotta go get Connor and Nova out of the studio." Amelia crossed the deck to Rain and Levi. She held out her hands. Rain didn't hesitate to clasp hands with the girl. Levi looked uncertain, but finally he shrugged and took Amelia's other one. Together, they went inside to find her cousin and Levi's little sister.

"Do you need to answer your call?" Frey asked. Being Gargoyle, he had heard Lor's phone going off.

"It's not important." The world could be ending down in Brazil, and Lor still wouldn't care.

By the time Amelia had opened all her presents, Lor's phone had buzzed several more times. Frey arched an eyebrow, and Lor shook his head. This was Amelia's day. She might not be Lor's daughter, but she was the closest he had to one, and he wasn't going to miss a second of her party.

Rafael was standing close by when his own phone rang. The King's mood had been strained ever since he arrived. So had Kaya's for that matter. Lor held out his arms for Sebastian so Rafe could take the call. Bas was getting so big, and Lor loved his chubby cheeks and toothless grin. He swayed the baby in his arms while keeping an eye on

Amelia, Rain, and Connor. The kids were safe with all the other Goyles in the house, but he'd watched after them for months, so being attentive was ingrained.

"Fuck," Rafael muttered. He had taken the call outside, but his voice carried enough for the shifters in the room to hear. Lor continued rocking Sebastian while he waited for his King to return. When he did, Rafael's face was a mixture of worry and fury. Instead of ruining the party, Rafael ignored the questioning looks from his Clan.

Priscilla called out to the kids. "Amelia, how about we move the party into the dance studio?" The beloved housekeeper had been with Rafael a long time, and she knew enough about Clan business to understand when the King needed a minute alone with the Gargoyles.

"I'll take Bas," Abbi offered since Katherine was currently snuggling baby Jonathan. Lor handed the Prince over while the other females rounded up the kids and took them and the babies out of the room. Before Rafael could explain the phone call, Tessa stormed through the front door with Gregor trailing behind. Both looked ready to take someone's head off.

"We have a problem," Gregor said after looking around the room.

"Yes, we do," Rafael responded. "I would say let's take this conversation outside, but I'm not sure it's safe."

Tessa flipped her long, red braid over her shoulder. "You already know?"

"About Dante? Yes."

"Fuck! He was attacked too?" Gregor asked.

Rafael reached back and rubbed his neck, blowing out a deep breath. "As was I."

"Why the fuck didn't any of you call me?" Frey asked, his voice booming through his living room.

Rafael held up a hand. "Calm down, Cousin. I didn't call because I handled it. I heard the slide of the rifle bolt and took off running toward the shooter. There was no way

20

I was giving the man a chance at aiming toward the house. He managed to hit me before I reached him, but it didn't stop me. I knocked him out with a solid punch and left him tied to a tree. I wasn't about to call you away from Amelia's party. Gregor, what happened to you?"

"Fucker shot at me through the windshield. If he had been two seconds quicker..." Gregor growled, his fangs dropping.

"Gregor would be without a mate. I leaned over to kiss him and had barely returned to my side of the Hummer when the shot hit," Tessa explained.

Trevor gasped. "But you're okay, right? I mean, you're standing here so obviously you are, but Jesus H, Tessa!"

Tessa's ire softened minutely at Trevor's fussing over her. "I'm okay, Nerd Boy. Gregor made me wait in the car while he went after the bastard. Needless to say, he didn't bother tying this one up. Fucker's not going anywhere except into a grave." Tessa looked around. "Where are the kids?"

"Priscilla and the other mates took them to the studio."

Tessa turned to Rafael. "What about Dante and Belle? Are they all right?"

"Yes. Apparently, Connor had a vision last week, so Dante had Julian set motion detectors around his property, then brought Connor here to spend a few nights. Dante was able to reach the man before he got a shot off. He took his shooter to the Pen, and they're on their way here now."

"Seriously?" Frey threw his arms in the air. "He knew this was coming and didn't tell anyone but Julian?" Frey turned on his brother. "Why the fuck didn't you tell anyone?"

"Frey," Rafael warned. Lorenzo was on Frey's side, though. If someone was gunning for their Clan, they all needed to be cautious, especially those with kids.

"No, Rafe. We all need to watch our backs. This had to be a planned attack if the three of you were targeted the

21

same day. And now we're all together? Fuck." Frey took off out the back door, and Lorenzo went with him. If someone was out there, he and Frey would find them. After reaching out with their senses, neither one found a stranger lurking near the house or on the surrounding property.

When they reentered the house, Julian got in his brother's face. "I didn't tell anyone because Dante didn't let me in on why he wanted the motion detectors. Not specifically. He just said he was being cautious. Now calm your fucking tits so we can talk about this rationally." Julian wasn't nearly as large as Frey, but he wasn't backing down from his brother.

Frey nodded and gripped Julian's shoulder. "Yeah. Sorry."

"Let's look at what we know," Rafael said. "The man who came after me had a high-powered rifle as did the one Dante took down." He looked to his brother. "I'm assuming yours did as well?"

Gregor nodded, his face grim. "That means they don't know we aren't human."

"Could this be the mystery hacker hiring mercenaries?" Lor asked Rafael. A few months back, someone had attempted to take down a jet carrying several mates and the kids who were headed to Kai's homeland of New Samoa after some of their homes had been bombed. If it weren't for the fact that Julian had designed the cabin on the jet to be an ejectable pod, things would have ended in tragedy. Lachlan Rokesby was the main suspect, but Henry assured them it wasn't the Goyle behind the attack. Lachlan went on the run after incapacitating Hunter, his mate as well as one of the other guards at the Pen. Lor wasn't sure what was worse – having a mate break your neck to put you out of commission or... Nope.

Rafael shrugged one shoulder. "Could be. Since they haven't been able to get past Julian and Henry, it's possible they're coming after us a different way."

22

Frey widened his stance and crossed his arms over his chest. "But who are they? We've taken out the Greeks. I don't see Drago's lackeys having the funds to put out a hit on one of us, much less three."

Tessa rubbed one of Gregor's hands wrapped around her middle. "If it is the hacker, they have the means to get their hands on the cash. Who else have we pissed off lately?"

"That's just it," Rafael said. "The Greeks are the only ones we had trouble with. I agree with Frey; those who are still in the States don't have the means. Kallisto is behind bars, so it's not her. We have our own male heading up the Goyles in Greece."

"But," Tessa inserted, "there are those who were loyal to Alistair who could have pooled their money together or got it by unscrupulous means. And let's not forget about Lachlan."

"Henry assured me Lachlan wasn't behind the attack on the jet," Rafe said.

"No, but he did incapacitate his own mate to get away," Tessa argued.

Remy, who had been silently leaning against the wall, spoke up. "I don't think it's him. He was pleading with Hunter to give him a chance to prove himself, but then Hunter released Lachlan from their mate bond. The male was devastated."

Lorenzo understood that. "Have you heard from Donovan lately?" Donovan Lindholm was the Goyle who had taken Alistair's place once the Greek King was killed.

Rafe shook his head. "No, but I guess a call is in order. I'll do that now." Rafael stepped away from the group.

Lor's phone vibrated again, and Frey told him, "You might want to see who that is. Just in case."

"It's my mother. There's nothing she has to say to me I want to hear."

"Are you sure? Is it possible she knows something that

23

would help us?" Frey asked.

"From Brazil? I don't think so." Lorenzo was being obstinate, but on the off chance this was about the Clan, he needed to put aside his own feelings for just a moment. "Excuse me." Lor left the room and headed out the back door. He took a deep breath and checked his phone. There were several missed calls and texts from his mother along with a number he didn't recognize. It was that voicemail he listened to first and wished to the gods he hadn't.

"*Lorenzo, your mother has been trying to get in touch with you.*" Jordana's voice cracked before she continued. "*You need to come home. The King... Leo is dead, and Marcos ... Damnit, I have to go.*"

Lorenzo sank onto one of the patio chairs, dropping his phone onto the table. He ran his hands through his hair and closed his eyes. *Leo is dead.* As much as Lor hated the male, he was still his brother. Then why didn't he feel worse about the news?

You know why.

His beast was right. Lorenzo knew exactly why he wasn't going to mourn the death of his sibling. The male had taken everything from him all those years ago, and in Lor's mind, in his heart, Leo's actions were unforgivable. His mother had said she understood Lor's need to leave the family, so why was she calling now? Lor wasn't about to hop a plane to South America. Even if his North American Clan wasn't in the middle of a crisis, he wouldn't return to Brazil for his brother's funeral. Leonardo had a son to take his place. Lor wasn't needed. Still, he picked up the phone and returned his mother's call, rising from his seat so he could pace the length of the deck.

"Lorenzo! Finally. *Filho*, you need to come home. It's your brother."

"*Mãi*, I'm not coming to Brazil. That hasn't been my home for many years."

"But Lorenzo, he was executed," she whispered.

24

"Maybe he deserved it," Lor muttered, but with his mother being a Goyle, she heard him.

"You don't mean that! Leo was your brother," his mother argued.

"Leo stopped being my brother the moment he took away my future. I'm truly sorry for your loss, *Mãi*, but I'm not coming to Brazil. I have a family here that needs me."

"I need you," she whispered. "There are things you must know."

"You have your grandson and Jordy, uh, Jordana." Old habits died hard. "Me being there will only be awkward and cause more heartache." *To me.* "I need to go. I truly am sorry for your loss." Lorenzo hung up before his mom could guilt him into returning to the one place he vowed never to see again.

A text came through almost immediately from his mom. *"You called her Jordy. She needs you. We're in trouble."* Jordana had mentioned a Marcos, and Lor tried to remember anyone with that name. Not that it mattered. If someone had taken the throne, Lor's mother would be given a stipend and removed from the house. Jordana and Diego, well, he didn't know what would happen to them, but they weren't his concern.

Lorenzo shoved the phone in his pocket without powering it off. Yeah, he knew why he hadn't, and Lor considered himself ten kinds of a fool for it. He leaned his forearms against the wood rail of the deck and let his head hang. When Lorenzo left his home at a young age, he broke all ties with his family, which hadn't been easy. His father was King of the Gargoyles in the eastern part of South America and had eyes everywhere. It was only because those same eyes were in attendance at the wedding that he was able to slip away unnoticed. Like humans had to rubberneck at a car crash, Lor had to check on any news of his family over the years. That was until he found out Leo had been crowned King, and Jordana became Queen. After several years of waiting on Jordana to leave Leo, Lorenzo finally gave up. He thought he was over her, then his mother let it slip that he was an uncle. Jordana had borne Leo a son, albeit quite a long time after the wedding, but it had been the one thing that allowed Lor to finally put his mate out of his mind. Mostly.

Lor only gave himself a couple minutes to stew in misery before heading back inside. His family needed him. Not the one in Brazil who hadn't cared enough to do the right thing, but the ones who had taken him in and made him part of their Clan. By the time he returned to the living room, Rafael had ended his own call.

"Donovan had nothing to offer. Those Greeks who remained on the island are happy with him as King. He couldn't assure me those who followed Drago to the States aren't up to something."

"Then we're back to square one," Urijah said. Banyan wrapped a beefy arm around his mate. Jasper and Trevor stood off to the side of the room, quietly taking it all in.

Kaya sat down and leaned against the arm of the sofa. "Are we ever going to catch a break?" she asked no one in particular. Tessa crossed the room and lowered herself next to the other female. Tessa clasped Kaya's hand but remained silent for once.

Frey stepped up to Lorenzo. "Everything okay with your mother?"

Lorenzo shrugged one shoulder. "Not really. My brother was killed." Lorenzo left out the fact that his brother had been King because that would have been an entirely different conversation.

"Lor, I'm sorry for your loss. Do you need the jet to go home?"

Lor turned his gaze to the large Goyle. "Thank you, but no. This is my home, and everyone here is my family." Lorenzo didn't want to explain what happened all those years ago, and thankfully, Frey let it go. He clapped Lor on

26

the shoulder and squeezed, offering his silent support. The other Goyles in the room gave him nods and brief smiles of condolence. Lor didn't need them though. He was fine. Still, he couldn't help but think about Jordana. What if Lorenzo had it wrong? He had been a young Goyle just coming into his shifter when he met the female. He had been so sure she was his mate, but then Leonardo, a few years older, claimed the female as his own. Lor had been heartbroken. Jordana tried to explain how she wasn't given a choice, but Lorenzo had been too pissed to listen to any explanation. On this date almost one hundred years ago, his mate married his brother, and Lorenzo fled Brazil.

Kaya looked up at Rafael. "So, what now?"

"We remain cautious."

Frey turned to Julian. "Please set up motion detectors at every home. Rafe, I'll come back with you and take the shooter to the Pen with the one Dante captured."

Tessa rose from the sofa and stepped into the safety of Gregor's arms. "I think you should let Tamian come with you." Tessa's clone had abilities none of the rest of them had, so Lorenzo thought that was a good idea.

Frey's fangs dropped, and he pointed to them. "I have a feeling these will be enough to get the information we want, but if not, I'll call him. In the meantime, I want everyone to have extra security at all times."

The front door opened, and Dante and Isabelle entered. "Where are the kids?" Isabelle asked, looking around the room.

Tessa strode across the living room to meet her cousin. She gripped Isabelle's biceps and gave her a once-over. "They're in the studio. Are you okay?"

"Yes. Thank the gods for Connor's visions or..." Isabelle shook her head.

"I have to ask. Was it only your house he saw? Because shooters came after Rafael and Gregor too."

"What?" Isabelle ran a fingertip down her cousin's face.

"You were hurt."

"It was just a little glass, but it was still way too fucking close for comfort."

In that moment, several phones pinged at the same time. The owners pulled them out and looked at them, then at each other. "I don't like this," Rafael said.

"Neither do I," Dante agreed.

"What the fuck?" Gregor muttered.

Tessa released her grip on Isabelle and returned to her mate's side. "What is it?"

Gregor handed the phone to her. "It looks like a contract taken out on us. But why would someone send a copy to us?"

Rafael shook his head and took a breath. "The contract was for Gregor, Dante, and me specifically."

Kaya jumped to her feet. Their Queen was recovering remarkably well after the explosion at the manor. "Rafe—"

Rafael pressed two fingers to Kaya's lips. "At least we now know the rest of the Clan is safe, and the three of us have a reprieve. We will let Julian install the motion detectors while we'll all have extra security with us until we find out who's behind the contract." Rafael tapped a few times on his phone. "I sent that to Ryker. Not that he can do anything with it other than share it with his own handler."

"Why Ryker?" Remy asked.

Rafe scrubbed a hand down his face and blew out a harsh breath. "For those of you who don't know, some of the Hounds are mercenaries. While Sutton and Rory work to take down the Ministry, others work to eliminate the vilest men and women in the world like pedophiles, human traffickers, and rapists. Those who have enough money to buy judges and continue living their lives with no repercussions. Ryker is in charge of that aspect of their lives. I'm going to give him a call and see if this came across his handler's desk." Rafael placed the call to Lucy's uncle. After disconnecting, Rafe recounted Ryker's side of the conversation for Kaya. "He said there are different handlers and mercenary groups. Unless one group failed to get the job done, it's doubtful this would have come across his handler's desk, but he's still going to call her."

Tessa turned to Gregor. "Why just you three? Since they didn't know you are Goyles, they can't be going after the throne because then they'd need to take out Sin too. And..." Tessa shook her head. They all knew what she was thinking but couldn't bring herself to say it. They'd go after Bas, too.

"That's a good question." After pocketing his phone, Rafe turned to Frey. "Let's go grab my shooter and get him to the Pen. Kaya, please keep Bas here. Right now, I think there's safety in numbers. I don't want you anywhere near the manor."

Kaya stepped up to her mate, and Rafe wrapped his arms around her, kissing the side of her head. Kaya leaned back. "I don't think you should go. Not with your name on the contract. I think Frey should take lead on this so you, Gregor, and Dante can stay put."

"I agree, Brother," Dante said. He looked over at his assistant. "Trevor and Simon can handle the morgue in my absence."

"Absolutely," Trevor agreed.

Dante continued, "Deacon has the Pen covered. But instead of remaining here and putting everyone else in danger, I think the three of us should take our families and move to an undisclosed location."

"I know just the place," Tessa said. "Dad is in Italy for the World Council Delegation, and Mom went with him. Their home is practically a fortress. Say yes, and I'll call Tamian to get his plane ready. No offense, but I don't want to take a chance on the Clan jet being targeted again."

Rafael looked down at Kaya. She pressed a hand to the side of his face. "I know what I said earlier, but this changes things. If you feel we should go, then that's what we'll do."

Rafael stared into Kaya's eyes, then turned to his

cousin. "Frey, looks like you're in charge again."

CHAPTER THREE

JORDANA HEARD EVERY word of the conversation, so she already knew Lorenzo wasn't coming. Still, Francisca shook her head. Her mother-in-law didn't look a day over forty, yet with her oldest son's death, she seemed to have aged overnight. "I'm sorry," the female whispered.

Wrapping her arm around Francisca's shoulder, Jordana led her to the nearest chair. "I didn't expect any other outcome." But she had hoped. Jordana hoped and prayed to the gods that after a hundred years, Lorenzo would have happily rushed home to Brazil knowing they could be together. Maybe if Leo had kept his word about letting her go once she gave him an heir, things might have been different. Or maybe it was the gods who had intervened. Or the fates. Jordana eventually gave up on Lorenzo coming home. For years, she waited. When it didn't happen, she resigned herself to her fate and offered her body to her husband, but only to try for a child. It took over seventy years after their wedding for Jordana to give him a son.

The longer it took, the angrier Leonardo became. He accused Jordana of sorcery, doing something to keep from giving him an heir. She argued that was not the case, reminding him of his promise to release her from her vows once a child was born. They sought specialists who assured them there was nothing wrong with either of them, and sometimes, the universe just didn't cooperate. Diego, now twenty-seven, should have been heir to the throne, yet the one who struck down his father made it clear he would do

31

the same to Diego should the male interfere.

Jordana's son was a fighter, but he was still young in Gargoyle years. Marcos Ruiz had hundreds of years on Diego, and the Goyle was ruthless. Captain of Luiz's, then Leonardo's guard, the male had trained Diego himself. Why he turned on Leo was an unanswered question. One Jordana wasn't sure she wanted the answer to. The male had always made Jordana uneasy with the way he leered at her. The way he made sure he was the one to guard her whenever she was left alone at the family estate. Now the male was King, keeping Jordana, Diego, and Francisca locked down in their own home. If he knew they were reaching out to Lorenzo, he would probably take their phones and... Jordana sighed deeply because she didn't want to think about what else he would do.

The only decent thing Marcos did after taking Leo's head was to allow them to have a small funeral. Leo was laid to rest in the family mausoleum next to his father and his father before him. It was a small structure at the back of the property, having been in the family a few thousand years. That had been three days ago, and since then, Marcos had insisted Jordana join him for meals. When she first refused, he threatened Diego's life, and she capitulated. Jordana would do anything to keep him safe.

There was a knock on the door, and Francisca shoved the cell phone between the chair and cushion where she was sitting. Jordana prayed it was Diego. She hadn't seen her son since the funeral. Marcos explained Diego's mourning period was over, and his place was in the guard. She was used to going days without seeing Diego, but now... Her prayer was squashed when Marcos's face appeared.

Ignoring Francisca, Marcos stepped into Jordana's space, running a fingertip down her face. Jordana jerked back, crossing her arms over her chest. "You need to pack a bag. I have to travel south for a few days, and you will accompany me. Make sure to bring at least three dresses as

32

we will be having dinner with important families."

"I'm not going anywhere with you. I am not your Queen. You are not my mate to dictate my actions. As a matter of fact, Diego, Francisca and I would like our stipend so we can get on with our lives."

"Leonardo wasn't your mate either, yet you were his Queen and gave him a child. There will be no stipend. Francisca is welcome to leave, but you will be my Queen and will act as such in all ways, or your precious Diego will meet the same fate as his father. Are we clear?"

"As mud," Jordana muttered.

"What was that?" Marcos rose to his full height, but Jordana didn't cower. She would never give this male the satisfaction of intimidating her.

"We're clear." Jordana shoved her hands behind her back to hide her claws. Her beast was roaring in her head, but they were no match for a Goyle male.

"You have fifteen minutes." Marcos turned on his heel and strode from the room, leaving the door open. Jordana followed behind and closed it.

She returned to a shaking Francisca's side and knelt beside the female's chair. She reached out with her shifter hearing to make sure Marcos wasn't lingering outside the room before taking her mother-in-law's hands in her own. "Do you have any friends on the outside who can help you?"

Francisca shook her head, tears streaming down her cheeks. "I don't want to leave Diego. Or you. Jordana, what are you going to do?"

"I'm going to bide my time until Lorenzo comes to help." When Francisca shook her head harder, Jordana gently gripped the female's face. "He will come. Wait until Marcos and I are gone, then call him again. Tell him we are being held against our will and that Marcos will rape me sooner or later when I refuse to give him what he wants. I know in my heart Lorenzo will do the honorable thing. He's

33

our only hope. Now, I better pack."

"Promise you'll be safe," Francisca pled. Their relationship started off badly, but the older female assured Jordana she hadn't been onboard with Jordana's marriage to Leo. With her own mother out of the picture, Francisca had won a place in Jordana's heart over the years. When Leo's father crossed over, Francisca busied herself with being the best mother and grandmother she could, passing the crown over to Jordana once Leo took his place as King.

"As safe as I can be." Jordana placed a kiss on the female's cheek, then rose to pack. When Marcos returned for her, Jordana strode out the door, leaving the male to grab her bags. If he wanted her to be Queen, then by the gods, she'd act like one. As they entered one of the heavily guarded cars she had ridden in hundreds of times, Jordana sent a prayer to the gods asking they keep Diego and Francisca safe. She also asked that Lorenzo do the right thing, because Jordana knew he was the only one who could save her.

THINGS WERE CHAOTIC once Rafael agreed to take Kaya and the others to Xavier's home in New York. Since no one knew how long they would be in hiding, Rafael, Dante, and Gregor came up with a plan to go home and pack one at a time while each one was accompanied by several guards. If it was only the three males, it wouldn't take long, but Rafael had his mate, son, and housekeeper to pack for. When Rafael suggested Priscilla remain in New Atlanta, the look she gave the King had Lorenzo biting back a laugh. The human might work for Rafael, but she also ran their home and helped take care of their son.

Growing up, Lor had never known of humans working for Gargoyles. Their servants had been shifters as well. His father was old-school in his beliefs that no human should be aware of their existence. He would never have gone along with the Goyles mating with humans. With unmated females being nearly extinct, it was why he demanded Leonardo marry Jordana. Lorenzo hadn't understood the politics behind his father's demand. He hadn't cared for the reasons his mate was taken away from him, nor had he forgiven his father. When Lor learned of his father's crossing over, he didn't grieve for one second. He didn't rejoice either. Lor put it out of his mind, because with his father no longer living, that meant Leo was the new King, and Jordana his Queen.

"Uncle Lor!" Amelia yelled when she ran into the room. Lor dropped to a knee and held open his arms, knowing the girl would want to be held. Her life started out roughly, but with Frey and Abbi adopting her, she was a happy, thriving ray of sunshine.

"Yes, Munchkin?" Lor scooped her up when she lunged at him.

"We're having a sleepover. Did you know?"

Lor banded an arm around her legs and stood. "I heard." Banyan and Uri agreed to let Nova and Levi spend the night since Connor was leaving.

"Connor has to go away. I want to go with him, but Daddy says I have to stay here."

"If you went with Connor, who would look after Jonathan?"

"Mommy. Duh."

"Duh," Lor mimicked, and Amelia giggled. His phone rang, and Lorenzo sighed. He ignored it until his beast pushed at him.

You should answer.

We both know who it is.

Something's wrong. I feel it.

Lor hated to admit it, but he did as well. He placed Amelia on her feet. "I'm sorry, Princess, but I need to

35

answer my phone." She took off running to where Rain was sitting with his parents. Lorenzo swiped his screen before it could go to voicemail. "*Mai*, I told you—"

"Marcos took Jordana. He threatened Diego if she didn't agree to be his Queen the same way your father threatened her all those years ago. Lorenzo, please. The male is vile. He killed your brother, and if you don't do something—" His mother choked back a sob. "Please. You don't have to forgive her, although she did nothing wrong. Please don't punish us for things which were out of our control."

Lorenzo's head spun. "What do you mean the same way Luiz did?" Lorenzo had long ago given up calling Luiz Santos "father."

"He told Jordana if she didn't marry Leo, he would have your head. I'm so sorry, Lorenzo. Sorry I wasn't strong enough, but he was my mate. The King. There was nothing I could do to stop him. I know you blamed me as well, but there was nothing I could do to—"

"*Mai? Mai!*" Lorenzo looked at his phone, but it had disconnected. The hair on his neck bristled. "Fuck!"

"Uncle Lor, that's twenty dollars," Amelia reminded him. Abbi had started a swear jar for when Matthew visited. He did his best to curb his language around his little sister, but whenever something slipped, Abbi made him pay up.

"I'm sorry, Munchkin." Lor pulled out his wallet and handed her a couple twenties. He was one of the few beings who preferred cash over plastic. It was a habit he began when he was hiding from his family. Not that they had credit cards that long ago, but he learned all the best ways to stay hidden, and paying cash helped for many years. After Amelia skipped off with her payment, he hit redial on his mother's number, but it went straight to voicemail. When that happened several times, he tried the number he had saved earlier. "Come on, Jordy. Pick up." It, too, went to voicemail. Lor didn't bother leaving a message. If what his mother said was true, Jordana was in trouble. The new King had probably destroyed her phone, or disabled it at the least.

"Julian," Lor called across the room as he strode toward the other Goyle. "I need you to trace a phone. It's in Brazil."

"Lor, what's going on?" Frey asked.

Lorenzo dragged his fingers through his beard, sighing. Amelia, Rain, and Connor were within earshot, so he inclined his head toward the kitchen. Frey and Julian followed him out the back door. "I told you my brother was killed. What I didn't tell you was he was the Brazilian Gargoyle King. Some male named Marcos is responsible for his death. Our mother, his wife, and son are being held at the estate. From what my mother said, the male threatened them all if Jordana didn't agree to be his Queen. I was speaking with my mother when her phone cut off. Now neither she nor Jordana are answering."

"You said your brother's wife, not mate." Julian arched an eyebrow.

Lorenzo looked out over the backyard as he found his resolve. "That's because she was my mate, but I was the younger brother. Long story short, our fathers came to an agreement. One in which Jordana would marry Leo since he was heir to the throne, and she was the only unmated female in our Clan."

"Damn, Brother. That sucks," Julian said. "Are you going after her?"

"I'm needed here, but—"

"But nothing." Frey clapped him on the shoulder. "I understand now why you said what you did earlier, but Lorenzo, this is your mate. Not was. Is. No matter what happened or why, that's in the past. I'm not saying everything will be wine and roses once you rescue her, but Brother, she is your mate. And it sounds like your mother and nephew are in danger as well. Julian, take Lor's phone and see if you can't get a lock on it. I've got things covered here."

"But the kids," Lorenzo argued.

"The kids are their parents' responsibility as your family is yours. I know you, Lor. You're one of the most honorable Goyles I've had the pleasure of being around. You might have had your heart shredded when you lost Jordana, but she needs you as do your mother and nephew. Once Jules gets a lock on the phone, I'll send Paxton and Oakley with you."

"No, Frey. You need everyone here to watch after the kids."

"We have plenty of bodies to remain here. I'm not sending you into a Clan as large as the Brazilians with no backup. If this Marcos was able to take down your brother, who I assume had guards, then you'll have your hands full in getting close to him. Damnit, the three of you will be outnumbered. Let me get with Dominic and Sin. Since the threat is here in New Atlanta, taking males with you from Cali and New Orleans shouldn't be a problem."

Lor swallowed hard as his emotions tightened. This was what family did for each other. No matter the crisis, they found a way to be there for one another. "Thank you, Frey."

"No thanks needed, Brother. You're family. Now, you and Jules head to the lab. Katherine will be safe here."

"Let me tell her where I'm going, then we'll head out." Julian strode inside to find his mate, and Lorenzo remained on the deck taking deep breaths while Frey started making phone calls.

Lorenzo didn't know how to feel about Jordy. If what his mother said was true, his mate had put her happiness aside to save Lorenzo. Sacrificed her life for his. If Lor hadn't been such a stubborn, heartbroken bastard and gone after her before now... No. No what-ifs. Nothing good ever came of wondering what could have been. Frey was right; putting the past aside, Lorenzo's family needed him, and he would do whatever it took to make sure they were safely removed from the male who killed his brother. If he had the chance to avenge his family in the process? He'd cross that bridge when he got to it.

When Lor and Julian arrived at the lab, Lor was surprised to find Lucy sitting with Henry. Both were tapping away furiously on their respective keyboards. Lucy had been holed up with Jonas for months working on a secret formula.

"Lucy? What are you doing here?" Julian asked.

"Tamian told me what's going on, and I also got a text from an unknown number with a copy of the hit. I was hesitant to open the text since I didn't know who sent it, but I was curious."

Julian cocked his head to the side. "And you know what they say about curiosity and cats, right?"

"Ooh, Jules got jokes." Lucy stuck her tongue out at him. "Since my family is neck-deep in the merc business, I thought I could help. I called Ryker since he's in charge, but Rafael had already called him. Ryker said Kyllian is currently watching over their handler, and he called him so he could make sure the contract hadn't gone through Quinn. I was sure it didn't because she's really good at doing her due diligence before offering jobs to her mercs. She assured Ryker it didn't come across her desk, so that leaves us looking for other handlers. I'm starting with Nexus, the agency my family worked with before. Natalia was able to give me a little insight into how their organization is run."

"Natalia?" Lor wasn't familiar with that name.

"She's my uncle Mav's mate. Former assassin for Nexus. Long story, but the short of it is both she and Mav were sent after the same mark. They may have tried to take each other out before figuring out they were better as lovers than fighting one another."

Julian plugged Lorenzo's phone into his own computer. "Where is a good starting point?" he asked.

"The estate is in São Paulo."

Julian thanked him, then got busy. Lorenzo was always amazed at anyone who could easily manipulate technology. He was good at searching the internet, but that was about it. The three beings in the lab could probably build a rocket ship if they put their minds to it.

"Any idea who sent the text with the contract?" Julian asked Henry.

"My guess is Lachlan. I've been getting redirects every so often. I'm pretty sure he's out there watching each keystroke while doing his own digging. It's almost as if whoever is behind the scenes is letting me know not to waste my time. The first time it happened, I continued on with my search and came up blank. The second time, I received the end information well before I would have gotten there on my own. After that, I took the hint and redirected my search."

"Do you think he's trying to keep us off the right track?" Lor asked.

Henry shook his head. "No. I honestly think he's helping. I know what he did to Hunter was shitty, but he also knew his mate would recover. He did what he had to do so he could have access to his own equipment instead of being relegated to the computers at the Pen. No matter how good you are, you can only do so much with limited equipment." Henry never stopped typing while he spoke. That was another thing that amazed Lorenzo.

If what Henry said was true, Lachlan was out there somewhere trying to help his mate by helping the Stone Society, even though Hunter had released him. At least Jordana hadn't released Lor all those years ago. He peered over Julian's shoulder as the male attempted to locate Jordana. A map of Brazil focusing on Lorenzo's hometown was on the monitor, and with each keystroke, the area became smaller. Lor didn't understand technology, but he had faith in Julian. After what seemed like hours, Julian finally got a lock on Jordana's phone, but the signal was moving. Had Jordana managed to escape, or was she truly in trouble as his mother stated? Lor couldn't see any mother running from her child, even if said child was an adult. Then again, he didn't know his mate.

Yes, you do.

Lor didn't want to argue with his beast, so he didn't respond. He knew the female she had been when they were young, and he doubted she'd changed at her core that much over the last hundred years.

"It stopped." Julian pointed at the monitor. A red dot was flashing in Curitiba, some four hundred kilometers south of São Paulo.

"Shit." Lor cursed, running his fingers through his hair.

Lucy stopped typing and gave him her attention. "Tell me what's going on." After Lor explained the situation, Lucy rubbed her belly. "If that were me and someone threatened my child, there's no way I would leave them behind unless I had family I could trust to help with the situation. Is that possible?"

"I doubt it. It was our fathers who insisted she and Leo marry. My father was King, and hers was a powerful businessman. No one would go up against either one of them back then, and I doubt that's changed. Jordy's mother is Renata Callas. Back then she was an opera singer, but I have no idea where she is now. The only Marcos I'm aware of was a lieutenant in my father's guard, but I don't remember his last name. If this is the same male, he would have been close enough to Leo to take his head." Lucy winced, and Lor shrugged. "Sorry, I know I should feel worse about his death since he was my brother."

"But he took your mate. I get that." Lucy tapped her fingers against her belly. When she noticed him staring, Lucy smiled. "Yes, I'm pregnant. We haven't announced it because I'm not that far along."

"Congratulations."

"Thanks. We're excited. Trying to figure out if she'll be a Goyle, a Gryphon, or a hybrid of the two."

"You're having a girl?"

Lucy held out her hands, palms up. "No idea, but I don't want to call the baby it, so I've chosen 'she' until I know otherwise. I guess 'they' would be more appropriate since she could identify as either or neither. Anyway." Lucy turned back to her keyboard. "Why don't you give me all your family's information, and I'll plug it in the system and see if I come up with any clue as to who Marcos is. If we can figure that out, maybe I can see if he has family in Curitiba or at least some connection. If I come up with anything, I'll text it to you."

"Thank you. Now that we have a starting point, I'm headed home to pack and meet up with Paxton and Oakley. Julian, great job as always."

"Good luck, Brother. Henry and I will be a phone call away should you need us." Lor said his goodbyes to the trio and headed home, calling Frey on the way to tell him what Julian found. Several of the West Coast Clan were already in the air on their way to New Orleans where they all would meet up with some of Dominic's Goyles. From there they would continue to Brazil. Lorenzo's stomach churned. He wished Frey was going to be with him since the male was well-versed in battle. Lorenzo had sparred with the other males during their training sessions, but that was the closest he'd come to fighting. Having spent his early years hiding from his family, Lorenzo had changed his name and kept off the grid as much as possible, moving from Brazil to the western part of South America, then north to the US. That wasn't until after the last military draft had expired. Not that he wished he'd seen war, but Lor would like to have some military knowledge. Or even tracking experience. He prayed the males Frey chose to go with him were better equipped at the cloak-and-dagger stuff. His mate's life was depending on it.

CHAPTER FOUR

LACHLAN TOOK A sip of coffee as he studied Henry Palamo's keystrokes. The young Goyle was good, he'd give him that. But he wasn't as good as Lachlan. Frowning at the cold sip, Lachlan stood and padded into the galley. His thoughts went back to the last time he and Hector – Hunter as he preferred to be called now – were on the boat together. Shaking his head, he dumped the cold coffee into the sink and poured a fresh cup. Thinking of his mate... No, not his mate any longer. Hunter had released him, and the pain was just as strong as the day Hunter stated the words. Everything Lachlan was doing now was to get back in Hunter's good graces. Breaking his neck might have been overkill, but it was the only way to get away from the male and away from his prison cell.

Yes, Lachlan deserved to be in the Pen, but he couldn't help the Stone Society from behind bars. Even if they allowed him to use their computers, the equipment wasn't extensive enough to do what he needed. It was probably stupid for him to live on his houseboat, which was closer to a yacht. Hunter knew the water was where Lachlan was most at home. All he had to do was give the information to Julian or Henry, and they'd start tracking him.

Sitting back down, Lachlan switched keyboards, leaving Henry to follow the recent breadcrumbs he'd sent the male. Lachlan could do all the work for the group, but he wasn't ready to leave his haven. Not yet. Maybe never. If things didn't go the way he hoped they would, Lachlan would set out to sea and never return. His life had been a

43

long one. Mostly fulfilling with the exception of not having Hector by his side. Lachlan was an only child who had lost his parents centuries prior. He had no reference for wanting to remain by a brother's side, much less a twin's, the way Hector did. When they first met, Hector didn't believe they could be mates since they were both male. In recent years, they had both encountered gay Goyles, but Hector had already put distance between them at that point.

When Lachlan outed himself as Achilles, he painted a target on his back and disappointed his mate. Hector chose Carter even before that happened, and now? Well, now all Lachlan could do was help the Stone Society take down the female who was after them. He should just send a message letting them in on the woman's identity. She had already tried to sabotage the Clan's jet filled with mates and children. That should have been enough for Lachlan to pull the plug on the female. Eden Wood, codename Whisper, was an expert hacker who helped run her father's business. Nexus was one of the largest assassin groups in the world from what Lachlan had uncovered. What he hadn't figured out was why she was after the Stone Society.

Rafael Stone was an honorable Goyle. He was a fair King. A good brother. Loving husband and father. His Clan loved him. If Eden were a Goyle, it might make sense she wanted the throne for herself, but since she wasn't, Lachlan had no idea of her angle. He was certain she wasn't aware of the Gargoyles since she sent armed men to take out the three brothers, so he didn't think she was getting revenge for the Greeks. But something happened to make the female see red. And since she was almost as skilled as Lachlan, the female was able to erase her footprint almost completely. Almost. There were a few instances where she had not erased her whereabouts. Had she not cared if someone found out about those weeks? Or had she been distracted and forgot?

What would make someone go after a group of

seemingly good guys? There were only two things Lachlan could think of – family and love. Since her parents were alive and well, that left a husband or wife, or a lover possibly? Lachlan hadn't come across a spouse in his digging, so that left a lover as the most obvious reason. After checking on Henry's research, Lachlan got back to what he did best – outsmarting the rest.

WITH BANYAN AND URI standing guard at Frey's house, Frey and Remy followed Rafael to the manor. The shooter was where Rafe left him bound to a tree. The human's eyes narrowed, and he grunted and squirmed. Trying to get loose was pointless considering Rafael had used his shifter strength to secure the man. When Frey approached, he let his claws extend to cut the rope, and the human pissed himself.

"I thought an assassin would have better self-control," Remy quipped.

Frey snorted a laugh. "You're not wrong, Brother. It probably won't be the last time unless he cooperates." Frey dragged the human up by the arm, took a step back, and punched him in the side of the head. Before the man could slump unconscious to the ground, Frey caught him and tossed him over his shoulder. Having trained in martial arts, Frey knew how to throw a punch to knock someone out without killing them. He also knew how to strike a fatal blow, but he wouldn't do that. Yet. He needed information from the man first. Remy strode by his side as they returned to Frey's truck where he tossed the human into the back seat. They then went into the manor to help Rafael finish packing. Once finished, Frey dragged his cousin into a bone-crushing hug.

"Stay safe, Cousin. Have everyone turn their phones off

and remove the battery before you get on the jet. I don't like the thought of you being tracked to New York. I'm going to get enough burner phones for everyone here. I'll send you the number once I get it, but unless it's an emergency, that will be the only time I contact you. I don't want you to worry. I'll handle everything here."

Rafael cupped the back of Frey's head. "I know you will. You did a fine job all these past months. It should have been you who was King. Not me."

"Bah. You're the best of us, Rafe." They touched foreheads, then Frey strode to his truck while Remy joined Rafael for the ride back to Frey's home.

Frey made the trip to the Pen lost in his thoughts about who would attack his family. The same questions swirled in his brain regarding the Greeks, but he was no closer to answers by the time he arrived. Deacon met him at the back entrance where they brought in Unholy they'd captured. With Isabelle and Dante having completed the serum to change the monsters into Reborn, the Clan had been busy not only helping rehab everyone held in the Basement but to also capture the few Unholy left around the city and do the same for them.

The warehouses they had remodeled to hold the Reborn were all but full. The project was going as smoothly as possible with only a few Unholy not taking to the serum. Those remained in the Basement where they would live out their days. It was a major undertaking, but the Clan had the means both in bodies and finances to help restore the lost souls to their former humanity. Remy had taken several batches of the serum to California and administered it to the few Unholy being held in the new prison there. Gregor had chosen well when he chose Remy Doucet to be warden for the newest Stone Society prison.

"I have a room waiting," Deacon said, holding the door open. He slid past Frey once inside and led him down a long corridor. Instead of taking the human to an open cell, they

46

placed him in a private room. The human didn't need to see the other assassin Dante had captured. Frey felt sure if the human had gotten a shot off and come close to killing Isabelle, the man wouldn't be breathing. Frey didn't fault Gregor for killing his shooter. He'd have done the same if he'd been in his cousin's boots.

Frey placed the man on a chair Deacon set in the middle of the room, then proceeded to bind his hands behind his back. He wrapped the thick rope around the man's torso before securing his feet to the metal legs. Since the human was still unconscious, Frey left him alone and followed Deacon down the hallway to another room.

Dante's shooter was awake. Not only was he conscious, but he was lying on his side, doing his best to loosen the rope binding him to his chair. Frey strode over and picked the chair up as though the man weighed nothing. He slammed the legs down and slapped the man with his palm. The human glared at Frey, muttering behind the gag.

Frey took a step back and crossed his arms over his chest. "Here's how this will go. I'm going to remove your gag, then you will answer my questions. If you answer truthfully, I'll let you live. If you give me any trouble whatsoever, I'll gut you where you sit. Nod if you understand." The man narrowed his eyes, not indicating he would cooperate. When Frey took a step toward the man, he leaned his head back and nodded.

Frey let a claw out and sliced the gag with one swipe. He may have cut the man's cheek in the process. It would heal. Eventually.

"What the fuck?"

"That's just a small example of what I'll do to you if you don't tell me what I want to know. Who hired you?"

"I want a lawyer. I get one phone call."

Frey looked over his shoulder at Deacon, laughing. "Can you believe this guy?" Deacon shared the laugh, then Frey turned back to the shooter. "Did someone Mirandize you? Give you any reason to believe you were under arrest? No, they did not. Who hired you?"

"I don't know."

"Wrong fucking answer." Frey let his fangs drop, and the man gasped.

"What the fuck! Let me out of here! Help!" he bellowed.

The scent of urine was strong, and Frey shook his head before slapping the man again. The human stopped yelling and licked at his split lip.

"Let's try this again. Who hired you?"

"I don't know who takes out the contracts. We never do. Our handler sends them to us, and we carry out the hit. I swear I'm telling the truth."

"Who is this handler? Who do they work for?" Frey circled the captor.

"Man, they'll kill me if I tell you."

"And I'll kill you if you don't." Frey stopped walking when he was once again directly in front of the man and waited.

The shooter closed his eyes and let out a deep breath. "Nexus. I work for a group called Nexus, and my handler's name is Whisper. I don't know where they're located. Everything is top secret, and all the jobs come through either text or email." That tracked with what Ryker told Rafael about how things were done.

"And you don't bother looking into the ones you're contracted to kill?"

The man shook his head, sweat beading across his upper lip. "It's the handler's job to vet the mark. I was assured when I signed on with the company that it would only be those who deserved it. The worst of the worst."

"Then you put your trust in the wrong fucking handler, because the man you tried to take out this morning? He's as good as they come." Frey turned to Deacon. "Let's go see if the other one is awake. Maybe he'll have more to offer."

When they reached the door, the shooter called out,

begging them to untie him, but Frey ignored him. When they reached the other room, Rafael's shooter was awake and wiggling in his chair. Frey removed the gag without using a claw. This one had already pissed his pants once, and Frey's sensitive nose didn't care to add to the stench.

"I want a lawyer," the shooter blurted as soon as the gag was missing.

"What is it with you men? I sure as shit wouldn't hire a dumbass to take on jobs for me, so tell me, what's your name?"

"I'm not a dumbass, and I'm not telling you anything."

Frey smirked, then let his fangs drop. "I think you will. Your buddy in the next room spilled his guts, and he's alive. If you want to continue breathing, I suggest you tell me what I want to know."

"David. My name's David."

"Very good. Who do you work for, David?"

"They'll—"

"Kill you if you talk. Yes, I know. But let's get something straight, David. I'll kill you if you don't. And" — Frey extended his claws — "I think I'm a bigger threat at the moment. Don't you?"

"What the fuck are you?"

"Your judge, jury, and possibly your executioner, so tell me what I want to know. Now." The smell of piss hit Frey's nose, and he took a step back, even though it wouldn't help. "Fucking amateurs," he muttered. "I'm waiting."

"Nexus. The company's name is Nexus."

"And your handler?"

David bowed his head, his body trembling. When he looked back at Frey, he sighed. "Her name's Whisper. And no, I don't know her real name. Everyone at Nexus uses code names. It's supposed to keep us safer."

"Have you met this Whisper?"

"Yes. She approached me not long after I left the army. Made me an offer I couldn't refuse." Frey twirled his finger in the air, indicating David should continue. He did. "I couldn't find a job. Not many companies have a place in their ranks for a sniper. She offered me a lot of money with a bonus if I signed on that day."

"What does Whisper look like?" Without a name, it would be hard to track this female down, but at least it would give them something to work with.

"I haven't seen her in years, but when I met her, she had short, dark hair. She's about five-three and was dressed like she was ready to go out on the town."

"And the company; do you know where they're located?"

"No. She met me in a coffee shop close to the apartment I was renting. After I signed the papers, she gave me a secure phone and said all contracts would come via text or the email she had assigned me. I take it this Rafael Stone is one of you, whatever you are. One minute I had him in my sight, and the next I was on the ground."

"Rafael is no longer any of your concern." Frey turned to Deacon. "Lock him and his cohort up."

"Wait! You said if I gave you the information, you wouldn't kill me."

Frey looked over his shoulder at David. "And I'm not. But there's no way I'm letting you go. You tried to kill my cousin. He's a good, honorable male, and the contract was bullshit. Your Whisper should have done a better job vetting the hit." Frey strode to the door with Deacon following. When they were in the hallway, Frey asked, "Do you have somewhere to put them away from the other inmates?"

"Yes. I have two cells prepared in the Basement. Now that the Unholy are being released to the warehouses, we have plenty of room."

"Good. I need to get back to Julian with this information. I'll see you later, Brother." Frey clapped Deacon on the shoulder, then pulled out his phone to call Julian and Lucy. Hopefully, she would be able to offer some assistance since some of her family previously worked for Nexus.

JORDANA WIGGLED HER toes against the SIM card she'd removed from her phone and hid in her shoe. Even if Marcos found her phone in her bag, she'd at least have the card in case she happened upon another phone. She didn't know whether or not Francisca would convince Lorenzo to come for her, but she hoped he would. Jordana sat tall in the back seat, not looking at Marcos. Instead, she gazed out the side window of the large SUV she'd ridden in often. It was specialized in that it was fully armored with shatterproof glass. Leo had it made especially for her since she didn't have the impenetrable skin like the males. He should have paid more attention to those he had guarding him instead.

"I expect you to go along with everything I say in these meetings," Marcos said. She turned to the male then and sneered. "And that right there? If you look at me that way or in any manner other than a devoted Queen, your son will meet the same fate as his father."

"Don't worry. I know how to pretend to be the devoted female." Jordana turned away and once again studied the scenery.

"Ah yes. The Ice Queen knows how to play the game." Marcos chuckled. The moniker had been whispered over the years, but it didn't bother her. Jordana was kind to their Clan. Kind to everyone in their employ, especially since she didn't believe in having servants for every little thing. Jordana spent time in the kitchen learning to cook. She helped wash and put away her clothes that didn't need to be dry-cleaned. Before being forced into a loveless marriage, Jordana had been a good daughter and better friend. Over the years, her heart hardened except for Diego. She doted on her son when he was younger, but when he transitioned, she had no choice but to turn his care over to Leo.

Jordana was not a fighter. Hell, neither was Leo, but he'd had to learn to be a stern but fair ruler once he inherited the throne. Diego learned the sword as did all Gargoyles. He had the best tutors money could buy because being the heir, he wasn't allowed to go to school where he couldn't be guarded twenty-four seven.

"This time, it better not take seventy years to give me a son." Marcos's phone rang before Jordana could respond. She willed her claws to stay put. There was no way she was having sex with the male, much less giving him his own heir. Jordana listened to both sides of the conversation. Marcos didn't attempt to hide his business from her. He probably figured she would meekly comply with every demand. She would, for now. She would play the game until Lor came for her.

When they arrived in Curitiba, the driver continued through the city until they pulled into an estate that rivaled her own. Considering Marcos was now King, she probably shouldn't think of it as hers any longer. Whenever Leo's father passed the crown down, he also passed ownership of the estate over to him as well while moving from the master suite into a different wing with Francisca. What he didn't do was allow Leo to rule in his own way. Luiz continued on as advisor against Leo's wishes. It wasn't until Diego was born that the male completely turned loose of the reins. Jordana didn't know what happened to her father-in-law for him to cross over, but she was glad when it happened. She felt nothing but ire for the male after he and her father made her marry Leo.

Jordana had to endure seeing her own parents over the years. They moved away from São Paulo soon after the wedding, but they visited often. Her mother was too invested in her career as a singer to worry about Jordana, and her father was the same bastard he'd always been. It wasn't until Luiz crossed over that her parents stopped coming to visit. Knowing how she felt about them, Leo made it clear they were no longer welcome at the estate. With him being King, they had no choice but to abide by his decision. She hadn't heard from either of them in almost thirty years.

When the car stopped, the driver – Miguel – got out and came around to open Marcos's door. He stepped out, then held out his hand for Jordana. She refused the offer and got out on her own. Marcos stepped into her space, but Jordana didn't move back. She squared her shoulders and said, "I will abide by your rules while in the presence of outsiders. But when we are alone, you will not touch me."

"You forget your place, Jordana. You are Queen in name only, and I am in charge. Always. You would do well to remember your precious son's life depends on your fealty, as does yours. You wouldn't want Diego to be an orphan, would you?"

Jordana tamped down her shifter and stared back at the cold eyes of the male before her. "I do not forget my place, but you should know I'm not afraid to die. By your hand or my own. I would rather slit my throat than to have you put your hands on me."

Marcos glared at her, more than likely weighing the truth of her words. Instead of responding to her, he told the driver to grab Jordana's bags and check them for a phone, then turned on his heel and strode toward the house. Jordana wanted to lean against the car and steady herself, but she wouldn't let Miguel see her as anything less than confident.

"I'm sorry about all this," Miguel whispered as he leaned over and searched her bags for a phone. When he found it, he slid it in his pocket before pulling her luggage from the trunk.

Jordana pretended to take in her surroundings, and when her back was to the house, she answered, "I appreciate that." Since she had no idea whether the male was being honest, she didn't say anything further. Miguel was a Goyle but one she hadn't met before that day. She didn't know who to trust, so she went with her gut and didn't trust anyone. After he closed the lid, she followed him to the house. Marcos was nowhere to be seen, but his voice echoed through the cavernous foyer as he gave instructions to someone.

"I'll show you to your room," Miguel said, moving past her toward a grand staircase. When they reached a lavish suite on the second floor, Jordana entered the room and crossed the thick carpet to peer out a window. The property boasted a large pool and stunning landscaping. In another life, she might have enjoyed the outdoor setting.

As Miguel placed Jordana's luggage on the floor, he whispered, "I'll try to get you a new phone." In a normal tone, he said, "Marcos has meetings scheduled with several influential males over the next week beginning tomorrow evening. You are to accompany him to dinner each night. Until then, you are free to make yourself at home. Eliana is an excellent cook, and she would probably love to make your acquaintance. If you need anything, pick up the phone and dial *one*." Miguel gestured to the same type of phone one would find in a hotel. She had no idea how old the male was, but when he spoke next, he reminded her of how a caring father would sound. "I would not choose this life for you, My Queen. I wouldn't choose this for any female. Eliana and I will do our best to make your stay here as easy as we can, but you have to know we are no better off than you. Leo was a fair King, but I'm afraid things aren't going to be fair for any of us going forward." His voice wavered, and Jordana had the urge to hug the male. She wasn't the only one whose world had been turned upside down.

Footsteps sounded on the stairs, and Miguel took a step toward the door. "I'll leave you to unpack." Miguel stepped out of the room just as Marcos reached the door.

"I hope you find the room to your satisfaction. Mine is across the hall." His cold eyes softened. "I know we got off on the wrong foot, but I'm hoping with time you will find I have your best interests at heart. My ways may seem archaic, but I think you and I could be a formidable couple. I do not wish to force myself on you. Ours will be a long life together, and I regret how it has begun. Please accept my apologies. While we are here, feel free to become acquainted with the staff. They have been instructed that your word is law as long as you aren't contradicting my wishes. Our first guests will be here tomorrow for dinner. Tonight, I have instructed Eliana to serve you either in the dining room or here in your suite, whichever you prefer." Marcos paused, staring at her. When she didn't say anything, he inclined his head and left her alone.

His change in demeanor wasn't fooling her. If Marcos were an honorable male, he would allow her and her son to choose a life away from him. He would find someone else to be Queen. Marcos was a handsome male. Tall and broad. Broader than Leo had been. But no one could hold a candle to her mate. Jordana hadn't seen Lorenzo in so long. Not since he was a young male coming into his Goyle. She had no doubt he favored his brother. Leo had been stunning, and if they had been true mates, she would have found herself blessed to be chosen for him. Actions and attitude were so much more powerful than a handsome face, and if Marcos thought his lip service was going to thaw the Ice Queen, he was wrong. Like she told the male, she knew how to play the game, and this time, Jordana was playing to win.

CHAPTER FIVE

INSTEAD OF HIDING out in the bedroom, Jordana decided to explore the house. Any intel she could gather, whether from the cook or just by being observant, couldn't hurt. She knew she was no match for a male Gargoyle, but she was no wilting flower either. Given any opportunity to run, she would. Marcos might have taken Leo's head, but what he hadn't taken was her Clan's loyalty. You didn't rule as Queen for close to thirty years and not know your people. Then again, Leo had ruled for the same amount of time and hadn't realized someone in his guard was after the throne.

Twisting the knob, she cracked the door and listened for any sign of movement. When she didn't hear Marcos in his bedroom, she slipped out and padded quietly down the hallway toward the stairs. She paused at the top, opening her senses. The large house was eerily quiet save for the sounds of humming. Jordana moved in that direction and found a cook stirring something on the stove.

"My Queen." The female smiled and bowed her head. "I am Eliana. Miguel didn't expect you to leave your room, but I'm glad you did. I am preparing your dinner. It should be ready in about half an hour. Until then, may I get you something to drink?"

Jordana waved her off and walked over to the refrigerator. There were several pitchers of what looked like the sweet tea drink her mother preferred. "What is this?"

Eliana stepped closer, and when she saw what Jordana was pointing to, she wrung her hands. "It is *Chimarrão*." Eliana lowered her voice. "Marcos requested it for tomorrow's dinner."

Jordana found it interesting the female didn't refer to Marcos as the King. "Speaking of, do you know where he is?" Bypassing the tea, Jordana opted for a bottle of water. She didn't trust the open container not to be poisoned. Even if it wasn't, she had lost her taste for the sweet drink a long time ago.

"Miguel only said he had business to attend."

Jordana lowered her voice to barely above a whisper. "How many guards are here?"

"Currently, five," Eliana whispered. "He took two with him. There are two by the gate, and the others are stationed at the doors." She inclined her head toward the back of the house. Jordana turned her gaze that direction to find a large male with a sword strapped to his back standing guard.

"And those he is entertaining this week know of Gargoyles?" Why else would Marcos have males armed with swords and not guns? The guard wasn't wearing a coat, so unless he had a handgun strapped to his ankle, the blade was his only weapon.

"My Queen," Eliana started, but Jordana held up her hand.

"Please call me Jordana. I'm not feeling too royal at the moment." When Eliana frowned, Jordana continued. "I am here against my wishes, and if Miguel was being truthful, you are too."

Eliana's eyes widened. She looked toward the guard, so Jordana did as well. They were still whispering, but Gargoyle hearing was extraordinary. The cook grabbed Jordana's hand and led her deeper into the house. "You are correct, My— Jordana. Miguel and I had plans to retire and travel. We have been in your family's employ for over fifty years, but once Marcos took over, we were informed our retirement was not granted."

"My family? I'm sorry, but I know everyone who helps at the estate."

"Not the royal family. Your parents."

Jordana took a step back. *No, no, no.* "You…" Shaking her head, she turned to retreat to her room, but Eliana caught her by the wrist.

"Please listen to me," the female begged. "I know your story. I know they made you and Leonardo marry against your wishes. I have listened to your parents speak of you over the years, and My Queen, your father is still pulling strings. Whose house do you think this is? Marcos was a guard and no doubt paid handsomely, but enough to own something to rival your own estate? Your father was beyond angry when King Leo banished him from your home. This very room had to be remodeled after your father finished taking out his ire on it. His was – is – a long game. With you as Queen, he was important in his business circles, but once Leonardo cut him off, that power waned."

"Are you saying my father ordered Marcos to take Leo's head?"

"That's exactly what I'm saying. You're in more danger now than ever before, as are Miguel and I. But we stayed with your parents for one reason only – to gather all the information we could. Only we didn't get to Leonardo in time. He did meet with Marcos here, but your father was careful not to discuss in detail what he required of Marcos. He informed him if his plan succeeded, he would turn the keys to the estate over to him. We didn't know what plan he referred to. I'm so sorry." Eliana's eyes filled with tears, and Jordana felt the truth in the female's words. She didn't hesitate to pull her into her arms.

"It's not your fault. Somehow, I will get out of this mess, and when I do, I'll take you and Miguel with me." Jordana didn't dare mention Lorenzo. If Eliana didn't know Francisca had reached out to him, she couldn't be forced to say anything. No, Jordana kept that hope to herself. As she held the cook, she prayed to the gods her mate did the right thing. Releasing the older female, Jordan took a step back.

"Am I right in assuming our guests tomorrow night are my parents?"

Eliana nodded. "How did you know?"

"By the *Chimarrão*. It was always my mother's favorite. She said it helped her throat. I have to ask, though. If you and Miguel worked for my parents for so long, why are you here instead of with them?"

"Along with the estate, we were a 'gift' to Marcos for a job well done. He plans to move here full time, gathering his own staff."

That made sense. When the throne was turned over to Leo, he had Jordana do the same thing. Those who had served his parents were given a retirement gift to go live a life of their choosing if they didn't wish to remain at the estate. Jordana had asked the former staff if any of their family were interested in taking over the vacated positions. It was considered an honor among most to work for the royal family. If any of those in her employ wished to move on, Jordana gave them a monetary gift and wished them well. She never held anyone against their will. It was one reason her people adored her. That and she didn't treat them like hired help. To her, they were family.

And now that she was looking at the house with the knowledge it had been her parents', Jordana should have recognized the furnishings and garish colors. Her mother did have a flair for the dramatic.

Jordana was taking a big risk, but she felt she could trust the cook. "I hate to ask this, but do you have a cell phone? Marcos had Miguel take mine."

"Come with me." Eliana returned to the kitchen and walked into the large pantry. Jordana made sure the guard wasn't watching and followed. Eliana reached up to the top shelf and pulled down a box of cereal. She removed the contents, and hidden at the bottom was a phone. "Will this one work?"

"It's perfect. Thank you so much." Jordana shoved the

device into her bra while Eliana put the cereal back.

When they exited the pantry, the guard was looking through the window, and Eliana padded to the stove. "Your dinner will be ready soon, but you have time to freshen up beforehand."

Jordana kept her face impassive. "If you don't mind, I'd prefer to eat in my room."

Eliana inclined her head. "As you wish."

Jordana didn't look the guard's way before heading back upstairs. Once in her room, she removed the SIM card from her shoe and replaced it for the one in Eliana's phone, thankful it was the same model Jordana had. She then hid the phone in the bathroom between two towels. Once that was taken care of, Jordana went to the window of her bedroom and looked out over the property. Knowing her father was behind Leo's death changed things. She would have to be even more guarded. The estate was massive, so it didn't make sense to her that Marcos would only have seven guards, unless he was so cocky he didn't think anyone was brave enough to challenge him. *Please, Lorenzo. Please be brave.*

It was well past midnight when Marcos returned. Jordana knew this because she refused to sleep until he was back. After eating the delicious meal Eliana prepared, Jordana roamed the house. Either her parents didn't spend much time there, or they had moved all their personal belongings out before handing it over to Marcos. All the bedrooms were still full of furniture, but there was little in the way of artwork on the walls. There were no statues or floral arrangements to give the house any character. Not that her mother's tastes would do much to add to the hideous color scheme. Leo had allowed Jordana to decorate however she saw fit once they took over their estate, and she chose soft colors for the rooms she redecorated. With Francisca remaining there, Jordana didn't bother changing any of the rooms in her mother-in-law's area.

Marcos found Jordana sitting in the kitchen with a cup of coffee when he returned. He lingered only long enough to ask her how her evening was. She didn't ask the same of him because she couldn't care less. Marcos bid her goodnight and left her to her drink. Jordana finished her coffee, rinsed the mug, and put it in the dishwasher before making her way upstairs. She closed her door not bothering to lock it. If Marcos wanted in, he would get in easily. Jordana stood by the window, staring out as she waited until Marcos was in bed and his breathing evened. Only then did she dare try to sleep herself.

SINCE RAFAEL AND the others had taken Tamian's plane, Lorenzo and those going with him to Brazil were on the Clan jet. He knew the males – Gannon, Everett, and Thane – who had joined them from the West Coast, having lived there many years before heading to New Atlanta. The Louisiana Clan – Malone, Rasmus, and Fallon – were eager to join Lor, Paxton, and Oakley in the rescue. As they traveled through the sky, each one of the NOLA Clan regaled them with tales of living in or near New Orleans and what it was like to have a pirate as their leader. Lorenzo liked Dominic Dubois, but he adored Lilly and their new twin girls, Solaris and Luna. Lor had never met a witch before meeting Lilly, but he admired her craft. She had saved both Jasper and Desi with her knowledge of spells and potions, and Lor was grateful to the pretty blonde. He was also grateful for the males filling the time with idle chatter.

Lor's mother had reached out again, only this time, she told him Marcos Ruiz was now King and had taken Jordana away for a few days. She cried as she told Lor what Marcos planned for Jordana if she didn't cooperate. Lorenzo had

Julian trying to find any information he could on Marcos, but Lor knew enough to be wary. The male had been one of the lieutenants in his father's guard, and Lor had no doubt Marcos had remained such when Leo took the throne. As a guard, he was formidable. As King? He would have his own guards at his beck and call while being able to hold his own against the small group heading his way. The only things they had on their side were surprise and the specially coated blades of their swords. Urijah made sure to have plenty of the weapons forged and ready at all times. Lor informed the males with him who Marcos was.

"If Marcos is in Curitiba, would it make sense to stop off in São Paulo to retrieve your mother and nephew first while the male's focus is elsewhere?" Gannon asked.

Before Lor could answer, Paxton jumped in. "How much do you look like your brother?" When Lor narrowed his eyes, Pax continued. "I'm asking because if you favor quite a bit, you could use that to your advantage."

"How? Leo is dead. And to answer your question, I'm not sure. I haven't seen him since I left home as a teenager."

"What are you thinking?" Rasmus asked Pax.

"If they favor enough, it could allow Lor to pretend. Pretend Leo is still alive at least until we reach his mother and nephew. Or," Pax continued, "those who lost their beloved King might see Lorenzo and be willing to aid us in rescuing Diego and Francisca. From what Lor remembers, Marcos isn't a nice male. He's not going to rule with fairness the way Leo did."

Oakley shook the ice in the now empty tumbler of whiskey he'd been sipping. "That's true, but they will probably be leery about pissing off the new King, especially if he is ruthless. He could see their help as treason."

"I agree. Either is a dangerous game. We don't know who is on Marcos's side." Lor twirled his phone in his hand. He paused the motion and sent his mother a text.

Lor: *Do you have a current photo of Leo?*

It took only seconds before she responded. Instead of words, Lor stared at a photo that looked so much like himself he gasped.

"What? What's wrong?" Gannon asked. Lor turned the phone around, and the male sucked in a breath. "Guess that answers that question." Lor showed the photo to the others.

"Ask your mom if she knows how many are on Marcos's side. If this were our Clan, it wouldn't be a high number," Rasmus said. Lorenzo did as requested, and his mother responded with she wasn't sure, but she doubted it was many. She then asked what he was planning. He didn't want to put her in more danger than she currently faced, but they needed all the help they could get.

"If we do this and we have to fight, taking Marcos's head means I would become the next King. I don't want that. My life is in the States," Lor admitted.

"Then let me be the one to fight the male. I've lived in Louisiana for almost a hundred years. I could do with a change of scenery, and São Paulo is a lovely place from what I remember," Fallon offered.

"Dominic wouldn't mind?" Lor asked.

"No. He entrusts the territory to me whenever he and Lilly are in New Atlanta," Sully informed them. "If Fallon wants to move to Brazil, I have no issue with that. Not only do I not mind, it would give me somewhere to vacation."

"And if I were to become King, that would allow your family to either remain there in the city or move on and not be held prisoner. You would be free to court your mate."

"Yeah, that's not going to happen," Lor muttered.

"Lor—"

"No, Gannon. Let's worry about rescuing them first. If our plan, whatever we come up with, fails, the rest is moot."

Gannon sighed, then inclined his head. "Find out everything you can from your mother. See if she can determine ahead of time where Marcos is keeping Diego. Once we go in, we're going to need to be quick about it."

"As Rasmus said, the number of males with Marcos is probably going to be low enough that we can take them down with the element of surprise," Fallon said. "Have your mother speak to the servants first. I have found over the years they are the ones with the most knowledge of what goes on within a household. Once we have the lay of the land, we can determine the best course of action."

"I'm betting it's more than nine of us want to go up against," Lor said.

"Ten," Bryce called out from the cockpit. "I am more than a pilot. I served with Frey in the military."

Lor sent his mother another text asking for any intel she could gather, then bid her be careful. He might not be close to her any longer, but she was still his mother, and he didn't want to see any harm come to her.

"I just pray Marcos doesn't take his frustration out on Jordana," Lor admitted aloud.

Everett clapped him on the shoulder and gave a quick squeeze. "From what you told us, your mate has been a pawn for far too long. However, she is Queen and has been for a long time. If anyone can figure out how to stay alive, it would be her."

Lorenzo stood and walked over to the small bar, pouring himself another drink. "How? She is Goyle, but she's a female. I know they are strong mentally, but physically they are no match for males. Instead of waiting to see how Marcos reacts, I think we should meet him head-on in Curitiba. He may have taken guards with him, but I don't want to leave Jordy's fate in his hands too long." When he returned to his seat, all eyes were on him and several of the males were smirking. Ugh.

Thane, being the mature one, ignored the slip and leaned forward in his seat, propping his forearms on his thighs. "I have to agree. Even if your mother is able to ascertain an approximation of those on Marcos's side, we won't know for sure what we're up against. I think taking

Marcos down first is the safest bet for Jordana. We get her to safety, then we can show up at the estate and declare Fallon to be the new King. First, we need to know if her cell phone has moved."

"I'll call Julian." Lor could text, but having a conversation would save him from facing Gannon's smugness for a few minutes. Before he could dial, Julian's name popped up with an incoming call.

"Julian?"

"Jordana's location hasn't changed. In fact, it's static, so either they found her phone, or she isn't carrying it around. The good news is I have a satellite image of the estate. It took some digging, but Lucy was able to find ownership. Lor, the estate belongs to Jordana's father."

"You have to be shitting me. If she and Marcos are—"

"Lor, stop," Gannon said sharply. "Julian, send everything you have to Lorenzo's email, and we'll take it from there."

Julian stopped tapping his keyboard. "Lor, I have to agree with Gannon. From what your mother said, Jordana was taken against her will. You need to give her the benefit of the doubt until you hear her side of the story. She is your mate whether or not you want to claim her. I know what it's like to have a mate in the middle of a shitstorm. You have to trust the fates on this, Brother. They wouldn't give you, an honorable male, someone unworthy. Trust them if you don't trust her."

"You're right. Shit. Okay, send the information, and we'll do what we can with it."

"Sent. Good luck, Brother." Julian disconnected, and Lor shoved his phone into his back pocket.

Gannon stepped up beside Lor. "The way I see it, Jordana has always been a puppet in her father's schemes. Since you weren't around these last hundred years, you don't know if that remained the same. Like Julian said, don't disregard her until you have the facts."

Lor scrubbed a hand down his face, then blew out a breath. He should feel blessed that he might get another shot with his mate, but Gannon was right about one thing; a hundred years was a long time. He often wondered what would've happened if he hadn't run off. Would Leo have done the right thing and let Jordana go? Or was he their father's son and did whatever he wanted to get ahead? Lor grabbed the laptop Julian had sent with him, then opened the email containing the information Lucy had gathered. He wouldn't get any answers until he had Jordana away from Marcos.

JORDANA ENDURED BREAKFAST with her captor the next morning. He was cordial to Eliana, even going so far as to compliment her cooking, taking both her and Jordana by surprise. Afterward, he announced he was leaving and would return promptly at seven with their dinner guests. Jordana wanted to call Francisca and ask if she'd spoken to Lorenzo, but she didn't want to risk removing the phone from its hiding place.

With several hours to kill, Jordana spent most of the day with Eliana, watching her cook. Jordana offered to help, and the look on the older female's face was priceless. "I do help out at home. Always have," she said. "From the day I married Leo, I planned on being free from him at some point in my life. I wanted to learn as much about cooking and housework as possible so I wouldn't be useless on my own."

Eliana's smile was sad. "You are so very different from your mother."

"I'll take that as a compliment." After that, Eliana motioned for Jordana to come around the island and help with the preparations until it was time for Jordana to shower and change.

Jordana was dressed in her best when familiar voices sounded downstairs. She made sure the small SIM card was safely in the toe of her shoe just in case she was removed from the premises. She pulled on her Ice Queen façade and headed downstairs before Marcos could come for her. When she reached the bottom of the stairs, she took a deep breath before continuing into what her mother always referred to as the receiving room. It was large enough to accommodate at least fifty guests comfortably.

Let the games begin.

Three sets of eyes turned her way. Renata was as beautiful as ever, and Pedro still held the same evil glint in his stare. She didn't stop until she was standing next to Marcos, slipping her hand around his arm. Her gesture must have surprised him because his eyebrows dipped. Smiling sweetly, she turned to those who had brought her into the world.

"Pedro, Renata, it's been a long time. How have you both been?" Jordana asked, her smile never wavering.

Pedro scowled. "You dare call us by our names? You are still our daughter, Jordana."

"No, Pedro. I am your Queen, and as such, I am allowed to call you whatever I choose."

Her father sputtered, his face turning red. Marcos slipped his arm around Jordana's waist and squeezed. "I have to agree with my Queen. She deserves your respect. After all, you were the one who insisted she be given the title."

Jordana had observed Pedro interact with Leo's father when he was still King. It always amazed her how Luiz bowed to Pedro's wishes as though he were the one in charge. Maybe Marcos's backbone was sterner. Or maybe the male was more ruthless than even she gave him credit for. Whichever was the case, she had to watch her back where both were concerned. Turning to her mother, Jordana asked, "Renata, are you still singing?"

Instead of answering, her mother asked, "What happened to you?"

"Your mate happened while you stood by and did nothing. You took the life I should have had with my own mate and tossed it away, and for what? Power I'm assuming, because it's an evil beast. Once you get a taste of it, it tempts you. Taunts you until you get more. Then? It consumes you until it's all you can think about." Jordana turned her attention to her father. "You wanted what Luiz had, but the throne has been in the Santos family for generations, so unless you took Luiz's head, you had to play a different game and insisted I marry Leo. What you failed to realize is I was the stronger of the two of us. Now it seems you're still playing a game without knowing the players. You might think you know Marcos, but you definitely don't know me."

Pedro pointed a claw at Marcos. "You and I have an agreement, so you should think carefully about how you proceed."

Marcos released his grip on Jordana's hip, pushing her behind him. "We did, and I got what I wanted out of that agreement. Jordana was right; you made the mistake of not knowing the players. Guards." Four of the guards stepped into the room, their swords at the ready. "I will allow your mate to walk away unharmed, but I'm afraid this is where we part ways, Pedro."

"Jordana, do something!" Renata cried.

"Can I get you some *Chimarrão*? Eliana made some since she knew it was your favorite."

"What? No, I don't want some damn *Chimarrão*. I want you to save your father. Marcos, please! We'll leave, and you'll never see us again."

"Shut up, Renata. I will not have you beg on my behalf. If this fucker thinks I'll cower before him, he's sorely mistaken." Pedro dropped to his knees with his arms spread. "Take my head, but know this – I have plans in place you're unaware of. When I don't return home, my attorney will go to the authorities, and you will spend your life in a human prison."

Marcos laughed. "He'll go to the authorities with what? You have no proof of our agreement. There is no paper trail."

Pedro sneered. "Do you take me for a fool? I recorded every interaction you and I ever had." He tapped the button on his suit coat. "Technology is amazing in this day and time."

Marcos held out his hand to the nearest guard for his weapon. When he gripped the sword, Marcos turned to Jordana. "If you do not wish to see this, you should return upstairs."

"Jordana! No!" Renata dropped to her knees in front of Pedro, but he pushed her aside.

"For the gods' sake, stop acting like an idiot."

Jordana almost felt sorry for her mother. If Marcos hadn't said he would let Renata go, she might have intervened. As it were, she shrugged and strode toward the steps with her mother screaming her name.

"No! Get your hands off me. Jordana!"

Jordana did turn to see Renata being held back by the unarmed guard. She should feel bad about what Marcos had planned, but Pedro had ruined Jordana's life. He was still interfering for his own gain with no consideration for her. She rushed up the stairs and closed the bedroom door behind her. She strode to the window and looked out. With Marcos busy, now would be the perfect time for her to escape. There were four guards downstairs, so that left three somewhere on the estate.

A flash of silver caught her eye, and Jordana peered into the waning daylight. When the male holding the blade stepped out of the shadows, her breath caught. "Lorenzo."

CHAPTER SIX

LOR AND CREW landed in São Paulo since it was more populous. Bryce rented two large SUVs, then they drove the rest of the way to Curitiba. Instead of hitting the estate immediately, they spent all day hiding out at *Mirante do Passaúna,* a large park heavily laden with trees. The group split up into pairs so anyone visiting wouldn't alert the police to ten large males strolling along the paths. More than once, Everett had to talk Lor off the ledge. His beast fought with Lor to go rescue Jordy instead of waiting until dusk.

Some ten hours later, Lorenzo was hidden in the shadows, ready to make a move. Lor and the other Goyles had waited until close to dark to move in on the estate, watching to see if the number of guards changed. He wanted to storm the house as soon as they arrived, but the others talked him down. When he stopped by the armory to retrieve the specially coated swords, Lor also picked up the communication devices Julian perfected for the Clan's use in patrolling Unholy. The comms were coming in handy as the ten of them were scattered around the property, and their targets were all Goyles as well.

The conversation inside shouldn't make sense, but it did. Jordana's father was still as ruthless as he had been a hundred years ago. He was still using his daughter as a pawn, or at least he was trying to. When Jordana's icy voice met Lor's ears, his beast wanted to roar. When Marcos called Jordana his Queen, Lor didn't know if he was referring to the fact that she still held the title as Leo's wife or if the male was claiming her as his own. Lor fisted his sword tighter. That didn't matter, or it wouldn't in the long run. By the end of the night, Marcos would be no more, and Jordana would be free.

Each was able to hear the conversation inside, and when Marcos called forth his guards, Bryce said, "Now." They had counted seven guards in total, and only three were watching the entrances.

Lor stepped out of the shadows, and movement in an upper window caught his attention. His breath caught. The female he remembered was gone. In her place was an older, more sophisticated version of his mate. She was looking right at him when her mouth moved. *"Lorenzo."* Jordana placed her palm on the window.

"Lor, are you with us? Lorenzo, check in," Gannon said.

"I'm here. I have eyes on Jordana."

"Perfect. You protect your mate. We'll handle the others," Bryce instructed. With the pilot having prior military experience, the rest of their group deferred to his expertise in leading the mission.

Before Lor could take a step, Jordana opened the window. "What are you doing?" he whispered, knowing she would hear him.

"Getting the hell out of here. Are you going to just stand there?" Jordana put one leg over the windowsill, not caring she was wearing a dress, and that was enough to break Lor out of his stupor. Before he took a step, Jordana was grabbed and pulled back into the room. A large male peered out the window and sneered.

"Oh, hell no." Lor released his wings, shredding his shirt, and took flight, praying the window opening was large enough to accommodate his size. Lor flew fast and true, retracting his wings at the last second. The guard backed up, and Lor yelled, "Jordy, run!" He made it through the opening, scraping his back, then tucked his head and rolled into a crouch. The guard had one arm around Jordana's neck and his blade pointing at Lor.

His beast pushed to the front, ready for battle. "Let her go," he seethed. "You'll not make it out of this house alive."

The guard frowned. "My King? Marcos said you were dead."

Lorenzo took advantage of the male's confusion. "As you can see, he lied. Let the Queen go. Now."

"Please forgive me." The male released Jordana, and she ran to Lor's side, but he pushed her behind him. Lorenzo strode forward. "On your knees." The male complied, still thinking Lorenzo was his brother. "No one threatens my mate." With one swift stroke, Lor took the male's head. When the body didn't immediately fall, Lor pushed it with his boot. As soon as he turned to check on Jordana, she rushed into his arms.

"I knew you'd come." Jordana grabbed Lor's head and pulled him down for a kiss. She didn't waste time shoving her tongue in his mouth, and Lor couldn't resist. He returned the passion as their mouths moved, tongues stroked, hands wandered. He had thought of this moment thousands of times, certain he would be able to keep her at arm's length, but what foolish thoughts those had been. She was his mate, and his beast was onboard with claiming her then and there. Lor hadn't been celibate over the years, but never had he allowed anyone to kiss him. He had used females in his younger days to try and forget the pain of losing his beloved. It hadn't worked, so he finally kept to himself, using only his hand to slake his needs.

Jordana leaned back, her hands stroking his beard. "You're really here. I—"

"Lor, Jordana is needed downstairs," Everett said through the comm. "We need to know how she wants to proceed with the staff as well as her mother."

Jordana leaned her forehead against his chest and sighed. "My mother can kick rocks, but I promised Eliana I would help her and Miguel. Lor, I—"

"We can talk later. For now, we have a mess to clean

up." Lor's heart was torn. All the years of heartache hadn't disappeared just because Jordy was in his arms, but she was his mate, and that trumped everything. Not able to stop himself, he kissed her forehead, then took her hand in his. He didn't have Dante's ability to push peace into others, but as with most Goyles, Lor could read Jordana's emotions. She was thrumming with adrenaline. Whether from being near him or the chaos inside the house, he didn't know. They followed the sound of a woman wailing, and when they reached her, she launched herself at Jordana, but Rasmus captured her around her waist, preventing her from taking another step.

"You could have stopped this! Now my mate is dead. How could you do that to your own father?"

Jordana's mood shifted from happy to furious. "He stopped being my father the day he threatened my mate. He took my life away, so you'll have to forgive me if I feel no remorse. As for you, you need to remember I am your Queen, and your life is now in my hands."

While Jordana chastised her mother, Lor took in the room. Two males without their heads were bleeding out on the carpet. Another two of Marcos's guards were slumped against a wall being watched over by Lor's team. A couple, presumably staff members, were huddled together on the sofa, the male holding the female closely. Lor assumed the rest of the guards were also dead like the one upstairs.

"My life is over! Your father was everything to me. Without him..." Renata choked on a sob. "I'll do as your father threatened and go to the human authorities. Queen or not, your life will be wrapped up in —"

Jordana slapped her mother hard enough to split her lip. Then, when Renata started to speak, she slapped her again. "I don't think so. You were aware of what Pedro was doing all this time. You're no better than he was. As far as I'm concerned, you committed treason by conspiring against the King. Now you're threatening the Queen."

Renata spit blood at Jordana's feet. "Considering that male" — Renata pointed at Fallon — "took Marcos's head, you are no longer Queen, unless you plan on whoring yourself out to him as well. I will ruin you. I have your father's money now, and there's nothing you can do to stop me from telling everyone that Diego—" Before any of the males could move, Jordana released her claws and slashed Renata's throat. Renata's eyes widened as she choked against the blood loss.

The female on the sofa screamed, and Jordana turned to the female. "I'm sorry you had to see that, Eliana." Jordana retracted her claws as she went to sit beside the other woman on the sofa. "I'm not usually one for violence." Jordy shrugged a shoulder.

Eliana pulled away from the male and wrapped an arm around Jordana's shoulder. "There's nothing to be sorry for. You forget I worked for your mother a lot of years. I know how she was, and her threat was not an idle one. She would have tried to ruin you. I do have to ask, what happens now?"

Fallon moved closer to Eliana and who Lor assumed was her mate. "As Renata said, I am now King. My name is Fallon Silvestri, and you are?" He gestured to the male.

"I am Miguel Sosa, and this is my mate, Eliana. We have been in the Callas's employ for fifty years, but Pedro gave us to Marcos as a gift."

Fallon rubbed the back of his neck. "I'm going to need help considering my Portuguese isn't very good. I probably should have thought about that before now. I would like to offer you both a position in my household. Just long enough to get my feet under me. I'll pay you handsomely for your assistance. If at any time you wish to leave, I won't stop you. I'm not sure what type of King Leonardo was, but I vow to you both, on my honor, I will do my best to be fair and honorable. It is how my King, Rafael, leads our people in the States, and I can only hope to be half the leader he is."

Eliana grabbed Jordana's hand. "What do you think, my Queen?"

"Since Fallon is now King, I am no longer Queen, so please, call me Jordana. And I think the choice is yours. You and Miguel deserve the retirement you mentioned earlier, but I also don't see the harm in helping Fallon for a bit. You might find you enjoy the kind of life I believe he will offer you in his home." Jordana turned to Fallon. "Speaking of… Now that you're King, I would be indebted to you if you allow Lor's mother to leave the estate."

Fallon fisted his chest and bowed his head. "No debt is required, Jordana. You are Lorenzo's mate, and it was my honor to assist in your rescue. As for his mother, she and your son are free to leave as well. Or they will be as soon as we get back to São Paulo, and I take the lay of the land. I'm going to need your help with that. Considering I have no idea who was on Marcos's side in taking down Leo."

"Maybe they can help with that," Lorenzo said, pointing toward the males sitting against the wall.

It was Bryce who pointed a sword at both captives and asked in perfect Portuguese, "How many in São Paulo were with Marcos?"

The one on the left answered, pointing at Fallon. "Why should we tell you? He'll just kill us anyway."

When Bryce translated, Fallon crossed the room to stand in front of them. "Not if you help me. Tell me how many we're up against, then go back with us to recount what happened here so everyone knows I am truly King. You do that, and you're both free to leave the country. But you will leave Brazil. If you step foot back into the territory, your lives are forfeit. Or say nothing and die right here. Your choice."

The male sitting on the right said, "There should be about twenty who were with Marcos. There were almost thirty of us, but you've taken out a handful of those today. I'll help you, my King."

"And you?" Fallon asked, pointing his blade at the other male.

He pulled his knee to his chest and wrapped his arms around his legs. "I'll help as well. I'm not ready to cross over just yet."

Fallon dropped his sword to his side. "Very well. Jordana, if you would, I'm going to need as much information about the estate as you can give. I'd like to have a viable plan in place before we storm the palace."

"Anything you need." Jordana turned to Lorenzo with a smile, but he held up a hand. Her smile faltered, but Lor wasn't ready to hear what she had to say to him. That would come later when they were alone. Lor had no idea whether or not he could let the past go as easily as she seemed to.

Fallon frowned at Lor. Lor got it. All Gargoyles wanted their fated mate, and Lorenzo was brushing his off. He needed to get their current situation resolved first. "Why don't we take a seat? Jordana can tell us everything she knows about the estate, and the two guards can fill in the blanks about who is part of Marcos's team as well as where they're located. I know it's late, but I'd rather have a plan in place sooner rather than later. I don't want my mother held against her will any longer than necessary."

"Agreed." Fallon turned to Miguel and Eliana. "I take it there's alcohol in the house?"

Eliana jumped up from the sofa. "Yes. I'll gather drinks for everyone. Also, there's plenty of food if anyone is hungry. I prepared a meal thinking tonight was going to be a quiet dinner. I would need a few minutes to get it reheated."

Fallon smiled at the cook. "I could eat. If you would, see to getting it ready, and we'll move the meeting to the dining room." Eliana bowed her head, then rushed out of the room with Miguel following. Turning back to the captured Goyles, Fallon instructed, "You two, get up." As they were standing, he continued, "Have a seat at the table." Everyone moved to the dining room, and Rasmus and Sully stood behind their prisoners instead of sitting with the others. Lor didn't think the males were stupid enough to try anything, but it was better to be safe with Jordana in the room. Speaking of, she took a seat and looked up at Lor. Hope was evident in her eyes, and by the gods, he stupidly sat next to her. He might not be sure of what their future held, if they even had a future, but if anyone was going to protect her, it was him.

EDEN TYPED FURIOUSLY at her keyboard. She had sent three of her best assassins, and not one of them had alerted her to a task completed. Tapping into the GPS on their phones, what she found made no sense. Two of the men showed to be at the New Atlanta Penitentiary while the third was still at the home of Gregor Stone. How fucking long did it take to shoot someone? Their orders had been to take the three targets out at home, not follow them to the prison.

Her patience had gone out the window hours ago, so she broke protocol and sent a text to their encrypted phones: *Report*

Not a minute later, Eden's phone rang, and she grabbed it up, ready to lay into the man on the other end of the line until she saw who was calling. "Shit." Eden hit "ignore" and let her father go to voicemail. She had promised to check in with him, but she had bigger issues to worry with at the moment other than assuring Nexus she was fine. She sent him a quick text, hoping it would assuage his worry for the time being.

Returning to her computer, Eden searched the area around both Rafael Stone's home as well as that of Dante Di Pietro. It took over an hour, but she found security feed at the latter's home. Cameras dotted the perimeter of his property. When she attempted to hack into the server the cameras were linked to, she hit a firewall. Eden shouldn't have been so smug, thinking this would be a walk in the park given her expertise. After an hour of getting nowhere, she slammed both palms on her keyboard. It was as though someone were on the other end blocking each move she made. Slumping in her chair, Eden blew her hair out of her eyes. She knew there were those out there as skilled as she was, but she hadn't come across them until dealing with the Stones.

Her father's words from their most recent conversation echoed in the back of her mind. *"Maybe you should give up, Eden. This woman is in prison for a reason. I don't want you to end up in a cell next to her."* But Eden had never backed down from a challenge, and she wouldn't start now. She checked the GPS on the assassins' phones and found they hadn't moved in the last hour.

Turning her attention back to her computer, she froze. Someone, presumably whoever had kept her from getting into the Di Pietro security feed, had typed out a message.

"I see you."

Eden pushed her chair back from the desk hard enough to send it toppling. She looked around, searching for any sign of a camera. No one should know she was there in the rental house she leased under an assumed name. Even her father had no idea where she was. She spent the next half hour tearing vent covers off, checking the windows and doorways, looking into every nook and cranny where a camera could be hidden. Frustrated didn't begin to describe Eden when she came up empty. She wasn't using a laptop. There were no cameras on her computer equipment, so whoever sent the message must have not meant they could see her literally. But she had been careful to cover her tracks. Her IP address pinged in thousands of cities across the globe. Even if her assassins had been caught, they had no idea where she was. They didn't know her identity, only that the contract came through Nexus. "Fuck!"

Eden grabbed her phone and listened to her father's voicemail.

"Do you realize what you've done? I told you this had better not blow back on the company, and that's exactly what's happened. At this moment, the GIA is crawling around the Paris house. You need to stop this shit now, Eden. I know you think you love this woman, but I won't have you ruin my life's work anymore than you already have."

"No, no, no!" Eden drew back to throw her phone, but at the last second, she tossed it on the desk. Breaking it would only cause her more trouble. Her father's words pissed her off. She didn't think she was in love – she knew it. He'd asked her more than once if her feelings were returned. She never told her father the truth of her meeting with Kallisto. How they'd only spent one long weekend together. She had no doubt he would berate her for being foolish, even though he and her mother had fallen in love just as quickly.

Eden strode into the tiny kitchen and grabbed a bottle of wine. She rarely drank, but she deserved a little something to take the edge off. How in the fuck had the Global Intelligence Agency found out about Nexus? There was nothing in her father's house in Paris linking him to their company. They were both too smart for that, but somehow the Agency had come across James's name. That didn't bode well for either of them, because if her father was in their crosshairs, it was only a matter of time until they searched for her as well.

"I see you."

Fuck! Eden's life was imploding. Was Kallisto worth risking everything for? Setting the wine back down, there was only one way to find out. She needed to talk to her lover. Going to the prison was too risky. Eden couldn't show her face. Not yet. She went back to the office and opened a new, prepaid phone. Calling would be risky, too, but she had to know if what she was doing, what she had already done, was worth the cost of losing not only Nexus but her father's love as well. After finding the phone number for the prison, she dialed. When it rang, Eden held her breath.

"New Atlanta Penitentiary. How may I direct your call?" a deep voice answered.

"I'd like to speak to one of your inmates. Kallisto Vargas."

"She... Hold please." The line went silent. There was no crappy elevator music filling the void. Eden pulled the phone away from her ear to make sure the call hadn't been dropped. She paced the small room while she waited. Three minutes and forty-seven seconds later, the man picked back up. "If you'll give me your name and number, I'll have the inmate return your call in about five minutes. It'll take that long to have her moved from her cell."

Shit. She should have expected it wouldn't be easy. There was no way she was giving them her name, and even if they did have the number, they wouldn't be able to trace it. "My name is Eve, and she can call me back at this number." Eden rattled off the digits, thanked the man, then disconnected. She bit the side of her thumb while she waited. Five minutes. Three hundred little seconds and she would hear the voice she'd longed for all these years.

CHAPTER SEVEN

"DID YOU GET that?" Deacon asked Julian.

"I got it. It's a burner phone, but go ahead and let Kallisto return the call. Nobody is supposed to know she's at the Pen, so we need to find out who this Eve is and what she wants. Keep this line open while they speak, and I'll record it."

"Ten-four." Deacon put his phone in the front pocket of his shirt, turning the face toward his chest so Kallisto wouldn't see it was lit up. He made his way to the room she lived in and knocked on the door before unlocking it and stepping inside. "Come with me."

"What's going on?" the blonde asked.

"You had a phone call. Someone named Eve. You're supposed to call her back."

"Eve?" Kallisto frowned.

"It's what she said, but if you don't know anyone by that name—"

Kallisto snapped her fingers. "Eve, of course. I've been down here so long she slipped my mind. I'd love to speak to her." Deacon knew the female was lying, but he pretended otherwise. He held out a pair of handcuffs, and Kallisto rolled her eyes. "Are those really necessary?" They both knew they weren't, but Deacon wasn't feeling generous.

"You either wear them, or you can sit your ass back down."

Kallisto huffed, but she held her arms in front of her. Deacon snapped a cuff around her right wrist before turning her none too gently and tugging her left arm behind her. He urged her toward the door, then led her upstairs to a conference room. Once inside, he pulled out a chair, and Kallisto scowled at him. Deacon unlocked one of the cuffs, freeing her arms. He set the paper with the phone number in front of her, then stood off to the side.

"What? No privacy?"

"You know as well as I do I can hear the conversation from down the hall, so no. I'm staying right here." He leaned against the wall and crossed his arms over his chest. When Kallisto stared at the phone, he said, "Press one, wait for the tone, then dial the number."

Kallisto put the receiver to her ear and did as instructed. It only rang once before the other woman answered.

"Kallisto?"

"Yes, it's me."

"Oh, thank god. It's so good to hear your voice."

"Yours too, uh, Eve." Kallisto cut her eyes to Deacon, but he kept his gaze at the wall over the female's shoulder.

"Sorry about that. I didn't want to give them—"

"So, how've you been? And how exactly did you find me?" Kallisto asked, cutting the female off.

"When you didn't call me, I figured you needed time, so I gave it to you. It took a while to track you down, but after the weekend we spent together, I couldn't let you go."

"Our weekend… Eden?" Kallisto whispered.

"Of course it's me. I've missed you, baby."

Kallisto sucked in a breath, her eyes once again cutting in Deacon's direction. This time, he arched an eyebrow, and she turned her back on him.

"Kallisto? Are you there?"

"Yeah, I'm here. Listen, Eden, I'm not sure why you're calling."

"Like I said, I missed you. I had hoped you felt the same."

"That was a long time ago, and like I told you back

then, it couldn't be more than what we had that weekend."

"You can't tell me you didn't feel it, Kally. What we shared was special. I fell in love with you the moment I laid eyes on you. I want to spend our lives together. Tell me you want that too. Please."

Deacon almost felt bad for the other female. She obviously didn't know who Kallisto Vargas was or what she had been caught up in with her father.

Kallisto cradled her head in her free hand. "You know where I am, Eden. I'm not getting out of here anytime soon, so you need to forget about me. Get on with your life."

"Yes, I know where you are, and I also know who put you there, the bastards. I have a plan to get you out. We can be together. I have money. We can disappear—"

"Eden," Kallisto hissed. "They can hear you. They aren't human," she whispered. Deacon raced across the room. Just before he reached the phone, Kallisto rushed out, "Sorry, time's up." Kallisto slammed the receiver down, then stood and put her arms behind her back.

Deacon cuffed her wrists together. "That was a mistake."

Kallisto shrugged a shoulder. "I think it's time the world knew what type of monsters are hiding in their midst. Besides, it's not like I'm ever getting out of here."

Deacon pushed Kallisto down the hallway leading back to her room. After that stunt, he was sorely tempted to put her in a regular cell and take away her comforts. He waited until he had her secure in her room before pulling his phone out and asking Julian, "Did you get all that?"

"Yes. We have a female, Eden, who figured out where Kallisto is. She was smart enough to use a burner phone. This woman isn't someone to be overlooked, Deacon. I have a bad feeling about this."

"What are you thinking?"

"She said she knew who put Kallisto in the Pen. That would be Rafael. Gregor was warden at the time, and Dante worked there when they needed a doctor. Those are the three someone put a hit on. Coincidence?"

"Not likely," Deacon responded.

"I'm thinking this is a woman intent on freeing her one true love. It didn't sound as though Kallisto felt the same, but it could have been an act for your benefit."

Deacon rested his shoulder against the wall. "I don't think so. She seemed truly surprised."

"Either way, Eden said she knew who put Kallisto behind bars, and considering the hit on Rafael, Gregor, and Dante didn't go the way it was supposed to, I'd say someone is getting desperate. I think our mysterious hacker just tipped her hand. You need to make sure the Pen is locked down tight. No one gets in who doesn't work there. No visitors for a while. I'll call Frey and fill him in."

"What about the fact that Kallisto told her we aren't human?"

"That's the least of our worries. She has no proof, and if she were to tell someone, who would believe her?"

"Yeah, you're probably right."

"Be safe, Deacon, because I think the shit on the fan is soon going to be slung off."

Deacon peered through the small window into Kallisto's room. She was sitting at the small desk with a book in front of her, but after watching for a full minute, she hadn't turned a page. Deacon wondered if Kallisto was thinking about her weekend with Eden or if she was imagining being sprung from her cell. Julian was right; security needed to be tightened. He made his way to the communication room to begin just that.

JORDANA WAS BONE tired. Weary. Both her parents were dead, her mother by Jordana's own hand. She should be elated. After a hundred years, she had her mate in her life, but it wasn't the happy reunion she'd imagined. Lorenzo had kissed her back when she threw herself at him, but now? Now he acted as though they were strangers. They were; she knew this, but damnit, she didn't want them to be. She wanted to get to know the male he'd grown into. Know what he looked like in the early morning light with sleep heavy in his eyes. What he sounded like when he was balls-deep inside her. Know what his dreams were for the rest of their long lives. That wouldn't happen if she didn't find a way to be alone with him. Something Lorenzo made sure didn't happen.

They spent part of the night planning what would happen when they arrived in São Paulo. Eliana had been a godsend, keeping them fed and full of drink. After taking care of the many bodies, the males sat around the dining table hashing out the best way to handle Fallon announcing he was now King as well as getting those who had sided with Marcos to bend the knee. If that had been Lorenzo's father or Marcos, there would be no negotiations. Of that Jordana was certain. They would go in swords swinging. But Fallon made a good point when he said if he wanted his new Clan to see him as fair, he needed to give the males a shot at falling in line first.

It was the middle of the night when Lorenzo texted his mother and told her the gist of what had gone down, letting her know help was on its way. That was one of the few times he spoke directly to Jordana. He had asked her where Francisca's room was. Lor was familiar with the layout considering it had been his home in his early days. He avoided asking about her life with Leo. He never once mentioned his brother. She knew why. Lor felt Leo was the enemy, and in a way, he had been. Leonardo had stolen Lorenzo's mate, even if it hadn't been his idea. Jordana didn't know if Lor would ever forgive her, but he hadn't let her down when she needed him most, so she held out hope he would eventually let her explain the last hundred years. When she told him the truth, maybe he would be able to let go of the past.

One of the things Fallon asked her to do was to contact her father's lawyer. Instead of admitting how they actually died, Fallon came up with a plausible tale. One in which Marcos had slain both Pedro and Renata. It had seemingly been his plan anyway. Miguel and Eliana agreed to the story. Neither one held any loyalty to Jordana's parents, not after the way they had been treated. With Jordana being their only child, she didn't know if she would inherit their assets. Not that she wanted them. But with Diego no longer being heir to the throne, she would offer him and Francisca whatever homes she was given, if that were the case, because Jordana didn't intend on staying in Brazil a second longer than necessary. She planned to follow Lorenzo back to the States. She would wait as long as it took for him to give her a chance.

"Are you ready?"

Jordana turned from the window and smiled. She couldn't help it. Lorenzo was her mate whether he acknowledged her or not. "Yes. I want to get this over with so we—"

"The others are waiting." Lorenzo turned and left the room without another word. Jordana sighed and hung her head. She had her work cut out for her, but as she tried to tell him, she was eager to put the past behind her and see what her – their – future held. She grabbed her luggage, having packed what she had unpacked less than two days before. Jordana had no intention of ever setting foot in the house again.

"Here, let me get those," Miguel offered. He didn't give her a chance to argue, taking both suitcases and gesturing for her to precede him down the stairs.

When Jordana reached the living room, Gannon and Everett were the only two males there. Everett walked over and opened the front door. "They're waiting for you outside." Jordana muttered a thank you and walked out into the dark. Fallon wanted to arrive in São Paulo before the bulk of the guards were fully awake, thus leaving at two. The new King stood next to an SUV holding the passenger door open. She looked around for Lorenzo and noticed he was already seated in a different vehicle. "Sorry about that," Fallon said. "He's a stubborn one."

Jordana waited until they were both buckled in to respond. "Yes, but he has nothing on me. I have waited a hundred years for Lor to come back into my life." She stared out the side window as the estate disappeared and the road leading to São Paulo came into view. Fallon didn't attempt to make small talk with her. He and Rasmus chatted about how Fallon's life was going to change now that he was King. His biggest hurdle would be the language barrier. Miguel and Eliana agreed to interpret for him, and he readily agreed. Jordana thought he was brave for trusting the couple when he'd only met them the night before, but she had a good feeling about them and had told Fallon as much when he asked her opinion. She had only just met them as well, but knowing they had endured her parents for so long, Jordana was willing to give them the benefit of the doubt.

As far as plans went, the one Fallon and the others came up with was sound as far as Jordana was concerned. The two males they captured were gathering Marcos's other followers as soon as they arrived. Jordana wanted to go to Francisca, but she was part of the plan. She was there to bear witness to what happened in Curitiba as well as act as translator. It didn't hurt that Bryce also spoke the language. The pilot was ex-military and carried himself as such.

As discussed, the two captives strolled into the estate like they belonged there with Fallon and Bryce at their sides. Once all Marcos's men were gathered, Jordana and the others joined them.

"My name is Fallon Silvestri." Fallon paused for

Jordana to translate. Most everyone spoke English as well as their native tongue, but there were a few older Goyles who never bothered. "Marcos Diaz is dead by my hand, making me the new King." When Jordana spoke the words in Portuguese, the air turned dark as Marcos's followers began rumbling between them. Fallon gestured for the two captives to step forward, and once they told what they witnessed, the followers calmed down. "I understand Marcos promised you large sums of money to help overthrow Leonardo. Here's what I propose; I will pay each of you five hundred thousand reais. The money will be transferred into your accounts today. You'll then pack your belongings and leave Brazil. Should you return, I'll take your head the same way I took Marcos's."

"That's not enough. Marcos promised two million each," one of the followers said in English.

"That's my offer. Take it and leave, or I take your head. Your choice."

"If you think you can best me, you can try." The male puffed out his chest, but the male next to him grabbed his arm.

"Shut up. He bested Marcos," his buddy whispered harshly. Bryce translated for both males.

"Are you challenging me?" Fallon asked, reaching behind his head to grip the sword strapped to his back.

"Fuck. No, just give me my money so I can get out of here."

"One more thing," Jordana interrupted. "Where is Diego?"

The one who told his pal to shut up offered up where Diego was being held. After being given the location, Jordana instructed one of her loyal guards to retrieve Diego while the meeting adjourned to her office. Being Queen, she was privy to the financial side of things. Leo hated dealing with money and had tasked Jordana with it early on. While Jordana transferred the money over to each male's account,

Lor went to check on his mother. Jordana had wanted to be with Lorenzo when he went to see Francisca, but he let her know her presence wasn't needed.

"You have a job to do, and you probably want to spend time with your son." Lorenzo's tone was harsh, and Jordana's heart shredded even more at his dismissal. She needed Lor to know the truth, but she couldn't tell him what she'd done all those years ago until they were alone. If she ever managed to get him to spend more than thirty seconds in a room with her without someone else acting as chaperone.

It took over an hour for the money transfers for those leaving to go through, and in that time, Lorenzo didn't return. Fallon and Lor's friends made sure everyone packed their belongings and left the estate. Rasmus, Everett, and Gannon agreed to remain in Brazil for the time being to help Fallon acclimate to his new role.

Jordana was reunited with Diego. She told him of the past few days and how he and his grandmother would be free to leave the estate if they so chose after she settled her parents' affairs.

"What about you?" he asked.

"After I get the accounts transferred over to Fallon, I have to call my parents' attorney and see about getting all their assets turned over to me. Once that's done, we'll have plenty of money. If you wish to remain here with Fallon, I'm sure he'd love to have you in his guard, but your future is wide open. You can go anywhere, do anything you'd like. But first, I need to make that phone call. How about you go check on your grandmother? I know she's been worried sick about you. Once my business is finished here, I'll come find you."

Diego hugged Jordana tightly, kissing her temple. "I love you, *Mai*."

"And I love you. Now go." Jordana watched as he strode out of the office. Her heart was sad as it always was whenever she thought too closely about their relationship. Every time he called her mother, she checked her emotions. Tamped down the fear. Shaking herself, Jordana contacted her parents' attorney with the news of their deaths. If she did nothing else for Diego Santos, it would be to set him up for a future of his choosing.

The attorney's assistant put her on hold, and after almost a minute, he came on the line. "Jordana? This is unexpected. What can I do for you?" The male didn't refer to her by her title. That in itself told her where his loyalties lay.

"There's no easy way to say this, so I'll get right to the point. My parents are dead."

"*Meu Deus*! Are you sure?"

"Positive. I was there when it happened. They were both slain by Marcos Diaz."

"Diaz? But he and your father... This is terribly upsetting. Pedro and I were more than attorney and client. We were friends." Jordana didn't offer her sympathy to the man. If he knew how she truly felt, he might not be eager to help. "I realize you are Queen, but you will understand when I say I'm going to need proof of their crossing over before I begin to settle their estate."

"If you'll give me an email address, I'll forward a photo to you. If that won't suffice, I can take you to the bodies. They're at the estate in Curitiba. The one my father offered to Diaz in exchange for his treason against my husband."

"Treason is a harsh word, Jordana. In our world, leadership changes hands with challenges. You know this."

"I am well aware of our ways, but you'll have to forgive me if I disagree. It was my husband who was slain after all."

"But he wasn't your mate. You spared no love for the male."

"Do not pretend to know my feelings based off whatever fallacies my father offered you. I was with Leo a century. I gave him a son. None of that is here and now.

90

There is a new King, and he has been gracious enough to allow me to remain at my home until my parents' estate is settled. The sooner that is handled, the sooner my son and I can get on with our lives."

"Marcos is letting you leave? I thought…" Rocha cleared his throat, catching the fact that he was about to admit to being privy to the deal Marcos made with Pedro.

"Oh, did I forget to tell you? Marcos is also dead." Jordana ignored the attorney's gasp and continued. "Fallon Silvestri from the States somehow caught wind of the plot against Leo. He arrived too late to save my parents, but he did save me from a miserable existence with Marcos. Now, is there anything further you need?"

"I do have to ask what you want to do about your father's various businesses."

"I'm only interested in the cash and properties right now. Send me the prospectuses on those, and I'll look them over later. For now, I'm sure each one has a CEO in place to continue until I make those decisions. Or, if there is a board of directors in place, they can do with it what they will. For now, I would ask you to begin the process of switching over the assets."

"I'll begin right away. Give me your email address and I'll send the forms you need to sign. There's no need for you to come to my office. The process will take approximately two weeks, but I'll do what I can to get everything changed over before that time."

"Thank you. I'll be sure to mention your cooperation to the new King." They exchanged email addresses, then Jordana disconnected and sat back in her chair. "One problem down, one more to go."

CHAPTER EIGHT

KAYA PERCHED ON the edge of the sofa, tears pricking her vision as she watched Tessa play with Sebastian. She wanted so badly to be on the floor with her son, but her hips wouldn't allow it. Tessa sat cross-legged, encouraging Bas to scoot to her on his bottom. Usually, the action had Kaya laughing at his antics, but today, all she could do was smile and wipe the moisture from her cheeks. And of course, that was when Rafael entered the room. More than likely, he felt her sadness and came to check on her. Damn Gargoyle bond. Kaya was grateful to be alive. Thankful she was able to walk. Thankful she was strong enough to carry her child and tend to all his needs. Mostly. If not being able to play with him on the floor was the worst of it...

"Andrea?" a male voice called out.

Tessa jumped to her feet. "Manny! I'm in here." She was met by an older man who pulled Tessa into his arms, hugging her tightly. "I thought you and Larry were on vacation," Tessa said when she pulled back far enough to see the man's face.

"We were, but when your mother called and told me you and Greystone would be hiding out here, I couldn't stay away. Speaking of... where is your mate?"

"In the kitchen with Myra. She's teaching him how to make macarons." Tessa hooked her arm through Manny's. "Come on. We'll go say hello." When they reached the doorway, Tessa asked, "Where is that fine husband of yours?"

Kaya admired Tessa for having so many in her life who

adored her, even if they insisted on calling her Andrea. Kaya had the mates, another thing she was thankful for, so why did she feel so jealous? Rafael sat next to her, taking her hands in his larger ones.

"Talk to me, Love."

"It's stupid. I have everything I could ever want in you and Bas."

"But?"

"I'm just feeling sorry for myself. Instead of being able to sit on the floor with him, I had to watch Tessa play with him. And she's got this big family who loves her. Not just the Clan, but both her parents and a brother. Even Manny and his husband rushed home from vacation to be with her." Kaya hadn't spoken to her own mother since her birthday, and that phone call had been awkward. "Like I said, it's stupid."

"It's not. You're allowed to feel whatever you're feeling. I can't say I know what it's like to be an only child, but I do know the loss of parents. And yes, your mother is alive, but you lost her when she moved. You really lost her before that. I remember you saying she couldn't abide you becoming a cop. As for sitting on the floor, you'll get there. And if you don't, Bas is growing so fast he'll be climbing on the sofa with you before you know it."

As if summoned, Sebastian scooted closer to the sofa, his arms waving toward Kaya. How could she stay melancholy when her son was so cute? Kaya lifted him onto her lap, and she snuggled her face into his neck, eliciting squeals of delight. Kaya laughed along with him. She turned her smile to Rafael. "No more pity party. This right here, the two of you, are all I need."

"Don't forget Seven. If our visions were correct, Bas will have a little sister. And who knows? They might end up with more siblings later."

Kaya grinned. "Seven. I think we might need to come up with an official name and let that be her nickname."

"I agree, but I somehow doubt Bas is going to call her anything other than Seven."

Kaya kissed Bas's sweet face. "I'm okay with that. I can already imagine the fierce older brother. With you for a father, he's going to be a force."

"He is, but it's also because you're his momma. Like I told you in Italy, your love is what will give him his true strength. Anyone can learn to wield a sword, but he needs your strength and guidance with the harder parts of life." Rafael sat closer, putting his arm around them both. "You, my mate, are the strongest being I know, and I am so fucking proud you are my Queen."

"Hear, hear," Dante said. Kaya hadn't heard him and Isabelle enter the room. "Pardon us for interrupting, but I couldn't help but overhear part of your conversation." Dante fisted a hand over his heart. "I'm not sure I've said this, but I am proud to call you my Queen, Kaya. You are the backbone of our Clan. You came to us at a low point in our lives, and you gave us hope. Then you gave us an ass-kicking when we needed it. You never back down when we need to hear logic. Your heart is pure, your ethics are strong, and your will to overcome adversity from your injuries has been nothing short of awe-inspiring. With you leading our children, I have no doubt the next generation is going to rule the world, not just our Clan."

Kaya didn't bother wiping the tears. There were too many, but they were the good, cleansing kind. Dante's words broke through the sadness she'd felt minutes before thinking she didn't have family. She did, and in that moment, she vowed to never take them for granted.

LORENZO FOUND HIS mother in the west wing of the estate, right where Jordana said she'd be. As soon as Francisca saw him, she jumped to her feet and ran to him, wrapping him in her arms. Lor allowed her to gush over him, even though he wasn't as happy to see her as she was him. Old wounds ran deep, and being around Jordana had split this one open wide.

"I can't believe you're really here." Francisca cradled his cheeks in her hands as she studied his face. "You look so much like—"

"It's over now." Lor stepped back out of her reach. "Fallon is the new King, but he's a good male. He'll give the three of you time to get your affairs in order before asking you to move on."

"What about Jordana?"

"She'll more than likely inherit her parents' money and properties. From what I understand, they were beyond rich, so she and Diego will be set for life. Fallon will surely be generous in giving you a stipend to settle somewhere else."

"And what about you?"

"I'll go back home. I did what I came here for. What you asked of me. Being here changes nothing else."

Francisca scowled. "It changes everything. She is your mate. You can't let this opportunity pass you by."

"I've spent my whole life without her through no fault of my own. She could have left Leo at any point in the last hundred years, but she didn't. She remained by his side, bore him a son, and only now that Leo's dead and she needed my help did she reach out. Doesn't say a lot about how much *she* valued our bond."

"It wasn't like that. She had no choice," Francisca argued.

"She might not have had a choice in the beginning, but she could have called me at any time afterward, and I'd have come for her."

"But Jordana—"

"Jordana made her choice, and it wasn't me. I have a life, a family back in New Atlanta. They need me. Jordana will inherit her family's money and assets. She has you and her son." Lorenzo swallowed hard. Maybe if Diego weren't in the picture, Lor could have found it in his heart to forgive her, but she had slept with his brother. Lived with him as his wife.

"You're still my son, whether you forgive me or not. I lost one son, and I don't want to lose another."

"You lost me a long time ago." Lorenzo wanted to take the words back when his mother blanched. "Look, you say you didn't have a choice. That Jordy didn't either. Maybe that was true in the beginning, but what about after Luiz crossed over? He was no longer around to tell you what to do. Or did Leo step into his father's shoes and demand you both remain by his side? If so, I feel even less remorse for his slaying."

"You bastard!"

Lorenzo turned to see who was cursing him. It had to be Diego. Lor could see the resemblance to Leo, to himself, but what he couldn't see was anything of Jordana in him. Diego might have the same bright blue eyes and curling brown hair, but he was not a large male. Both Leo and Jordana were tall, but Diego stood several inches shorter than six feet. What he lacked in height and breadth, he made up for in fire.

His nephew strode up to Lor, getting in his face. "Get out. Leave and don't come back."

"Diego, no," Francisca cried.

"It's okay, *Mai*. I was leaving anyway." Lorenzo bent and kissed his mother on the cheek, then pushed past the reminder that his Jordy had betrayed him.

"Lorenzo, please," his mother begged, but Lor kept walking. He didn't stop until he was outside where he could breathe easier. Fallon, with Bryce acting as interpreter, was talking to a group of guards. When he caught sight of Oakley and Pax, Lor strode to where they were.

"I'm ready to get out of here. How long is Bryce

staying?" If the pilot didn't plan on leaving soon, Lor would catch a commercial flight home.

"He was waiting on you. Miguel is ready to take over translating."

Bryce turned their way, having caught their conversation with his shifter hearing as had all the males within earshot. Lorenzo wasn't used to everyone being a shifter. Back home, the human mates and kids outnumbered the Gargoyles. At least it felt that way most days.

Fallon excused himself and Bryce, and the two walked over to where Lor was waiting. "I'm surprised you're leaving so soon. I thought you'd want to get reacquainted with your family."

Lor scowled at Fallon. "No. I came to rescue the Queen and save the Prince. I did that, and now I'm ready to be home." Fallon glanced over Lor's shoulder. Lor didn't have to turn to know Jordana was standing somewhere behind him. He could feel her as surely as he could his own heart beating in his chest.

"Bryce, if you're ready, then so am I. If not, I'll head to the airport and catch a commercial flight."

"Are you sure about this?" Bryce asked.

"Yes." Lorenzo was certain he had to get away from his mate before he succumbed to the pull. Maybe he should take a page out of Hunter's book and release Jordana.

Don't be so fucking hasty.

You shut up. You know what she did to us.

And you know why. She didn't have a choice. You should give her a chance to explain her side of things.

She slept with Leo. Gave him a son. That's unforgivable.

Is it really?

"Lor?" Bryce waved a hand in front of his face.

"Sorry. I was having a little chat with my beast."

Bryce grinned. "Arguing more than likely. They think they know better. Ungh." Bryce shook his head. "And mine just tried to bitch-slap me. I'm ready when you are."

Fallon held out his hand to Lor. When Lorenzo clasped it, Fallon said, "Don't worry. I'll take care of your family."

Lorenzo's Goyle growled, but Lor ignored the beast. "I'm sure they'll be fine. Congratulations again on becoming King. I know you'll make a fine one."

Rasmus, Gannon, and Everett decided to remain in Brazil. Rasmus to assist Fallon in his transition, and the other two to vacation for a while. Lorenzo expected Jordana to chase after him. His beast hoped she would, but she didn't. She did remain in the doorway, watching him walk away.

See? She doesn't really care that we're leaving. If she did—

How many times would you want to be turned away?

No. Lorenzo wouldn't think about her feelings. She had never cared about his. Without looking back, Lor made his feet keep moving steadily, even though his heart was breaking all over again.

"STUBBORN MALE." JORDANA wanted nothing more than to run after her mate and demand he listen, but his pride demanded he walk away from her. She got it. Didn't mean she liked it. For now, she would let him go. She had things to take care of in Brazil before she could go after him. Once Lorenzo and the others were out of sight, Jordana went in search of Diego and Francisca. They had things to discuss. When she got to her mother-in-law's suite, she found the older female crying, and Diego was making it worse.

"It's for the best. He turned his back on the family, and what he said about Papa was unforgivable."

Jordana could only imagine what Lor had said about Leo. "Diego, stop," she chastised. When he rounded on her, she held up her hand. "No. You don't know the whole story, only the version your father told you." Jordana pushed past him to kneel beside Francisca. She cradled the older female's hands in her own. "I've spoken to Pedro's attorney. It will take a couple weeks at least, but he assured me all my parents' assets will be turned over to me as their only child. Fallon has agreed to allow you and Diego to remain here as long as needed, but the house in Curitiba will be available once I have it cleaned. The two of you can move there if you wish. Or you can take the money and move somewhere new."

"What about you?" Diego crossed his arms over his chest, his face furious.

"I'm going to the States and talk to your uncle."

"Why would you do that?" Diego asked. "Lorenzo is an ass."

Jordana stood and faced her son. "It's time you knew the truth. How about we take a walk and let your grandmother rest?"

Diego shifted from one foot to the other. He was gearing up for a fight, and she needed him calm. It was Francisca who managed to get him to listen. "Your mother is right. You need the truth, and you need to listen to what she has to say without interruption. Can you do that for me?"

Diego's gaze softened. He and Francisca had always been close. Being the only grandchild meant she had doted on him his whole life. "For you, anything." Diego kissed his grandmother's cheek, then followed Jordana from the room.

"Let's go to the garden. It should be quiet there now." With Fallon being introduced to everyone at the estate, the garden in the back of the property was vacant. Jordana led Diego to a bench beside a pond, the place she found herself most often when she wanted time alone to think. Diego crossed his arms over his chest, looking anywhere but at Jordana. She patted the seat next to her, and he sat but kept his gaze on something in the distance.

"When I was twenty, I found my mate."

"I know this. You married my father."

99

"No, Diego. Please just listen. Your father was not my mate."

He snapped his gaze her way then. "But—"

Jordana placed her fingers against his lips. "No. Leo was not my mate; Lorenzo is." Diego's eyebrows shot up, but Jordana continued. "He was younger. He had just transitioned into his Goyle, and my beast recognized he was our intended. I was elated. I knew I would have to wait for him to age a few years before we could be together, but what's a few years in our long lives? Except your grandfather and my father had other ideas. They were both of the mind that I would be the perfect Queen for Leo. Since I was the only unmated female they knew of in Brazil, they decided I would marry Leo knowing Lorenzo was my mate. They didn't care. It was all about bringing two powerful families together."

Jordana clasped her hands in her lap. "I begged, threatened, and even ran away, only to be brought back by your grandfather's guards. Then I was threatened. Only they used Lorenzo's life as the bargaining chip. Either I marry Leo, or they kill my mate. In that moment, I hated everyone, your father included. We were married, and when we returned here, Lorenzo was gone. I had promised him I would find a way to be together, but I understood him not wanting to stay here and watch as Leo and I lived as husband and wife. Your father made a deal with me. Stay with him long enough to give him an heir, and he would give me a divorce. He felt remorse in the beginning. He understood the mate bond. Understood that my heart belonged to his brother. At first, I refused. How could I allow another male to touch me? Back then there were no cell phones. No computers. I had no way of knowing where Lorenzo was. Where he had gone. If he were still alive. Years went by, and he never returned. I was despondent. Angry. So damn angry. But eventually, I caved and began trying for a child."

Jordana treaded the topic carefully. She would tell Diego the truth but not all of it. "Fast forward to you being born, and technology had become a thing. Your grandmother, as much as she loved Leo, missed her youngest son. She came to me and begged me to help find Lorenzo. What she didn't know was I had already begun searching. What I didn't know was Lorenzo had been doing research of his own. He contacted Francisca. She was overjoyed at hearing his voice, but she didn't realize that by telling him how wonderful things were here, she pushed him further away. He took my giving your father an heir as the ultimate betrayal and told her to lose his number."

Jordana brushed a wavy lock off Diego's forehead. "One day, you'll find your own mate, and maybe then you'll understand better."

Diego's shoulders slumped. "So much makes sense now. Like how you and Papa were never affectionate and why you kept separate bedrooms. Did you ever love him?"

"No. I tolerated him for your sake."

"Why didn't you leave? And please don't say because of me." Diego turned and grasped her hands. Jordana blinked back the tears threatening to fall. Before she could answer, he said, "I love you. You've been the best mother a son could ask for, but I want you to be happy. You did your part as Queen, but like you told me, with your family's money, we can go and do whatever we want. I don't have to ask what you want. I can hear it in your voice."

"What do you want? Do you wish to stay here and be part of Fallon's guard? It's what you've been training for."

"No. I only did what Papa expected of me. Truthfully, I'd like to go to college. Maybe travel a bit. I'll take *Avó* with me so she doesn't waste away from grief. Then in a few years when you've managed to get Lorenzo's head out of his ass, I'll come visit. Who knows? I might enjoy America. Might find my own mate there."

"You're amazing, you know that?" Jordana whispered.

"I get it from you." Diego bumped his shoulder against hers before sliding his arm around her. He wasn't as tall as she was, so it was slightly awkward, but she leaned into him all the same. They spent another hour chatting about his future, but Jordana's mind was on her mate and how she was going to get him to talk to her. To give her a chance to make things right. Jordana had a long life ahead of her, and if it took hundreds of years, she would get Lorenzo to give her that chance.

CHAPTER NINE

WHEN LOR ARRIVED back in New Atlanta, he drove straight to Frey's home. He needed the familiarity of friends and the comfort of children. Not that Pax and Oakley weren't friends, but Lor wasn't as close to them as he was Frey and his family. Oakley headed to the Pen after calling Deacon, and Pax said he was going to the station even though he wasn't on duty. Lor understood wanting to keep busy. Without mates to distract them, they used their time keeping their Clan, their city, safe.

We have a mate.

Lor ignored his beast. It was all Lor could do to keep his shifter under control as they left Brazil. It had been decades since he and his inner beast were so at odds. When he first left home, it had been close to impossible to remain in control. Having only just transitioned, Lorenzo didn't have his family to help guide him through the intricacies of dealing with the shifter side. The longer he was gone, the farther away from Jordy he got, the easier it became. After a while, the beast settled down, practically ignoring Lor. But now, having been in Jordy's presence, inhaling her scent, feeling her in his arms, his shifter was pissed.

Even with the two-hour time difference, it was late when Lor pulled into the driveway. Lor sat in his car until Frey opened the front door wearing nothing but sleep pants and motioned for him to come inside.

"I'm sorry to come by so late, but I didn't want to go home to an empty house."

"I get it. Do you want to talk?" Frey rubbed his chest.

Lor had clearly woken the male.

"We can do that tomorrow. You should go back to your mate."

"You're welcome to the guest room if you're ready to sleep. If not, help yourself to whatever you want. Abbi put leftovers in the fridge."

"Thanks, Brother."

Frey left Lor to his own devices with a clap on the shoulder. He wasn't ready to go to bed, so he ambled to the kitchen for some of Abbi's cooking. Lor wasn't all that hungry, but Abbi was a goddess in the kitchen, and he couldn't pass up anything she made. He took the reheated plate out to the deck and stared out into the darkness as he devoured chicken and dumplings along with a huge slice of cornbread, washing it down with a glass of sweet tea. Setting the empty bowl aside, Lor slid down in his chair, tipping his head back to gaze at the stars. Technically not the same stars Jordana could view if she were outside at the same time from thousands of miles away, but the thought was a nice one.

A giggle woke Lor the next morning. He opened his eyes, grinning at Amelia. "What's so funny?"

"You are. You should have slept in a bed, silly."

"I didn't mean to fall asleep out here." Lor sat up and stretched. Voices and laughter sounded inside.

Amelia held out her hand, and Lor allowed the little girl to lead him inside. He was surprised to find the house full of family early on a weekday.

Lor relished the familiarity of being home. The scent of Abbi's cooking. The friendly squeeze of Frey's hand on Lor's shoulder. Trevor's snark as he cracked a joke. Matthew laughing at his ridiculous friend. Lydia cooing in her mother's arms. The house Lor lived in was just that – a house. This was home for him. Lorenzo stepped up to Sophia. He didn't have to ask. She offered Lydia to him, and he snuggled the baby close, pressing his nose to her downy hair, inhaling deeply. Life went on around them as if their worlds hadn't been rocked only a couple days before. Worlds, because this one was separate from the one in Brazil. He had no doubt Jordana would come for him, but Lor wanted a little normalcy before he faced her.

Lor relaxed as Frey caught him up on the phone call Kallisto received at the Pen. "Julian thinks this Eden could be behind the attacks on Rafe, Gregor, and Dante. He—" Frey's phone rang, and everyone quieted.

"Julian?"

"Hey, Brother. Henry received some information. We're pretty sure Lachlan sent it, but it's about Eden and her father, James Wood. James owns Nexus, the assassin organization the Lazlos worked for."

"Thus, the men sent to take out Rafe and the others."

"Not only that, but Eden is their computer specialist, and from what we're reading, she's beyond capable of the attack on the jet."

"If that's the case, then she'd be able to track Tamian's jet to New York."

"I've been looking into that, and all traces of the flight plan have disappeared. I think Lachlan was behind that as well because none of us here at the lab were responsible."

Frey ran his free hand through his hair. "I wish we knew where he was and if he is truly helping."

Julian sighed. "I'm just glad he *is* helping. We wouldn't know all we do without him. I realize this doesn't erase his past, but it goes a long way with some forgiveness."

"I agree. Forgiveness is often the hardest thing we can offer someone. Since Lachlan is behind the scenes watching out for us, why don't the three of you take a break? Abbi cooked enough for an army, and I know Kat would love to see you outside the lab. Have Lucy and Henry grab Tamian and Kili, then head this way."

"That sounds wonderful. Henry's mate is off on a girl's trip with her sister, but I'm sure Tamian would love to join

105

us. It'll take at least half an hour, so don't wait on us. We can eat when we get there."

"See you soon." Frey disconnected and replayed Julian's side of the conversation for the humans.

"Maybe you should turn Kallisto loose," Trevor said. "Use her as bait."

"That's not a bad idea," Nikolas agreed, his eyes on his daughter in Lor's arms. "If Eden's hellbent on getting to her, better she be outside the Pen than in. Who knows what the female has planned next?"

"Breakfast is ready," Abbi announced. "Let's table this discussion until later. Please."

Frey cradled Abbi's face and kissed her gently. "You heard my mate. Let's eat."

Sophia reached for her daughter, but Lor shook his head. "You go ahead. I'd like to just sit here for a few minutes with Lydia if you don't mind."

Sophia's smile was soft and understanding. "I don't mind at all."

As everyone bustled around filling their plates and settling at the large dining table, Lorenzo thought about what Frey said. Forgiveness was hard to offer. Would he ever be able to forgive Jordana? He didn't know what she had endured all those years. Hadn't been willing to listen. Now that she was free from Leo, was he going to go the rest of his long life without his mate? Lor studied all the couples. He glanced down at the innocent baby in his arms. The longing he felt when around them all, the chance at having what they all had was within his grasp if he could somehow get over the past. If he could swallow his pride and at least listen to what Jordy had to say… Lor closed his eyes and leaned his head against the sofa. What harm would it do to give her a few minutes of his time? His heart was already shattered. Maybe, just maybe, she could stitch it back together. His beast didn't argue. It gently pushed against his mind, reminding him how good it felt when she flung herself at him back in Curitiba. For that one moment, everything had felt right.

Making up his mind to call Jordy, something settled within Lorenzo – peace. For the first time in decades, peace washed over him.

Amelia, sans her tutu, plopped down on the sofa and leaned her head against Lor's arm. He glanced down at her, unable to see her face. "What's up, Buttercup?"

"I miss Rain. He went back to California. I want to go to California."

Rain and his parents had returned home so Remy could get back to running the new prison. Lor had been pleased to see them again so soon after they moved across the country. It hadn't been much of a surprise, though, considering how close Rain and Amelia were.

"I think your dad is planning on taking you for spring break." With this latest threat, it might take longer to get to the West Coast, but Lor wouldn't say that to Amelia.

"But that's soooo far away." Amelia reached over and took Lydia's hand gently so as not to wake her. "I can't wait for Lydia to get bigger so I can play with her."

"Are you going to teach her to dance?"

Amelia shrugged. "If she wants me to. She might rather color with Connor." The little girl sighed. "Babies are soooo boring. It's a good thing she's cute."

Lorenzo stifled a laugh. Her father, however, did not.

"Come on, Little One. You need to eat." Frey held out his hand, and Amelia slid off the sofa. She bent over and kissed Lydia on the cheek before taking her father's hand. Lor's heart clenched every time he watched one of the males with their child. He wanted what they had.

You could have it if you weren't so fucking stubborn.

Yes, he could. Then again, it had taken Jordy over seventy years to give Leo a son. Was something wrong with her? Would it take that long for them to have a child if they were to mate?

107

You can always adopt. Look at Amelia and Frey.

His beast was right. Frey didn't love Amelia any less than Jonathan just because she wasn't biologically his. And there were plenty of children who needed loving homes. Even if he and Jordy didn't get together, there was no reason Lorenzo couldn't be a single parent. With the Clan at his back, he would have plenty of help.

But wouldn't it be better to have a loving mate at your side?

Lorenzo sighed. He knew his beast was right. Again. Lor leaned sideways, careful not to jostle the baby too much, and tugged his phone out of his back pocket. He pulled up the number he'd saved when Jordana called and stared at it. He had planned on giving her time to get her parents' estate settled, but he didn't want to wait that long to see her. Lor should have stayed in Brazil so they could talk, but his emotions got the better of him when confronted with Diego. The young male would always be part of Jordana's life, and Lor would have to deal with that. Would Diego want to come to the States with his mother? Or would he stay in Brazil with Francisca? Regardless, he was Jordy's son, and Lor would need to put aside his hurt. It wasn't Diego's fault he was a reminder of what Leo had taken from Lor. Closing his eyes again, Lor knew he owed the young man an apology, or at least an explanation of his hurtful words regarding Leo's demise.

A text would be too impersonal, but Lor didn't want to call Jordy where his family could hear their conversation. As if Sophia knew something was up, she approached Lor.

"Let me take her so you can eat." Sophia didn't give him a chance to argue. She lifted her sweet girl from Lor's arms and inhaled the baby's scent. Lorenzo joined those still at the table and filled a plate. Eating would give him more time to think about what he would say to his mate.

EDEN WOKE EARLY the next morning. She replayed the conversation over in her mind as she waited on the coffee to perk. Kallisto had been unsure at first. It had been years since they were together. She hadn't declared her love for Eden, but she hadn't said otherwise either. And what the hell was the part about the guards not being human? At least she assumed Kallisto was referring to the guards. Eden figured their call would be monitored, but that didn't make sense. If only they had been allowed more time to speak.

She had to move quickly. Her father had called again, leaving another hate-filled message. If he lost Nexus because of her, he would never forgive Eden. Then again, they both had more money than they knew what to do with. Her father could disappear. Take her mother and buy an island where they could spend the rest of their days together. It was what Eden planned with Kallisto. She already had their new identities ready to go.

Instead of focusing on Kallisto, Eden went to her computer to look into why the GIA was targeting her father. If she could figure out who alerted the authorities, she could put a stop to it.

When she awakened the monitor, Eden's blood ran cold. There on the screen was a photo of her and Kallisto from their weekend together in Greece. Only this picture wasn't one of them having dinner on the patio. Or strolling the village as they chatted and got to know one another. This one was much more intimate. It was a still frame from one of the videos she had taken to remember their weekend by.

"What the actual fuck? This is impossible!" she screamed into the empty room. Those videos were stored on a private server only she had access to. Except someone had found them. And if they could hack into that server, it was possible they could find everything else.

As much as she loved Kallisto, Eden didn't want to end

up in a cell next to her. That was not the way she wanted them to be together. Even though someone had access to her files, she deleted them anyway. She wouldn't allow the government to find proof of what she'd done in her possession. Eden didn't have time to focus on helping her father. She sent him a text urging him to take her mother and disappear because that was exactly what she planned to do.

But first, Eden checked to make sure her other supposedly secure server was still unnoticed. Finding it was, she blew out a breath and mentally pumped her fist. She had never come up against someone as skilled as she, so she took this as a small victory. Next, she checked in on Henry and Julian. As she tracked their keystrokes, something odd happened. In the background of Henry's code, someone else was overriding his progress. "Who are you?" she muttered to the unknown hacker. Eden brushed her hands together, then began typing in her own algorithm. She had to mask it to look like it was something Henry was doing. She needed to know who was helping them. Whoever it was had to be behind the cryptic messages.

Once that was in place, Eden returned her attention to the prison. Security was tight, but it was nothing she couldn't work around. She hacked into the feed and searched for her assassins. She rewound to the day they were supposed to take out Rafael, Dante, and Gregor. "What the hell?" When she caught sight of Grim, she froze the screen. Her assassin was being carried into the prison. "Fuck!"

LACHLAN SHOULD FEEL bad about sending the GIA after James Wood, but he didn't. The man should have a tighter rein on his daughter. Then again, Eden was a woman in love, and if anyone knew about doing something crazy for the one they wanted, it was him. After hearing the phone call to Kallisto though, it didn't seem her affection was returned. He also knew all about that. Pushing back against the ache in his chest, Lachlan sent the latest information he'd gathered to Henry. Lachlan wanted to be the hero. Wanted Hunter to know he was the one gathering intel on the Clan's attacker, but Hunter had released him from their bond, and Lachlan doubted even capturing Eden would be enough for his mate to forgive him.

Rafael and his brothers were safe for the time being, but if Lachlan could track their movement to New York, Eden probably could as well. The female was one of the best Lachlan had ever come across. After the conversation with Kallisto, she would either be devastated and give up the task of taking down the Stones, or she would be more determined than ever to spring her former lover from the Pen. Lachlan replayed the call. Kallisto had told Eden to forget about her and move on, but he somehow doubted Eden would. Not after all the trouble she'd already gone to in exacting her revenge. And Lachlan wouldn't give up on stopping her. This would be his last good deed.

Lachlan felt the male's presence before his muffled footsteps sounded on the carpet just inside the door. "How did you find me?" he asked, keeping his eyes forward.

"You were always predictable." The smell of metal mixed with Hunter's natural scent. "Except for you snapping my neck. Can't say I saw that coming."

"I had to get away so I could prove my innocence." Lachlan refused to turn around. Refused to see the condemnation in his mate's eyes. Yes, Hunter had released him from their bond, but to him, the gorgeous male would always be his mate.

"You haven't been innocent in a long time."

"Truth, but in this case I am. Here, take a look at this." Lachlan pointed at the screen to his right. When Hunter didn't step closer, Lachlan sighed to himself. If Hunter were closer, he wouldn't have room to swing the sword. "That is Eden Wood. She's behind the recent slate of trouble the Stone Society is having."

"Why should I believe you? What makes you think I would believe anything you have to say?"

Lachlan turned his head so he could at least see Hunter's outline. "Because I have never lied to you. Not once in all our years have I ever spoken one word which wasn't true."

"Except for the fact that you were Achilles? And you helped Alistair? Lying by omission is still lying."

"I've spent every day since I outed myself to Frey in making that right. Have I paid my penance? Probably not enough to satisfy their Clan. Definitely not enough to satisfy you if that sword is any indication. But I'm trying. That's why I did what I did to escape the Pen. Eden Wood is better than both Julian and Henry. She's behind the jet going down. She aided Drago and his little human hacker with the bombs. She's also behind the latest attempts on Rafael's and his brothers' lives. She's not done either."

"Then why are you here in the middle of the ocean instead of stopping her?" Hunter seethed.

"Who says I'm not doing just that?" Lachlan waved his hand at the numerous monitors. "It's the reason I'm here instead of sitting in prison." One of his screens beeped, and Lachlan focused on the keystrokes. "What are you up to now?"

Hunter moved closer. "Where is that?"

"It's the Pen. Eden called Kallisto earlier. It seems the two of them had a brief dalliance one weekend in Greece, and Eden fell in love. All of this, everything happening to the Stone Clan, is because Eden wants her lover free from her prison cell. She wants Rafael to pay for imprisoning Kallisto."

"But why is the feed going so fast?"

"She's hacked into the security feed. Eden is looking for... There. That's one of the assassins Eden hired to take out Rafael and his brothers." The feed stopped on Frey's face. "Shit. Either she's planning on busting the assassin out as well or—"

"Or she's going to target Frey next."

"I'm on it." Lachlan copied what was on the screen and shot it over to Henry.

"That's not fast enough." Hunter pulled out his phone. "Damnit. There's no signal. How can I not have service when you've got all this equipment running?"

"Hang on." Lachlan knew he was taking a big chance letting Hunter make the call, but he had already decided after helping save Rafael's Clan he was ready for whatever happened to him. "There. It should work now."

Hunter held onto the sword as he stepped away from Lachlan. It hurt that his mate didn't trust him, but then again, he'd not given Hunter reason to. Hunter relayed what they'd observed with the security feed. When Hunter mentioned Lachlan's name, Frey didn't sound alarmed. Instead, he said he would be safe and disconnected.

Tapping the edge of the sword on Lachlan's shoulder, Hunter said, "You're coming with me."

Lachlan finally turned to fully face his mate, the tip of the blade inches from his neck. "I know you don't trust me, but I can better help from here. If I leave now, that's hours Eden will have where I can't track her movements."

"Henry and Julian—"

"Are no match for this female. They have been five steps behind her, and if I give up my post for even one hour, that's too much time for her to get that much further ahead of the game. Stay and watch over me or go help the Stone Clan. Either way, I will turn myself back over to you once she's taken down."

"It isn't me you need to answer to."

"Isn't it?" Lachlan ran his hands through his hair. "You

113

are the only one I want forgiveness from. No one else matters. I have waited centuries to be with you. I can wait a few more."

"And I released you," Hunter reminded him.

"Banyan released Urijah, yet they found their way back to one another. Banyan killed Urijah's human husband. Is what I've done worse than that? Are my sins so great..." Lachlan turned his back on Hunter. He didn't want the male to see his tears. "Go. Stay. I don't care. But I'm not leaving until I've helped take Eden down."

Hunter wouldn't take his head, but his indecision on whether to leave or not was evident by the unpleasant noise he made. Lachlan blinked the tears from his eyes and focused as best he could on the monitors. Having Hunter so close was doing a number on his beast. It wanted Lachlan to demand Hunter forgive them. To look at him with tenderness the way he used to. Lachlan cleared those thoughts from his mind. They only made the heartache worse.

"I'm leaving so I can help guard the others, but I will be back." Hunter quietly made his way outside, and Lachlan turned to watch him go, wanting one last look at the male he would never have again.

CHAPTER TEN

FREY WAS LEADING Amelia to the dining room when his phone rang. "Go sit with your momma," he urged his daughter before answering.

"Deacon?"

"We've got a big problem. The power's off at the Pen. I sent Aldredge out to check, and it's only off here. The backup generators kicked on, but if someone can shut the power off..."

"Then they can possibly manipulate the cell doors. Hang on. I'm going to conference in Julian."

After a beat, Julian answered. "We're on our way. Did you need me to pick something up?"

"Julian, I just got a call from Deacon who's also on the line. The power is off at the Pen, and it appears it's only at the prison. Hunter called me a few minutes ago. He's with Lachlan who has identified Eden Wood as the hacker."

"Who placed a call to Kallisto at the Pen," Julian said.

"The very same. Hunter also said Eden hacked into the security feed at the Pen and froze on an image of me carrying one of the assassins inside. I need to get my family to safety since I have no doubt she knows where I live."

"We can detour to the Pen instead of your house," Julian offered.

"No. I need you and Henry to head back to the lab."

"What do you need me to do besides see if I can locate the cause?"

"Just that. If Lachlan's right, which he usually is, Eden's the culprit. See if either of you can track down her location.

115

Deacon, I need you to call in all off-duty guards. I'll have Nikolas contact every available Gargoyle in the area and send them to help. If whoever's behind this manages to get the cell doors open, we need as many males as we can get to keep the inmates contained."

"At least there are only a handful of Unholy left." Julian cursed, then said, "Hang on. Tamian asked if you want him and Lucy at the Pen or to come guard you?"

"I have Lor, Nik, and Jasper here, so have them go to the Pen. Is Tamian sure he wants Lucy in the fray?"

Lucy answered in the background, "I'm a Gryphon, so yes, he does." Tamian mumbled something Frey didn't catch. He probably had no more control over his mate than Gregor did Tessa.

"Let's get on those calls. Julian, you all watch your backs."

"And you watch yours. It looks like you're the one in Eden's sights now."

"I think that target just widened to include all our family. Once I figure out where to send our mates, I'll let you know."

Lorenzo and Nikolas came to stand by Frey before he hung up. After he disconnected, Lorenzo spoke up. "I think I know the perfect place – São Paulo."

"Your home? I don't want to endanger your family."

"That's the thing, though. Everyone there is Gargoyle, and I doubt this Eden has me on her radar. Not only that, but Bryce said he would keep the jet fueled up and ready in case anyone needed to leave quickly."

"Fuck. With Rafael out of town, I need to stay here." Frey grabbed his hair and pulled.

Nikolas grabbed Frey's shoulders. "Then let Lor and me do this. We'll take Sophia, Abbi, Katherine, and the kids to Brazil so you can focus on what you need to."

Frey gripped his brother's wrists, relishing the contact. "Eden already tried to take down the jet once. What if she tries it again?"

Lorenzo pulled his phone out of his pocket. "I think I know a way. Let me make a call to Jordana. She's in the process of gaining access to her parents' estate. With as much money as he had, I'm sure her father had a jet of his own. If she can get her hands on it, we can drive down to the coast, and she can have the plane meet us there."

"You sure you want to do that? I know you aren't happy with your mate," Frey asked.

Lorenzo squared his shoulders. "She and I have things to work out, but this is more important."

"Yeah. Make the call. Thank you, Lor."

Frey didn't want to let Abbi out of his sight again, but she would be safer thousands of miles away.

JORDANA SPENT THE morning with Fallon going over the accounts. When it was just the two of them, she admitted to taking money and investing it in private accounts Leo knew nothing about. Fallon said he appreciated her honesty, and since there was more than enough for him in the regular accounts, she should keep what she squirreled away. Since he wasn't a citizen of Brazil, he called someone named Julian to see about faking some documents. She didn't think anyone in their Clan would turn him into the government as long as he was a good King. Fallon was certain this Julian would produce documentation that was iron-clad. Jordana hoped so for his sake. They both were surprised when Francisca offered to stay and help Fallon. She explained that she had plenty of experience considering she had been Queen. Jordana never imagined Luiz trusting anyone with the accounts, even his mate, but Francisca proved her wrong. Just one less thing for Jordana to worry about.

Diego left right after supper, headed up to Rio. Leo had

taken him there several times over the years while Jordana remained behind. She told Leo it was so he and his son had time to bond, but in truth, Jordana did her best to keep from being seen with her husband just in case Lorenzo was watching. With Francisca in the office and Diego out of the house, Jordana went to her suite and began packing. It was a little preemptive since her parents' money wasn't yet in her own account, but she wanted to be ready as soon as it was.

She picked up her phone to check the weather in New Atlanta. Before the app could populate, the phone rang. Jordana fumbled it when she saw Lorenzo's name flash on the screen. Tightening her grip, she slid the answer icon. "Lor?"

"Yeah. Sorry to bother you, but we have a situation here, and I could use your help."

Jordana's heart tattooed a rapid beat within her chest. "Anything. What do you need?"

"Pedro had a jet, didn't he?"

"Yes. Two of them, but I don't have access to either one yet. The attorney is working on that."

Lor sighed. "Shit. Okay. I'll figure something else out."

"Wait. Let me give him a call. Just because they aren't officially mine doesn't mean I can't use one of them. Give me a few minutes to contact him."

"Okay. Thanks, Jordy."

"You're welcome. I'll call you right back." Jordana disconnected and placed the phone against her chest, closing her eyes. He called her Jordy. She shouldn't read too much into it, but hope was a strange thing, and like when she had Francisca reach out to him when Jordana was in trouble with Marcos, she held onto it again. Jordana walked through the bedroom to her sitting area and placed the call. She bypassed his assistant and dialed his personal line.

"Rocha," he answered gruffly.

"*Senhor* Rocha, I apologize for disturbing you, but I'm

118

in need of one of my jets."

"Going on vacation so quickly?"

Jordana ignored the snark. "Nothing like that, but I do need it immediately. Or rather, King Fallon has requested it." Jordana had no qualms throwing about the new King's name to get what she wanted for Lorenzo.

"In that case, I'll make it happen. I'll send you the pilot's name and phone number. I have already informed him of your father's death and told him you would be taking over possession of the planes. He is on standby should you need him."

"Thank you, *Senhor*. The King is appreciative of your cooperation." Jordana disconnected and muttered, "Asshole."

"I hope it isn't me you're calling an asshole," Fallon said from the doorway.

Jordana grinned. "Nope. My father's attorney. Lorenzo called asking for help. Something is going on, and he wanted to know if I had access to Pedro's planes, so I made the call. I apologize for using your title to get what I need quicker."

Fallon waved a hand in front of his body. "Use away. If Lorenzo called you asking for help, things must be escalating back home. I take it you were successful?"

"Yes. He—" Jordana's phone pinged with an incoming text. "That was the lawyer sending me the pilot's information. I need to call Lor."

"Of course." Fallon leaned against the doorframe and crossed his arms. Jordana would have liked some privacy, but it seemed he wasn't ready to give her any, so she made the call with him listening.

"Hello?"

"I got a plane. Do you want us to come to New Atlanta?"

"No. It's too dangerous. We will drive down to New Orleans."

119

Fallon crossed the room and held out his hand. "May I?" Jordana told Lorenzo to hang on, then passed the phone over. "Lor, it's Fallon. I'll have the pilot meet you at the Lakefront Airport. It's smaller. Who are you bringing with you?"

"Nikolas and I are escorting Abbi, Katherine, Sophia, and the kids."

"I will have rooms ready for your arrival. I'm handing you back over to Jordana."

"Lor, what's going on?" Jordana asked.

"It's a long story, but the short version is someone is after our Clan. She's a skilled hacker who can track almost every movement we make. She tried to take down the Clan jet with several mates and kids on it a few months back. This is the reason for my request. She isn't aware of you or my connection to you as far as I know."

"Damn, that's crazy. Okay, let me get off here and contact the pilot since the flight will take longer than your drive. Lor, please be safe. I'll see you soon."

"Thank you, Jordana. My King appreciates your help." The phone beeped indicating Lor hung up without giving her the opportunity to say anything further. When she laughed, Fallon arched a bushy eyebrow.

"He played the King card."

"He did, but he appreciates the help too. Give him time, Jordana. The mate bond will kick in, and soon you'll be together the way you should have been all these years."

"I hope you're right. Let me call the pilot, then I'll talk to Francisca about those extra rooms."

"I can handle the rooms. You need to get to the airport. I'll have Gannon and Everett drive you."

"I don't mind driving."

"Please humor me. Marcos's men haven't been gone long, and I'd feel better if you weren't alone."

"Okay, thank you," Jordana conceded with a smile. Fallon was a considerate male and would make the perfect leader for her people.

Fallon excused himself, and Jordana called the pilot. She then freshened up and dug around her closet for something more comfortable than her usual attire. Being Queen, Jordana had always dressed the part. As soon as she got some free time, a shopping trip was in order. Maybe one of the women Lorenzo was traveling with would be up for going with her. Jordana didn't have any friends, only acquaintances.

She found Gannon and Everett waiting for her by the front door. It took close to an hour to get to the small airport where her planes were housed. Gannon escorted her to the private jet where she introduced them.

"Salvador?" When the male nodded, she said, "This is Gannon Hopkins. He will be traveling with us."

"Please, call me Sal. It is my honor to fly you, Jordana. Gannon, it's a pleasure to meet you."

The two males shook hands, then Gannon followed Jordana up the stairs. On the drive, he explained he would accompany Jordana on the flight per Fallon's request. They didn't know the pilot and therefore wouldn't expect her to travel such a distance with no one to watch her back. Jordana was in awe of Lorenzo's friends.

When Sal joined them, he introduced them to the flight attendant. "This is my mate, Connie. She will take good care of you both. If you'll take your seats, we'll be in the air momentarily."

When Rocha texted Jordana with Sal's information, he informed her the pilot was a Gargoyle. She had figured as much considering her father, but it was good to know she and Gannon didn't need to hide their true selves. After they were in the air, Connie asked if she could get them anything.

Jordana asked for coffee with cream, and Gannon requested whiskey. Connie was efficient, if quiet. Jordana couldn't help but notice the sideways glances the other female shot her way. After passing out their drinks, the female remained standing by the door to the galley.

"Connie, why don't you grab yourself a drink and sit with us?"

"Oh, I couldn't."

"Sure you can. It's a long flight."

Connie turned and fixed herself a coffee, then took the seat closest to Jordana.

"How long did you and Sal work for Pedro?" Jordana asked.

"Almost twelve years. He hired Sal when the last pilot wasn't available at a moment's notice." Connie ducked her head. "I'm so sorry."

"What for? Pedro was an asshole, so it doesn't surprise me he expected everyone in his employ to be at his beck and call."

Connie gasped, and Jordana grinned. "I would apologize for my language, but seeing I'm no longer Queen, I don't feel the need to guard my words. I hated my father. He and King Luiz made me marry Leo who wasn't my mate. Leo's younger brother was. Lorenzo left home during the wedding, and we've only recently seen one another again after a hundred years. Lorenzo is who we are picking up in the States. Him and several of his Clan. They're having security issues, and we're bringing three mates and their children back with us for safeguarding."

Connie gripped her mug firmly in both hands. "So you're finally with your true mate?"

"Not exactly. It's a work in progress. Lor hasn't yet forgiven me for marrying his brother, even though I wasn't given a choice. I'm hoping with enough time we'll get there. Tell me about you. Do you and Sal have children?"

Connie's eyes lit up, and her frown lifted into a brilliant smile. "Yes. We have three sons and two daughters. They're all scattered around the world, but with technology, we are able to see them over video chats."

"Have you thought about retiring so you can travel to see them?" Jordana asked.

"We would love to but..." Connie frowned again.

"But Pedro wouldn't allow it, I'm sure. Don't you worry. As soon as the trouble with Lorenzo's Clan has passed, you and Sal can either take a long vacation or retire altogether. I have no doubt you've earned it."

Connie's eyes filled with tears. "Thank you. Sal and I are yours as long as you want us, but a vacation would be lovely."

Jordana planned on letting the couple retire, but she needed them for the time being. Jordana asked to see pictures of Connie's kids and grandkids. It passed the time and kept her mind off Lorenzo for a while. When Jordana asked Gannon about what was going on with their Clan, he explained all the trouble they'd had over the last several years, from King Rafael's uncle trying to tear them apart to the latest issues with the hacker.

"And I thought Pedro was an ass. I'm glad Alistair and Drago met their ends. So much death and destruction all because of human mates?" Jordana hadn't known Gargoyles could mate with humans. Even if they had been aware of the fact, she had no doubt her father and Luiz would have still insisted Jordana marry Leo to keep the bloodline pure.

Gannon stood and helped himself to more whiskey. Connie moved to get up, but he waved her off. "If you'd asked me a hundred years ago, I might have scoffed at having a human mate, but after meeting the ones our Clan has found? They are some of the strongest beings I've ever encountered. You'll see what I mean when we get to the States. Sophia is a half-blood, but Abbi and Katherine are human."

Gannon filled Jordana in on the little he knew about the mysterious hacker while Connie fixed them something to eat. When his plate was scraped clean, Gannon made his way to the cockpit to sit with Sal, and Jordana got to know the other female a little better.

"Please forgive me for saying, but you're nothing like your parents," Connie said.

"I'll take that as a compliment. I'm under no illusions as to how horrid both Pedro and Renata were. Renata was only interested in her career, and Pedro, well, he was greedy. I may have inherited everything, all the money, the houses, the jets, but I'd give it all back to have had parents who loved me. Who allowed me to be with my mate instead of forcing me to marry his brother. I never wanted to be Queen. I only wanted to be with Lorenzo and live our best lives."

Connie reached out and patted Jordana's hand. "Maybe you still can."

Jordana was counting on it.

FREY ARRIVED AT the Pen to find a mess. And by mess, he meant fucking chaos. Eden, assuming the hacker was responsible, had not only shut off the lights, but she had managed to open all the cell doors. Frey had never struck a female in his life, but when he got his hands on this one, he wouldn't hold back.

Getting inside proved to be harder than expected. Nik had managed to call in over fifty extra Goyles on top of all the guards Deacon contacted, but not all were on the inside. He opened the door to find a handful of males holding back a horde of inmates, all doing their best to push their way to freedom. Frey instructed several shifters to guard the door in case any humans managed to slip through the barricade of Goyles. He pushed his way inside while keeping his beast at bay. It wouldn't do for an inmate to see what he and the others truly were. Frey wasn't sure how to get the inmates back to their cells without harming them.

A loud whistle rent the air, causing the inmates to freeze momentarily. "Go back to your cells, now!" Tamian's voice brooked no argument, and Frey could only stand in amazement as the inmates turned and walked away from the door.

He knew Tamian was special, but that was some next-level shit. "Brother, am I glad to see you," he said to the half-blood. "Where's Lucy?"

"On the roof." When Frey frowned, Tamian explained, "She's keeping an *Eagle* eye out for any escapees."

That explained how the female got to the top of the Pen. It wasn't common knowledge among their Clan that Lucy was a Gryphon, but her secret was safe among those in the know.

Deacon grabbed Frey's attention. "We need to get to the Basement."

Frey turned to Tamian. "I'll take a group down while you stay up here and work your magic." He took twenty males with him, leaving the rest upside with Deacon and Tamian. Frey hurried to the Basement to contain the Unholy who hadn't responded well to the Reborn serum. Aldredge, along with a few others, were holding the door as the Unholy did their best to batter it down.

Frey got the males' attention. "We're going to have to fight. I would say try to push them back without killing them, but I have a feeling that won't work. Let's get this over with." Frey motioned for Aldredge to open the door, and Frey led the charge. Without their swords, Frey and the others relied on their claws to fend off the monsters. They did their best to coral the Unholy, but after being locked up so long, the beings fought with everything they had trying to escape. In the end, they were no match for the Goyles, and the Basement was covered in blood and dead bodies. Not a single Unholy had been spared. Neither had Eden's two assassins.

"Fuck. Fuck!" Frey roared. Taking a life was never easy,

even when it was self-defense. This was another reason to end Eden fucking James. He pressed his back to the cool, concrete wall and got his beast under control. Frey surveyed the others who were all heaving as heavily as he was. Each had sustained injuries, but the gashes from Unholy claws were stitching back together. No one said a word as they stood among the bodies. There was nothing to say. The weight of killing was a heavy shroud. Pushing away from the wall, Frey strode out the door and led the way back upstairs.

As he and the others marched through the corridors, the inmates stared from inside their cells. The doors stood open, but the humans didn't move to get free. He wouldn't either if he were them, not with twenty-something large males striding past covered in blood. Frey's phone rang, and he was surprised it had managed to remain intact during the fight. He didn't recognize the number, but with Abbi on the road, Frey wouldn't take a chance on not answering.

"Hartley," he answered. As he did, the cell doors began closing.

"Frey, Lachlan. I've managed to override Eden's computer for the moment, but I can't guarantee she won't try again. Do you have eyes on Kallisto?"

Frey wanted to rail at the male, but for the moment, it seemed Lachlan was on their side. "I don't, but I'll find Deacon and get an update."

"I know you have no reason to trust me or listen to any advice I have, but if I were you, I'd turn Kallisto loose. She's the reason Eden is causing trouble, and if you let her lover go, Eden might stop targeting your Clan. At the least, it'll give you breathing room, and you can always follow Kallisto. She might lead you to Eden."

Frey blew out a breath. Trevor had suggested the same thing, and after what just happened, it didn't sound like bad advice. Before he could respond, both Deacon and Tamian met him in the hallway. Their faces were bleak. "I'll take it under advisement." Frey disconnected and steeled himself for whatever bad news was coming. "What is it?"

Deacon's dark skin was pale. "It's Kallisto." Deacon swallowed hard, shaking his head.

Tamian squeezed the male's shoulder and finished saying what Deacon couldn't. "A couple of the inmates attacked her. Sergei somehow managed to find her in the chaos, and while he did his best to protect Kallisto from being raped... They're both dead."

"Fuck. And the inmates who did this?"

Tamian's eyes flashed an eerie color, and Frey barely refrained from taking a step back. "They're dead too. Turned on each other."

Frey had no doubt Tamian coerced the humans to do so. He didn't feel one ounce of regret about it either. Scrubbing a blood-covered hand down his face, he blew out a breath. "Let's go to the conference room."

Deacon led the way, and once they were away from the inmates, he asked, "I take it Julian got the cell doors closed?"

Frey propped against the long table. "Actually, it was Lachlan. That's who was on the phone when you walked up. He was able to override Eden's computer. He suggested we release Kallisto in hopes it would appease Eden, but now?" Frey rubbed his nape and cursed.

"Now she's going to be even more determined to take us down," Deacon finished.

"Then we don't let Eden know Kallisto is dead. I have an idea," Tamian said. "We give her what – or who – she wants."

"I don't think handing over her dead lover is going to make the female happy," Frey said.

"Jonas can make a prosthetic. I'll have Lucy don it and lure Eden out into the open."

Frey clenched his fists. "You'd risk your mate?"

"She's a Gryphon," Tamian said at the same time

127

Lucy's voice said, "And she's right here. What are you signing me up for?"

Tamian snagged Lucy around the waist and kissed her forehead. "Kallisto is dead, so I suggested having Jonas devise a prosthetic of Kallisto and use it to lure Eden out into the open."

Lucy pumped a fist in the air. "Yes! I've wanted to wear one of those ever since he showed me how he made them. We just need to get a recording of her voice for the modulator." Lucy turned to Deacon. "Do you happen to have a copy of the call she had with Eden?"

Deacon looked from Lucy to Tamian to Frey, his eyes wide. "We're seriously considering this?"

"Why wouldn't we?" Lucy asked, her face a cross between determined and pissed.

Frey saved Deacon from Lucy's wrath. "I'll ask Julian about the call, but we need a solid game plan. Eden is batshit crazy. One slip, and Gryphon or not, she could hurt you. Or worse." Frey looked at Tamian, begging him silently to reconsider.

"I won't slip. And if I do, I'll just voice her. Hell, I'll do that anyway. This bitch is going down," Lucy vowed.

"Voice her?" Deacon asked.

"It's a Gryphon thing. Well, and a Tamian thing. Gryphons have the ability to manipulate minds." Lucy held up her hand when Deacon's mouth fell open. "Don't worry. We don't use it willy-nilly. Only when dealing with bad guys or when the wrong person finds out our true nature. We make them forget what they saw. It's how Gryphons have kept off the human radar since we came to be."

Deacon cocked his head to the side. "That's useful."

Lucy nodded. "It is. So, who has spent the most time with Kallisto? Would know her mannerisms? Isn't her sidekick here as well?"

"Sergei died defending Kallisto, so he's out," Frey responded.

128

Tamian took Lucy's hand and threaded their fingers. "That would be Isabelle, but she's not here."

"We could get on a teleconference. I'll get Henry to help me set up a secure line." Lucy turned to her mate. "Tam, contact Jonas and tell him what we need from him. Frey, you come up with a plan on how to lure Eden out, and I'll head back to the lab to get in touch with Isabelle."

Frey grinned at the female. "Yes, ma'am."

Lucy grinned back, then tugged Tamian's hand. He halted her steps toward the door and asked Frey, "Do you need help with cleanup?"

"No. We got this. You two—"

"Deacon, there's a call on the main line. It's Eden asking to speak to Kallisto," Caleb interrupted.

"Bitch is probably fishing to see why her plan didn't work," Lucy muttered.

Frey agreed. "Tell her everyone is on lockdown at the moment, and we'll have Kallisto call back."

"But Kallisto's dead," Caleb said, not in on the scheme for Lucy to mimic the woman.

"She is, but we have the beginning of a plan." Frey turned to Lucy. "The first thing we need is a copy of that call. Get back to the lab and have either Julian or Henry work on that. We need to have 'Kallisto' return the call sooner rather than later, or Eden's going to try something else when she figures out this attack failed epically."

"We're on it." Lucy tugged Tamian's hand again, and this time he followed his mate out of the room.

"Gods help us," Deacon muttered.

Frey clapped the male on his shoulder. "Truth, Brother. Let us all pray to the gods this doesn't go sideways."

CHAPTER ELEVEN

LORENZO CHECKED IN with Amelia through the rearview mirror. Oakley and Paxton had secured two rental vehicles on the off-chance Eden was tracking their personal cars. Abbi, Amelia, and Jonathan were in the SUV with Lor while Katherine rode with Nikolas, Sophia, and Lydia. They had to stop several times for bathroom breaks and diaper changes. What would have been a six-hour drive turned into an eight-hour trip. Lorenzo didn't mind. The longer it took to drive, the less time they had to wait once they arrived in Louisiana. If he said he wasn't nervous about seeing Jordana again, he would have been a liar. At least on the flight to Brazil they would have plenty of distractions. He had no doubt once they got back to São Paulo, she would want to talk, and Lor was ready, but he wanted to be alone with her when they did.

"Uncle Lor, I need to pee," Amelia announced from the back seat. She had long ago stopped asking her mother if they could stop and began telling Lorenzo when she needed to go.

"We're almost to Dominic's. Can you hold it about fifteen minutes?"

"Sure. I'll just squeeze my legs together."

Lor glanced over at Abbi who was smothering a laugh. Since they would get to Louisiana several hours before Jordana, Dominic offered his house to them as a place to wait. He and Lilly had recently purchased a home in New Atlanta right before their twin daughters, Luna and Solaris, were born. Lorenzo was thrilled to see so many children coming into the Clan, even if he was a little jealous.

After a couple miles, he flipped on his blinker, and Nik followed. They had agreed Lorenzo should take lead since Amelia was with him, and she was the one who dictated how often they stopped. She needed more breaks than the babies. Sophia and Abbi took advantage of those breaks to change diapers and feed the little ones. He easily found Dom's home in the Garden District. Once they were parked, Lor helped Amelia out of the car and hurried with her to the door. He didn't know where the bathroom was located, but he rushed down the hallway until he found it. He flipped on the light for Amelia who was nowhere to be seen. Lor returned the way he came and found the girl gazing around a massive parlor. He didn't blame her. The room was reminiscent of a time long gone by.

"The bathroom's this way." Amelia held out her hand, still taking in the artwork, swords, and dark furnishings. At least the bathroom was modern. Voices sounded as the others found their way inside.

"Holy shit," Nik exclaimed.

"Language," Sophia chastised her mate. "But you're not wrong. I can see Dominic living here with his broody pirate image, but Lilly is all sunshine and rainbows."

"That's how you know it's true love," Nik responded, bouncing Lydia in his arms.

Abbi stopped in her tracks when she entered the room. "Tessa once told me about this house, but I thought she was exaggerating."

Katherine was right behind Abbi, carrying Jonathan's diaper bag. Her eyes widened when she got a good look at her surroundings. "This is so cool. It's like stepping back in time."

Lorenzo agreed. His own house had no culture. Nothing that set it apart from any other house. He had lived in New Atlanta a couple years and hadn't bothered decorating. Even the house he lived in back in California was as bland the day he moved out as it had been when he moved into it decades before.

When Dominic offered his home, he explained that not all rooms had electric lights. He liked the ambiance of oil lanterns. The kitchen and bathrooms were wired, but that was it. Dom had called ahead and had one of his friends light the lanterns and open the heavy curtains so the room wasn't completely dark. As cool as the house was, Lor couldn't imagine living that way twenty-four seven.

"Momma!" Amelia exclaimed when she ran down the hall. "Did you see this place? It's like a creepy museum."

Abbi cradled Jon in one arm and pushed Amelia's curly, black hair back from her face. "I saw it. Do you want to hold your brother while I go pee?"

"Sure." Amelia plopped down on the sofa and held out her arms. Once the baby was secure, Abbi disappeared down the hallway. Lor sat down next to the girl and touched Jon's soft cheek with his fingertip.

"Uncle Lor, why don't you have kids?"

Amelia's innocent question was a knife through his heart. Only it didn't hurt as much as it would have a few weeks ago. Lor had spent the drive thinking about meeting up with Jordana. About a future they could have together if he put his pride aside. She was his mate. He would never have another one, and he now had a chance at what had been stolen from them a century earlier. They were young enough in Gargoyle years they could still have a long life together if he accepted what happened to them was beyond either of their control. He spent so many years blaming Jordana, but after hearing her father talk to Marcos, Lor realized Jordana hadn't been given a choice in her life. She had explained that to him before the wedding, but Lor had been too distraught to listen.

He wanted to listen now.

Amelia patiently waited for an answer, and by the quietness in the room, the adults were as well. "Because I don't have a mate. Well, I do, but we've only recently found each other. Jordana, that's her name, she's the one coming to get us on her plane."

"If you get married, can I be the flower girl?"

"I doubt we get married since she's a Gargoyle."

"Is she a princess like Brynna?"

Lor smiled, although it was sad. "No, but she was a Queen."

Amelia scrunched her eyebrows. "But if you don't get married, how will she have your last name?"

Hoo boy. Lorenzo looked to Abbi, who had returned from the bathroom, for help. How did he explain it all to an eight-year-old?

Abbi smiled at him, then said, "Uncle Julian can do the paperwork like he did with Tessa and Gregor. They didn't have a wedding, but they have the same last name."

"But that's so boring." Amelia glanced up at Lorenzo. "Is there any food in this museum? I'm hungry."

Lorenzo laughed and tapped the girl on her nose. "Yes. Dominic had one of his friends fill the fridge. I'll go see what we have." He stood and headed toward the kitchen with Nikolas on his heels. Lor appreciated how the other males in the Clan didn't expect their mates to do all the cooking. Whoever Dom asked to ready the house had filled the fridge with several takeout containers. Lor and Nik got out several options, some Cajun cuisine and one less spicy option for Amelia. While the food was heating in the microwave, Lor found plates and cutlery, and Nik lit the lamps in the dining room. Even with the curtains pushed back, there was little light coming in from outside.

"Looks like rain," Nik muttered.

"Dominic warned me there could be a storm brewing. I hope Jordana doesn't run into any trouble getting here." Lor glanced out the window and frowned. It looked like more than rain. "Maybe we should check the weather."

"I agree. Let's get the food on the table, then I'll check."

Several minutes later, Nik told the mates the food was ready, then tapped away at his phone. "Yeah, this is gonna get bad. Like hurricane bad. The good news is it's coming up from the southeast. The bad news is it might get here before Jordana. I doubt they'll be able to land in this."

"Shit." Lorenzo scrubbed at his beard. "What are our options? If we leave soon, we can head west and hopefully outrun the worst of it. We don't have enough supplies to wait it out. We could go shopping."

"I'd rather meet them somewhere else if possible. If you would, get on the horn to Jordana. If they can reroute to somewhere farther west like Texas, we can meet them. I don't want to be stuck in a hurricane with the babies."

Lorenzo didn't either. Instead of calling, he sent his mate a text.

Lorenzo: *There's a hurricane headed our way. Probably best to meet somewhere farther west like Texas.*

Jordana: *Gannon and Sal just now notified me of the storm. I hate to ask you to drive farther with the little ones, but I do think it would be our best option.*

Lorenzo: *The babies are no trouble, and driving to safety is preferable to being stuck in a hurricane. Find out where the pilot can land, and we'll meet you there.*

Lorenzo showed Nik the text exchange while waiting on further instructions. Nik passed the phone back. "Good. I know it's not what we planned, but we didn't expect Mother Nature to pitch a hissy fit."

Lorenzo grinned at the male. Nikolas was one of the more laid-back Goyles. They hadn't spent much time together, but when they did, Lor enjoyed himself. His phone pinged, and he checked the next text.

Jordana: *Sal said one of the smaller airports in New Beaumont is still in service. It's the closest one to you across the Texas state line.*

Lorenzo opened the map app on his phone and checked the distance. Without the rain and kids, it was a four-hour drive. "They've chosen Beaumont," he said to Nikolas. "Four hours with no issues."

"With the rain and kids, better say five," Nik responded.

Lorenzo: *The mates are eating now, but we can be ready to head out in about thirty minutes. With the weather and Amelia, that adds a bit to our drive time, so say five and a half, six hours from now.*

While Lor waited on Jordana to respond, he fixed himself a large serving of jambalaya, then took a seat at the long table with everyone else. He had never been to Louisiana, but Priscilla had learned to fix a few Cajun dishes when Dom and Lilly made their way to New Atlanta. Lor was a fan. His phone pinged again.

Jordana: *Sal said our time is about five hours, so we'll meet you there. Please be safe.*

Lorenzo: *Will do.*

He wanted to say more. A lot more, but not in a text, so he left it at that. When he nodded at Nik, the male did the talking.

"Okay ladies, change of plans. There's a storm brewing outside, so we need to finish eating and get back on the road. Jordana's meeting us in New Beaumont, Texas. Another five hours in the car isn't ideal, but that's better than being stuck here during a hurricane."

Sophia pushed back from the table, gathering her empty plate. "No problem, Gorgeous. I think we all agree that's a better choice. If you'll take care of the containers, I'll wash the dishes right quick."

"Let me do the dishes, Sophia. You take care of Lydia," Lorenzo offered.

"She's fine in her car seat. But if you want to help with the dishes, it'll go faster, and we can get out of here sooner."

"Deal."

135

ISABELLE SHOOK HER head at Tessa and Manny's teasing. It had taken a while for her to get over her jealousy of Tessa being everyone's favorite, but Isabelle loved her cousin. It was hard not to. Now that Isabelle had come up with the Reborn serum, she was more secure in her own place in the Clan. For the longest time, Isabelle felt less than, even though she was an accomplished doctor. Being passed off to Maria and Rico had done a number on her younger self, and it still hurt, though not as much as it used to. Having a wonderful mate who adored both her and her son helped more than anything.

Connor was off somewhere reading. Priscilla was in the kitchen with Myra, and the rest of the adults were all hanging out in the sunken living area when Rafael's burner phone rang. Frey and Julian were the only ones with the number, but she and the others only had to wait a few seconds to know which one was calling.

"Hello?" After a beat, Rafe's face darkened. "Frey, I'm putting you on speaker." It was something he often did so that Kaya could listen in. All their moods darkened as Frey recounted what happened at the Pen. When he announced Kallisto was dead, a small sense of satisfaction bloomed in Isabelle's chest. If that made her a bad half-blood, she didn't care. The woman had wreaked too much havoc in their lives, and she wouldn't be missed. Except she would by this Eden character. Even from the grave, Kallisto was giving them grief.

"What about Gabriel? Did he get caught up in the fighting?" Isabelle knew her brother could take care of himself, but she still worried.

"He's fine. He stayed in his room the whole time, even going so far as to close his door when it opened. Listen, Isabelle, Lucy's going to don a prosthetic and pretend to be Kallisto," Frey said. "She's going to need your help."

"Mine?"

"Yes. Since you spent more time around Kallisto than anyone else, we hoped you would be willing to share what you know of how the human behaved. Lucy will need to sell the act."

Isabelle reached out for Dante's hand. "Yeah, sure. I can do that." She didn't want to relive her time being held in Greece, but if it would help capture the human responsible for all their latest woes, she would. Isabelle would do anything for their Clan. It was nice to be needed.

"Is my brother okay with this scheme?" Tessa asked.

Frey groaned. "It was his idea. Honestly, it surprised me, but knowing Lucy's special abilities, it does make sense she would be the one to do this."

"I bet War would disagree," Tessa said.

"Probably, but her father also knows Lucy's a grown female with a fierce mate. Tamian won't let anything happen to her."

Isabelle imagined Connor as an adult and doing something dangerous. It wouldn't matter how old he was, half-blood or not. She would always worry about him, and she had no doubt Warryck felt the same about Lucy. It would be years yet until they knew whether or not Connor would transition. Even though he hadn't seen a vision of his own future, Connor was adamant little Alyssa was his mate. She was out there somewhere living her own life, but one day in the future, Connor would go find her, and the next generation would take over. Isabelle wasn't ready for that.

Frey's voice brought her back to the present. "Lachlan's doing his best to counteract anything else Eden throws at us, and before you ask, yes, I trust him, if for no other reason than he wants back in Hunter's good graces."

Isabelle thought about her parents and the trust they had broken all those years ago. It was still a work in progress, but her resolve was softening with each passing day. It was also the reason she did her best to always be honest with Connor. Her son was young, but he was special and understood more than a child his age should. Speaking of the boy, Priscilla rushed into the room and motioned for Isabelle. Dante stood with her, and they both went to see what was wrong. When they reached the kitchen, Myra was wringing her hands as she watched Connor furiously drawing something. Having just met Connor, Myra wasn't aware of his visions. Maria, however, was sitting next to him at the counter, patiently waiting for the vision to pass.

Priscilla walked over and whispered something to Myra, and together, they left Isabelle and Dante alone with their son and his grandmother. Like Maria, she and Dante waited patiently, not interrupting. They knew Connor was okay, just focused. When he finally put his pencil down, he slid the paper across the counter. Dante picked it up, and after a quick inspection, he looked at Connor, then Isabelle with raised brows. Isabelle gripped her mate's hand. Tightly.

EDEN PACED THE room, fuming. Why had her plan not worked? Inmates should have been spilling out into the parking lot, yet not one had exited the building. A handful of guards should have been no match for all the men locked up in the prison. More than that, Kallisto was still inside. "Fuck!" When she called and asked to speak to her lover, the man who answered put her on hold only to come back and say the prison was on lockdown. How in the hell had they managed to control the chaos? And how had she been locked out of the security monitors inside? No, that she knew the answer to. Julian and Henry had help. It had to be whoever had gotten into her secure server. The same one taunting her with cryptic messages on her monitor. Eden had never encountered someone else as good as she was, but it looked like she had finally met her match. Once again,

Eden pondered whether or not Kallisto was worth all this trouble.

"They're not human."

Kallisto's words tumbled through Eden's brain. If those holding her lover hostage weren't human, what the hell were they? They couldn't be Unholy because those monsters weren't capable of coherent thoughts. Were they? Eden didn't know much about the disfigured creatures other than what she'd read in the news. Where did they come from? Who had created them, and how? When she thought about it, thought about what the Unholy looked like with their fangs and claws, was it possible they had been some evil mastermind's attempt at creating a sort of super soldier? And if so, where had the animalistic gene come from? From something else not human. If that were the case, then it was possible those in charge of the prison were a variable Eden hadn't planned for. How could she have when she hadn't been aware they existed?

Now what? Eden had done her level best to take down Rafael Stone and his family, yet they were all still standing. How did she fight something she didn't understand? Eden stalked to the kitchen and opened the freezer, pulling out a bottle of vodka. She needed to keep a level head, but she also needed something to calm her nerves. Taking a long pull of the clear liquor, she squeezed her eyes shut at the burn. If the world was filled with beings other than human, should she try to find a way to expose them? Could she? If they had lived among civilization and had yet to be discovered, they had to be good at hiding in plain sight. If they were capable of holding back an angry mob of inmates, they had to be more powerful than she could imagine. Did she really want to risk going up against something she had no idea how to fight?

Taking another drink of vodka, Eden wiped her mouth with the back of her hand. She should call her father. He would know what to do. Then again, he already thought

Eden had gone off the rails, and this would add another mark in the Eden-has-lost-it column. Her father had left several messages threatening to cut her off completely. He should know she had the means to make money without his help. She'd been doing it for years. Skimming money from large corporations, adding small sums to her own back account. Eden had been planning on spending the rest of her days with Kallisto on a remote island where no one knew who either of them were. She had the money to do it.

Now she wasn't sure that was a possibility. Her father's life's work was being threatened, and in turn he was threatening her. Eden loved her father. Loved both her parents, but didn't she deserve something for herself? Yes, she did, and that something was Kallisto. But was her lover worth it? How far would Eden have to go to retrieve the gorgeous blonde? Taking another swig from the bottle, Eden thought back to their short time together. While she had fallen in love, had Kallisto felt the same, or had Eden been nothing more than a fling to her? If that were the case, Eden was ruining a lot of lives for nothing.

No! Not for nothing. Her mind railed. Her stomach rolled. Eden dropped the bottle as she turned to the sink and threw up the alcohol. Damnit. When was the last time she had anything to eat? Eden turned on the water and rinsed the bile from the basin, then washed her mouth out. Grabbing a paper towel off the roll, she wiped the wetness from her face before sliding down onto the floor, leaning against the cabinet. Eden grabbed the overturned bottle. As she stared at what was left of the contents, her computer dinged from the other room. What fresh hell would she find if she went to look? Leaving the spilled mess, Eden pushed to her feet and trudged back to the office, hesitant to look at her computer. What she saw caused goose bumps to rise on her arms. She gasped as she watched the money in her father's account going backward. Stomach still sloshing, Eden sat down and furiously tried to stop the hack. Fuck, he was going to kill her. Her cell phone blasted with his ringtone, but she ignored it like she had the last fifty times he called. There was nothing good she could tell him. When trying to reverse the damage didn't work, Eden got busy trying to figure out who her nemesis was. Whoever it was? They were seriously pissing her off.

CHAPTER TWELVE

THE CLOSER THEY got to New Beaumont, the more nervous Lor became. His Clan was in the middle of another crisis, but the only thing he could focus on was seeing Jordana again. Seeing her now that he'd decided he wanted her. Had forgiven her. Although there was truly nothing to forgive. The only thing standing in his way of letting the past go was the fact that she'd given Leo a son.

That took over seventy years. Maybe she was waiting on you to come back and finally gave up.

He hated when his beast was logical, but Lor had thought about that as well. If he had put his pride aside years ago and gone back to Brazil, maybe she would have left Leo. It was possible Jordy had finally given up on Lor by that point. He wouldn't know until they talked. They wouldn't have a chance to do so until they were all safely back in São Paulo where the two of them had some privacy. Would they have a moment to themselves? Or would Diego form a protective shield around his mother?

"Lor Lor, I need to pee," Amelia announced again from the back seat. The little girl had been an angel on the drive, only requesting to stop a couple times. He figured that had as much to do with the rain as anything. None of them wanted to brave the storm to stop. It had taken hours for them to outrun the weather, and once they crossed the Texas border, it was as though Mother Nature decided the Lone Star State wasn't in need of watering. Add in the fact that Amelia had slept for quite a bit of the drive, and it had been peaceful. Not that he minded her incessant chatter and questions. He loved the little girl like she was his own, and Lor prayed to the gods if they saw fit to let him and Jordana find their way to becoming mates, he would have his own child to love.

"No problem, Munchkin."

Abbi called Sophia and let her know they would be taking the next exit. Not that Nik wouldn't know to follow, but Lor figured Abbi needed to hear her friend's voice. Abbi was a strong female, but she had left her mate home to deal with the Clan's mess. She put on a brave face, but her unease rolled off her in waves. That on top of Lor's own nerves was a heady mixture, almost to the point of stifling. While Nikolas escorted all the females into the rest area, Lor watched over Jonathan and Lydia as both babies slept in their car seats. Jonathan stirred briefly, his little eyes blinking in the darkness. Lor ran a finger down his soft cheek, and the baby blew a spit bubble before going back to sleep.

Nik and the females were exiting the building when Lor's phone buzzed.

Jordana: *We just landed. There's a separate waiting area for private jets. You should be able to follow the signs. If you get lost, let me know.*

Lor: *Just stopped to let Amelia use the bathroom. We should be there within thirty minutes.*

Jordana: *See you then.*

Lorenzo's stomach was full of butterflies. No, this was more like waves crashing against craggy rocks during a tempest. He took a deep breath and exhaled. There was no need to be nervous. This was his Jordy. His mate. Sure, they had a lot to talk about, but she was the one being the fates destined to be his, and they were meant to be, even if it had taken a century to get together.

"Everything okay?" Nik asked.

"Yes. Jordana and Gannon just landed. She said to meet them at the separate area for private planes."

"Yeah, I'm used to those. There will be signs." Nikolas often flew on the Stone jet, so it made sense he was familiar with the private area.

"Why don't you lead the way then?" Lor was nervous and afraid he'd miss the sign.

"You got it."

They loaded back up and hit the highway. Too soon, or not soon enough, depending on whether it was him or his beast thinking of seeing Jordana, they hit the exit, and Lor felt like he was going to throw up. He hadn't been this unsettled when he traveled to Curitiba to rescue Jordy. Then again, he hadn't been planning on anything more than seeing her safe at the time. When they parked, Lor asked Abbi if Amelia would be okay to fly right away.

"If the pilot doesn't mind, I'd rather get in the air. Amelia can sleep anywhere, and if Jordana's jet is like the Clan's, the seats recline, so I will be fine napping while Jonathan does."

"Okay. Let me go check with Nik." Lor got out of the vehicle, closing the door softly so he didn't wake the baby. When Nik rounded the front of his own SUV, Lor asked, "Are Sophia and Katherine okay to get in the air, or do we need to find a place for the night?"

"We were just talking about that. They're both okay to fly. Lydia's going to be up and down anyway. What about Abbi?"

"Abbi said they'd all be fine flying out straight away."

"I'll stay here while you go talk to Jordana and see if that's good with the pilot. If he's Goyle, he should have no trouble doing the trip back after he refuels."

Lor nodded and rubbed his hands on his thighs. Nik cocked an eyebrow, silently asking if Lor was okay. Lor gave a shaky smile. "I've got this."

JORDANA PACED THE waiting area. She had no idea what kind of greeting she would get from her mate. She didn't hold out hope he would rush to her with open arms. Two vehicles pulled up outside, and she whispered, "Oh, gods."

Gannon, who was reclined in one of the plush chairs, stood, but he didn't move closer. Jordana waited as Lorenzo and another male conversed once they exited their SUVs. Lor made his way inside, and when their eyes met, he gave her a tentative smile. She'd take it.

Jordana let out a little laugh. "Hi."

"Hey there." Lor ran a hand through his hair, ducking his eyes.

Before Jordana could process Lor's smile, Gannon spoke, "Hey, Brother. Where are the others?"

"They're waiting in the cars. I didn't want to disturb the little ones until I knew whether we were heading back out or if we needed to find a hotel."

Boom! Just like that, Jordana's ovaries exploded. Cliché? Maybe, but damn her mate made her want to tackle him to the floor. Or find the aforementioned hotel room, then tackle him. He was worried about the babies.

"Sal and I discussed it, and it would be better to get back in the air as soon as possible to avoid the bad weather headed this way," Gannon responded. "He and his mate are stocking the galley just in case."

"We're good with that." Lor glanced Jordana's way again, his mouth curling up on one side.

Gannon grinned. "I'll go tell him our plan then, and you two can…" Gannon waved a hand in the air and strode out the door, leaving them alone.

Lor toed at something on the floor. "Thank you for this. It means a lot to our family."

Jordana cheered on the inside. Her mate was adorable. "I'd do anything for you." When he met her eyes, she took a chance and held out her hand. Lor only hesitated a couple seconds before closing the distance and grabbing hold. "I want—" she started the same time he said, "We need—" They both laughed, and in that moment, Jordana knew they'd be okay.

Less than an hour later, they were in the air. The three females were kind, making Jordana feel like one of them instantly. Once they got the babies and Amelia settled, the women did their best to get some sleep. Jordana didn't want to rest though. She wanted to ask Lor if he was willing to give her a chance, but having Nikolas sitting close by, she decided to wait until they reached the estate where they could have some privacy. Lor sat next to her on one of the sofas and explained in full detail the situation with his Clan and why they were on the run. Gannon had told Jordana some of what was going on, but Lorenzo filled in the gaps. He spoke low so as not to disturb the females and children, and although Jordana had no trouble hearing him, she leaned closer. She would use any excuse to close the gap between them. And when they hit a patch of turbulence? She fell against his shoulder where she stayed until Amelia awoke and stumbled out of the bedroom.

The girl rubbed her eyes, looking around. Lorenzo held out his arms, and Amelia climbed onto his lap, resting her cheek against his chest. Jordana reached over and brushed a long, dark curl from the child's face. Seeing her mate hold the girl was bittersweet. She wanted him to hold their child. Jordana always wondered if she and Lor had been able to mate when they were younger if she would have given him a child easily. She wondered if she had trouble giving Leo an heir because they weren't mates. Thinking of Diego, Jordana's chest hurt as it often did when thinking about how he came to be. That was another topic she had to speak with Lorenzo about. He deserved to know the truth.

With Amelia settled on Lor's lap, their conversation was put on hold.

THE BABIES STIRRED, which woke the resting females. Amelia remained on Lor's lap while the mates chatted with Jordana about the children and other Clan members. Since Amelia was right there listening, talk was kept to lighter topics. By the time they touched down in Brazil, Abbi, Kat, and Sophia had welcomed Jordana as one of them.

Both Fallon and Francisca met them when they arrived at the estate. His mom ran to him and hugged him tightly, and Lor gently patted her back. He knew she held out hope he and Jordana would see their way back to one another, and it looked like she would get her wish. Fallon welcomed Nikolas and the others, telling them Lor's mother had prepared several rooms for them. Francisca led the way, and Jordana hung back with Lorenzo. As Francisca showed them where they would be staying, Jordana explained that the older female had moved out of her suite to a smaller room to give Abbi, Amelia, and Jonathan the space. Lor was surprised when his mother admitted she and Diego had cleaned out the suite Marcos had taken over, and that's where Nikolas, Sophia, and Lydia were housed. Katherine stayed in a smaller room on the same wing. Keeping them all together was ideal, and Lor thanked Francisca for her thoughtfulness.

While Lor's Clanmates settled in, Jordana excused herself to freshen up, but instead of leaving her to it, Lorenzo followed her. The walk to the other wing was done in silence, and Lor's nerves flitted in his stomach. They had a lot to talk about.

As soon as they crossed the threshold, Jordana closed the door and leaned against it. Lorenzo took a look around. "Was this yours and Leo's suite?"

"No. Just mine." Jordana sighed. "The one your mom put Nikolas and Sophia in was Leo's. He and I didn't live together as husband and wife after Luiz crossed over."

"But you have a child together." Lorenzo didn't want to talk about their sex life, but he couldn't stop himself.

"Lor, I made it clear to Leo that I would be Queen in name, nothing more. We spent our honeymoon in the same place, but we didn't share a bed. When I moved in here, I had to sleep in the same room to keep up appearances, but it was just sleep. He promised if I would give him an heir, he would give me my freedom. I couldn't do it. I couldn't have sex with him knowing my mate – you – were out there somewhere. I waited for you to come back. I waited years that turned into decades." Jordana's eyes filled with tears. "I told myself to give him what he wanted, then I could have my freedom and come for you. Only it didn't work as I planned." Jordana wiped the tears from her face and turned away, looking out the window.

Lor's heart broke for her. If he hadn't been such a selfish prick, he wouldn't demand to know the details of her relationship with his brother. "What do you mean?" Lor set his hands on her shoulders, pulling her back against his chest. "I'm here now, and I want you to talk to me."

Jordana leaned her head back against Lor's shoulder, grabbing onto his arms banded around her stomach. "I thought if I finally gave him a child, things would be okay, only I couldn't get pregnant. The longer it took, the madder he got, and the more I was lost inside. On the outside, I was the Ice Queen. That was the name I caught whispered about me. I had a smile and kind word for all our servants, but I hated Leo. Hated what he stood for. I didn't hide it."

"But you gave him a child." Lor didn't mean for his tone to be harsh, but the thought of his mate sleeping with his brother ate at him.

Jordana turned in Lor's arms, settling her cheek against his heart. "Sex was perfunctory. On a schedule. I saw specialists who told me which days of the month were optimal for getting pregnant. Only on those days did I allow

148

him to touch me, and it was only to try for a child. There were no passionate kisses. No tender touches. I refused to look at him. Refused to touch him while he... After the brief kiss at the wedding, which was for appearances sake, I never kissed Leo. Never held his hand. Never hugged him. I surely never told him I loved him. Hated him? I told him that often, although he knew it without the words. He told me until he had an heir, I wasn't going anywhere."

Jordana took a step back and went to the door. She opened it, looked both ways down the hall, then returned. Only she didn't move back into his arms. Instead, she wrapped herself in a tight hug. "One day, he was angrier than usual. He was ready to take over the throne, but Luiz wouldn't step down until Leo had an heir in place. When I suggested he get one from someone else, I meant from one of his mistresses. I knew he had them. I encouraged them. At first, he was appalled, but after about a week, Leo came to me and said he had the perfect candidate – my cousin. That way the baby would have some DNA in common with me. Then it was me who was appalled. Carlina had a mate and a couple of grown kids of her own, but Leo insisted she would do it for him." Jordana took a deep breath.

"Long story short, he approached Carlina. He offered her one million reais for her body and her silence. She agreed. It only took about a month before she got pregnant. He played it off with your parents that I was finally with child, but after having tried for so long, the doctor insisted I was at risk and needed to be under constant supervision. I went away to an exclusive resort. When Carlina began showing, she joined me. Talk about awkward. Anyway, she had the baby, and I brought him home as my own. Luiz stayed true to his word and handed the throne to Leo." Jordana looked up at Lor, eyes filled with tears. "But Leo didn't keep his word."

Lor couldn't stand the distance between them or the pain coming from his mate. He sat down on the sofa and pulled her onto his lap, holding her close. "You don't have to tell me the rest. I can figure it out."

"I was so stupid." Jordy rested her head against his shoulder. "Don't get me wrong. I loved Diego. Love him. But at the same time, he became the thing keeping me from finding you. He wasn't an easy baby except for when he was with me. I was the only one who could comfort him. Not even his own father could quiet the tears when he was upset. As much as I still wanted to leave and somehow find where you were, I just couldn't leave him. He was innocent."

"Of course you couldn't. I do understand that much." Lor kissed Jordy's forehead, and when she pulled back, her eyes were full of questions. Since they were having the hard conversation, they might as well address everything. "I was young when I left. So full of hurt and rage. I didn't understand the position you were put in or how you had no choice. I get that now. I'm not saying the hurt is completely gone, but I am saying I want you. I want you as my mate. We've lost too much time as it is, and if you'll have—"

Jordana's mouth covered Lor's, quieting his words. They had kissed briefly when he rescued her from Marcos, but this was different. This was a lover's kiss. Not that he'd had any of those, and if she had been truthful, she hadn't either. It didn't matter. Inexperience was overshadowed with the love he'd held onto in the deepest recesses of his soul. The feel of Jordy's lips against his, the taste of her tongue as it tangled with his could only be described as home. Lor was finally where he was meant to be after a century apart. He silently vowed to make up for lost time.

WHEN THEY CAME up for air, Jordana stroked Lor's beard. "I love you. I have loved you since the day I realized you

150

were my mate, and I've never stopped. I vow to you, on all that's holy, I will spend the rest of our long lives making up for the time apart."

Jordana was relieved. The truth was out there between them. Her phone rang, breaking their connection. She reluctantly stood to see who was calling. "It's Pedro's lawyer," she told Lor before answering. She didn't bother putting it on speaker since Lorenzo would be able to hear the whole conversation. "*Senhor* Rocha?"

"I fast-tracked the paperwork. Everything is now in your name. There are documents which require your signature. If you would come to my office—"

"No, *Senhor*. Anything that needs my signature can be sent electronically. I'm in the middle of something and do not wish to leave the estate."

The male hesitated before saying, "As you wish. I was your father's attorney for many years, and I would like to extend those services to you as well."

"I appreciate the offer. Let's get these documents finalized, then we'll discuss your roll in my life."

"Yes, of course."

"You have my email address, so I expect the documents soon."

"I'm sending them now."

"Thank you, *Senhor*." Jordana disconnected. "The audacity," Jordana spit. "There's no way in hell I'm using that male for anything after everything is processed."

Lorenzo held out his hand, and Jordana took it. Lor pulled her into his body and wrapped his arms around her, settling his cheek on her hair. Jordana instantly calmed down. This was what she had been missing all these years. The closeness, the tenderness, the love of a mate. Lor's heartbeat was steady and strong against her ear. How she had longed to hear it. To feel his strength. She looked up at him, and Lor leaned down, pressing their lips together. It was tender, yet full of so much longing. She wanted more.

As she deepened the kiss, Jordana pulled Lor's shirt from his jeans and slid her hands up his bare back, scraping her fingernails over his warm skin. Lor shivered. With one hand fisted in her hair, his other gripped her backside and pulled her flush against him.

It had been a century since Jordana felt lustful. Not since she realized Lor was her mate. She had tamped down on her longing back then because he had been so young, but now... Feeling his erection pressing against her brought those needs to the forefront. Her stomach quivered, and her core throbbed.

"I need you," she husked against his lips.

Lorenzo slid his other hand down her back and lifted her easily. Jordana wrapped her legs around his waist. Her hands were trapped beneath his shirt still, but the hold he had on her promised he wouldn't let her fall. Lor carried Jordana to the bed where he gently lowered her. With heated eyes, he removed her boots and socks. Jordana unbuttoned her pants, pushing them down her hips. Lor grabbed the legs and pulled them the rest of the way off. She wanted him naked, but her mate didn't make a move to remove his own clothing. Instead, he leaned over and pressed his nose to her inner thigh, inhaling deeply against her panties.

As he nipped at her clit through the silk, Lor slid his hands up her stomach, underneath her shirt, pushing her bra up over her breasts. He palmed both mounds, then toyed with her nipples. A zing went straight to her core, and Jordana arched her back, pressing into his face. "More. Please, Lor."

"Shh. I want to take my time with you."

"No, my love. Take your time later. I need you to fill me up and claim me. Make me your mate," Jordana begged, her claws and fangs extending.

"Jordy, my beast is too close to the edge. I'm afraid I'll hurt you."

"You won't. I trust you, Lor. I trust your beast. Mine is close, too, and it's demanding we do this now."

"Fuck!" Lorenzo pushed away from the bed and pulled his shirt over his head. His broad chest was covered in dark hair. She had seen Leo naked, but never had his bare body affected her. Seeing her mate uncovered had her panties soaking, and she hadn't even seen the rest of him. While Lor shed his boots and jeans, Jordana removed her blouse and bra. Lor's eyes flashed from bright blue to a stormy midnight, his beast showing itself. She was ready. She wanted fast. Hard. She wanted the bite.

Jordana moved to the head of the bed, spreading her legs in invitation. Lor stood before her, his body on display. She had always been repulsed by Leo's erection because it had been the wrong one. Lor's was a thing of beauty, long but not too thick, curled up against his stomach. She wanted to taste the pearl of liquid shining on the tip. Jordana licked her lips, and Lor growled low in his chest. He reached down with a claw and shredded her panties. He tossed the ruined garment before climbing on top of her.

"Are you sure?" he asked.

"Yes. Please," she begged again.

Lor didn't make her wait. Lifting her legs toward her chest, Lorenzo teased her clit with the tip of his cock, sliding it through her wetness.

"Hang on, *Preciosa*."

Jordana tensed, waiting for the pain that had accompanied Leo fucking her, but it never came. Lor eased his way inside before slowly sliding out. He set a slow tempo as he watched their bodies coming together for the first time. Jordana reached out to touch his chest. His nipples were tight little buds, and she scraped her fingernails over both. Lor hissed, his hips snapping forward, his cock going deeper. That! That was what she needed.

"I'm too close, Jordy." Lorenzo pulled out, and she groaned at the loss.

153

"What are you doing?" she hissed.

"I want to make this good for you," he explained as he slid lower to put his mouth on her clit.

"No, no, no. I want to come with you buried inside me." Jordana was losing her mind. She appreciated that he wanted her to get off too, but didn't he know she'd do that with him fucking her? Not that his tongue wasn't magical because holy gods. Jordana writhed against him because how could she not? But that wasn't what she needed. "Lor!" she whispered harshly.

Bright blue eyes found hers, his brow furrowed. What he saw on her face must have convinced him. He sucked hard on her nub one last time before kissing his way up her stomach, then latching onto a nipple. His teeth scraped the taut bud, and Jordana snaked a leg around his ass, putting his dick where she wanted it. Lor slid easily inside, and Jordana tightened both heels against his ass. She let her fangs drop once again, and Lor's eyes widened. Getting with the program, his own fangs came out, and he lowered to his forearms, his chest hair scraping seductively against her aching breasts. Using her feet for leverage, Jordana met Lor thrust for thrust.

"Jordy," Lor warned.

"Do it, My Love." Jordana tilted her head, baring her shoulder. This was it. This was the moment she'd waited her whole life for, and Lorenzo didn't disappoint. He hastened his thrusts, filling her with more than his cock. He filled her heart. Soothed her longing. Heat bloomed deep as her orgasm stole her breath. In that moment, Lor shouted right before sharp teeth punctured her neck, and Jordana gasped. Lor's wings were spread out behind him as he emptied his seed deep within her core. Jordana didn't wait. She sank her fangs into Lor's neck, sucking at the skin there. He shouted again, his body convulsing against hers. Their releases combined, slicking her passage further, and it was the most glorious feeling in the world next to the throb in her neck. After more than a hundred years, Jordana was home.

CHAPTER THIRTEEN

FUCK! LOR WAS sure he would pass out. Having thought about this moment his whole life, he never could have imagined how earth-shattering it would be to have his mate. To become one had been a fleeting fantasy, and it hadn't come close to reality. Her body was perfect. She clenched around him like a vise, gripping his cock tightly. He had planned to go slow. To make love to her, getting her off before slipping into her body. Lor didn't want to think about past lovers while with Jordy, but he'd always made sure they orgasmed before he took what he wanted. His female was different. He should have known she would be. The fates had chosen her for him, and in doing so, ensured their coming together would be perfect. And it had been. Until it wasn't.

"Mom!" Diego threw the door open, running into the room.

Jordy squealed, and Lorenzo lowered his wings to shield her body. "Diego, what the hell?"

"Shit, sorry. I heard shouting, and I thought... Never mind. Carry on. Or don't. Gods." The door slammed closed soon after his outburst, and Jordana laughed so hard her whole body shook.

"Next time, we'll have to remember to lock the door," Lor said, grinning. He retracted his wings. "I'm surprised he didn't haul me off you. I don't think he likes me."

"He doesn't know you, but we talked after you left. I told him everything."

"Everything?" Lor eased his half-hard dick from her

156

body and rolled to the side, propping his head on his palm, settling his other hand on the soft skin of her hip.

Jordy lowered her voice. "Not about where he came from, but about how I was forced to marry Leo when you were my mate." Jordana cradled Lor's cheek, running her thumb over his bottom lip. "He never understood why I couldn't stand his father. Why I was nice to everyone except Leo. Once I explained everything, he got it. I did my best not to speak ill of the dead, but there was no way to tell my side of the story without some displeasure coming through."

"I'm sure you were diplomatic."

"I tried to be. But now he knows you were – are – my mate. Oh my gods, you're my mate!" Jordana lunged, knocking Lor to his back. Jordana straddled his waist, her wet pussy rubbing against his erection. Yes, he was hard again, and Lor figured that would be a constant for a while now they were mated. Jordana reached between them and pressed the tip to her entrance. She rose on her knees, then lowered herself until he was fully seated inside. With sultry eyes, Jordana rode Lor's cock. He had never seen such a vision, nor had he ever felt anything as wonderful. Fucking her earlier had been about mating. Coming together for the first time to slake their needs and seal the bond. This? This was making love. Their connection was solid. Their beasts were happy, and Lor was ecstatic. He could have done without his nephew seeing his bare ass, but otherwise, the moment had been perfect. His mate riding him? Even more so.

When they both were sated a second time, Lor pulled Jordana into his arms. His mate was quiet.

"What's wrong?"

"I can't promise to give you children because it seems like that part of me is defective, but—"

"There is nothing defective about you. Having a child the old-fashioned way isn't important. There are plenty of kids out there who need a loving home, if that's something you'd be willing to do, but for now, I want time for just us. Once things with my Clan are less than chaotic, I would like for you to go back to the States with me. If you'd rather stay in Brazil, I'll consider it, but..." Lor sighed. He would do anything for Jordy, even remaining in South America although he didn't want to.

"No. There is nothing for me here. Diego is grown, and he'll know where to find me. He has his own life to figure out, and he doesn't need me to do so. I've planned to give your mother enough money to restart somewhere new if she wishes to, but it might be nice if you offer her a place in the States. With me leaving and Diego going off who knows where, she won't have family here. She loves you, Lor. Like me, she didn't have a choice in what happened."

This was the Jordana Lor remembered from so long ago – a beautiful female with an even more beautiful heart. "I'll ask her. My house is big enough for the three of us. For now. It isn't anything fancy. I haven't been in New Atlanta long. I spent a lot of years on the West Coast, and when I moved east, I took the first house I found. I have enough money to build us something bigger. Something that will be ours together."

"Money is something we'll never have to worry about. Not only am I inheriting everything from my parents, but I've been investing my own money over the last twenty-seven years. Leo was never good with the accounts, but I had a knack for it, so I was in charge of our finances. I'm also handy with a computer, so I may have put some money into investments he knew nothing about."

Lor gave a mock gasp. "Jordy, stealing from your own husband?" He grinned and kissed her perfect nose.

"Eh, I like to call it squirreling away for an emergency. And just so you know, I admitted as much to Fallon when I was showing him the accounts. He just smiled and told me to keep the investments since the rest is more than he'll ever need."

"Wow. I need to introduce you to Sixx. He's the financial wizard in our Clan."

Jordana stood and held out her hand. "I wouldn't say I'm a wizard, but I would say I'm hungry. Let's shower, then go join the others. They're in good hands with Francisca, but I want to get to know the other mates a little better since I'm going to be part of your Clan soon."

Lorenzo pulled her against his chest, nuzzling his face in her neck. "You already are."

Now that he had his mate where he wanted her, Lorenzo was loath to leave the bedroom, but as she reminded him, they had a long lifetime to make love. Begrudgingly, he agreed, and after showering together where he took her against the tiled wall, they made their way to the other side of the estate. When they walked into the living area hand-in-hand, they were met with knowing smiles. Abbi and Katherine might not have Goyle hearing, but it didn't take a shifter to know why they had been sequestered in Jordy's room for hours.

"Congratulations," Nik said, clapping Lor on the shoulder.

"Why congratulations? What's going on?" Amelia asked. The adults laughed, and the little girl frowned harder.

Lor turned loose of Jordy's hand and knelt beside his favorite girl child. "Jordy and I are officially mates."

"Still no wedding?" Amelia asked, pouting.

Lor glanced up at Jordy, winking. "I think we can have a small ceremony so you can be a flower girl."

"Yay!" Amelia launched herself into his arms. "You're the best, Lor Lor."

More laughter followed as Lor stood, cradling Amelia to his side. He would give the girl whatever her heart desired for as long as he could. For one day, she would be too big to carry on his hip. Too old to wear her tutus unless she was dancing. Too cool to be doted on by her Uncle Lor.

He would treasure these small moments with the child until then.

Amelia looked at Jordana. "If he's Lor Lor, that makes you Jor Jor."

Jordana scrunched her nose, and Lorenzo held his breath. Yes, it was a ridiculous nickname, but Amelia was important to him. His mate didn't disappoint. "Does that mean I get to call you Am Am?"

"No, that's just silly. You can call me Munchkin like Uncle Lor does," she said matter-of-factly.

"Munchkin it is. So, you want to be a flower girl, huh?"

"Oh yes. I'm the best flower girl ever. And I'll wear my tutu." Amelia turned to Abbi. "Mommy, did you pack my green one? It would be perfect for a wedding."

"I grabbed several, but I'm not sure if the green one was one of them. Why green?" Abbi asked.

"Because it matches Jor Jor's eyes." Amelia didn't tack on "duh", but it was intended.

Jordana stepped closer, placing her hand on Amelia's back. "I tell you what. If you didn't pack your green one, we can always go shopping for one. And maybe a new dress too? I know I need some new clothes as well as a new dress if I'm getting married."

"Shopping! Yay! Mommy, Jor Jor's taking me shopping!"

Lorenzo met his mate's eyes. He didn't think her smile could get any bigger. For just a moment, Lor pretended Amelia was theirs. His dream of having his mate had come true, and the only thing missing was a child of their own. After not being able to give Leo an heir, Lor doubted it was in the cards for them, but they could always adopt. Amelia was just as much Frey and Abbi's child as Jonathan, and she was loved no less.

"I could go shopping," Katherine said. For having been an exuberant reporter when she first came into the Clan, Julian's mate was much more soft-spoken now.

"And I'll watch Jonathan if you want to go too, Abbi," Sophia offered.

"Please, Mommy?"

Abbi was the sweetest female Lorenzo had met in his life. She was the best mate to Frey, the most devoted friend to the other mates, but most of all, she was the best mom to her children. Taking in her dead husband's illegitimate child was one of the grandest gestures Lor could imagine, yet Abbi loved Amelia as though she were her own flesh and blood.

"Shopping sounds fun, so thank you, Soph." Abbi turned her attention back to Amelia. "Before you go anywhere, you need a bath."

"Okay." Amelia wiggled, and Lor set her on her feet. When Abbi stood, he held out his arms for Jonathan. She didn't hesitate to hand the baby over before taking her daughter's hand and heading toward their room. Lor cradled the boy in his arms, breathing in his scent. When he felt Jordy staring at him, he turned her way. He didn't want to hurt her by reminding her she couldn't have a child of her own, but this was him. He was the guardian over the kids of the Clan, and he didn't want that to change.

"You're so good with them," Jordy said. Her face was lit up in joy, not a speck of sadness to be found.

"They were my job, at first." Lor rocked Jon in his arms as he told Jordana about watching over Matthew first, then settling in as the one who oversaw all the kids' safety when their parents needed an extra set of eyes. "In California, I oversaw the quarry there. A male named Finley was in charge of the one in New Atlanta. When Finley needed a change of scenery, we swapped places. I never really found my calling as a doctor or firefighter or anything important, so I did jobs the Clan needed doing. It wasn't until I began watching the kids that I found my passion."

Lorenzo didn't admit that he saw them as surrogates for the children he thought he would never have. He wouldn't admit that to anyone, especially his mate.

Jordana cupped his cheek, then rocked his world. "You're going to be an amazing father to our children someday." Lor leaned down and pressed a kiss to Jordy's temple as he blinked the tears away.

Once Amelia had a bath, they spent the next few hours shopping. Francisca and Eliana offered to watch the babies so Nik and Sophia could join in their excursion. Jordana bought not only a pretty dress, but also some casual clothes, explaining she was ready to not dress like a Queen. They stopped for lunch, then spent the rest of the afternoon searching for a green tutu. Lor held his mate's hand. He slid his arm around her in the back seat while Nik drove. He touched Jordana every chance he got. When they returned to the estate, he wanted nothing more than to take her back to her suite and make love to her again, but he refrained. Barely. Dinner was a lavish affair with Eliana helping Marcella, the cook who'd been with Jordana for years. Afterward, Jordana led Lorenzo to the garden where they sat on her favorite bench and stargazed while talking about the future. As much as he loved his family back in the States, Lor was content to remain in Brazil, only because it was where his mate was.

ISABELLE, WITH TESSA helping, told Lucy everything she could remember about Kallisto's mannerisms. Speech wasn't a problem since they had a recording of her voice to use with the modulator. With Tessa being the expert at using the device along with the disguises, she discussed that aspect of pretending to be someone else. The more they talked about the plan, the more Isabelle wanted to be the one to go after Eden, but there was no way Dante would allow it. Besides that, she was in New York while Lucy was

162

already in New Atlanta. Add to that was the fact that Lucy was a Gryphon. She was the strongest female Isabelle knew, and Lucy could voice Eden if it came down to it. Isabelle didn't doubt Lucy was ethical in her use of the ability the same way Tamian was with his.

After ending the call, Isabelle went to the bedroom where Connor was reading to Maria. It was something the two of them had been doing a lot of lately. Isabelle didn't think her surrogate mother was interested in the books Connor chose, but she never complained. Maria had always been Connor's greatest champion next to Dante and Isabelle, and Isabelle didn't see that changing anytime soon. Not until the day Maria left them from either old age or a human disease. Isabelle didn't want to think about that day, though. She cherished every moment spent with the older woman.

Things with her own mother were coming along. Not as swiftly as Caroline wanted, but Isabelle was spending at least one afternoon a week with her. She always took Connor with her as a buffer. Whenever conversation became stilted, Connor was there to talk about anything and everything that interested him. At the moment, he was focused on biology. Having two doctors for parents helped whenever he asked questions no seven-year-old should wonder. Except Connor was no ordinary child. Marigold did the best she could as his tutor, but it was apparent they would need to find someone whose intellect matched Connor's soon.

More than once, Isabelle wished Connor wasn't so special. His intelligence was one thing, but his special abilities were something else. Sure, his visions had saved his own life as well as others, but he shouldn't have to carry that burden. Not all his visions were life-altering, but some—

"Mom?" Connor said, louder than normal. By his frown, he'd called out to her more than once.

"Hey. What are you reading?"

"*Halt's Peril*. It's book nine in *The Ranger's Apprentice* series."

"Book nine? Already?" Isabelle wasn't really surprised. It was a series for children after all, and Connor read at college level. It was hard finding appropriate reading material for someone his age that didn't bore him.

"Yes. I finished them all earlier, but this is Mimi's favorite, so I'm reading it to her again."

Maria flashed a smile at Isabelle. After his earlier vision, Maria had requested Connor read her "favorite" just to get his mind off what he'd seen. The vision hadn't been a life-or-death situation, nor had it been another child destined to be born into the Clan, but it had been shocking, and they still weren't sure exactly what it meant. The drawing depicted an older version of Sebastian – she was sure of that because she'd asked Connor – standing alongside a grey wolf. Connor didn't know who the wolf was or what they meant to Sebastian, only that their futures were entwined somehow.

Isabelle and Dante had waited until Connor and Maria were safely inside his room reading before they showed the picture to Rafael and Kaya. While contemplating the meaning, Lucy had called Isabelle, and once they were finished talking, Isabelle had come to check on Connor.

"I'll take your place if you'd like," Isabelle offered.

Maria shook her head. "I'm enjoying the story. You go ahead."

Isabelle inclined her head to her friend, then left them to the book. When she reached the sunken living room, Dante held out his hand. Isabelle took it, allowing him to lead her to one of the sofas. Once seated, she leaned her head on his shoulder as Tessa hypothesized about the drawing.

"I say the wolf is a shifter,"

Gregor agreed with Tessa. "Why not? We always thought Goyles were the only shifters out there until we met the Gryphons. If there are two species, why not more?"

Rafael chimed in. "And with Lucy and Tamian being one of each, their child could possibly be a hybrid. What would that even look like?"

Kaya bounced Bas on her knee. "Are you going to change the world in more ways than one, my little Prince? Are you going to mate with a wolf?"

"Baba," Bas replied, and everyone laughed.

"Baba, indeed," Kaya responded. "I have a feeling the world will be a different place when our children are grown. And if there are wolf shifters, there are probably others we don't know about as well."

"And that would pose another set of problems in and of itself," Dante said. "Sebastian will be King of Gargoyles, but the other shifters will have their own rulers."

"Not necessarily," Isabelle countered. "The Gryphons don't have a King per se. Sutton is their leader in the northeast, but he isn't King."

Dante tightened his grip on her shoulder. "Truth. Hopefully, they'll learn to live together in peace. I'd hate for there to be wars between the species. We got lucky with the Gryphons. Lucy and Tamian being mates bridged that gap."

"Let's not borrow trouble," Rafe said. "We have many years ahead of us before we need to worry."

"Let's hope that's true. Sebastian is a teen in this photo. And he's so handsome, just like his papa," Kaya said, smiling sweetly at her mate.

Rafael kissed Kaya on the temple. "You're just biased."

"Nah, you're hot, and you know it. It's in the Goyle gene," Tessa said, and Gregor growled. "Oh, stow it, Stone. You know I only speak the truth."

"Yes, and sometimes the truth gets your ass spanked."

"Why do you think I do it?" she deadpanned, and again, everyone laughed. Isabelle didn't want to imagine what Gregor and Tessa got up to in the bedroom, but the thought of being spanked held a certain appeal. Not that sex with Dante was lacking in any way, but what if they changed things up a bit? They did have hundreds of years ahead of them, so why not think they would evolve in their relationship? Ever since he told her she was pregnant, Dante had been gentler in their lovemaking. Surely a little slap on the ass wouldn't hurt the baby. Right?

"You need to stop whatever it is you're thinking," Dante whispered in her ear. All those with Goyle hearing turned their way, and Isabelle felt her cheeks getting red.

"Ooh, Belle likes the idea of a little spanking? Am I right?" Tessa teased.

"Stop teasing your cousin, Red." Gregor tugged on Tessa's braid.

"We need to change the subject. As interesting as this is, I'll remind you my son is in the room," Rafe said.

Sebastian clapped his chubby hands together. "Baba."

Thankfully, Priscilla announced dinner was ready, so all talk of sex and shifters was put away. As Connor took the seat next to her, Isabelle thanked the gods for both the son beside her and the one in her belly. She prayed they both had peaceful lives, Connor with Alyssa, and Deklan with whomever the fates chose for their baby boy. Then she added an extra request for all the children to be as happy as Isabelle was with Dante. Now, if she could convince him to spank her.

LACHLAN WAS BOTH relieved and distraught. He had pushed Hunter away, telling him the Clan needed his help. While that was technically true, Lachlan had wanted some distance between them. He couldn't be around the male without wanting him. Lachlan missed all the nights they spent together on the houseboat wrapped in each other's arms, making love. Talking all night and sleeping in the next day. Those times were few and far between with Hunter spending most of his days with his twin, but Lachlan cherished each and every one of them. He knew it was his own fault for Hunter releasing him from the bond, but if he didn't accept it was true, did that make it so? Didn't they both have to agree?

Lachlan still felt the deep need to touch his mate, to bury himself deep inside Hunter and watch as he came apart. His cock lengthened at the thought, but he ignored it. Lachlan had gotten good at ignoring the longing for his mate during his time in prison. He hadn't been held in one of the regular cells. The Clan had put him in a room more like a dormitory than a small cell with bars. But he still didn't want to rub one out where any of the Goyle guards could hear. He wasn't an exhibitionist. It wasn't until he fled the prison and arrived on his boat that he gave over to the need for release. But that was all it had been. A simple biological need to get off. If he thought about Hunter while doing so, that was only natural. But that need had amplified as soon as Hunter stepped foot in the same room.

It had taken every ounce of his Gargoyle strength not to toss Hunter over his shoulder and take him to his bedroom. Hunter already hated him, and forcing sex on him would have only made it worse. Not that he would ever force Hunter to do anything. He loved the male with everything he had. He would do anything for him, even if that meant staying away. But the longer they were apart, the more despondent Lachlan became. If his mate refused their bond, what was the point of anything?

"Fuck!" Lachlan pushed back from the desk and went upstairs. He was at a standstill with Eden, and he needed fuel for the boat. Pulling the anchor and piloting his home to the nearest marina would hopefully give his brain a break. While there, he would head into town for groceries. Lachlan hadn't been eating much, and his beast wasn't happy about it. Where he once enjoyed cooking gourmet meals, now food was nothing more than fuel for his brain. Keeping up with Eden, he needed to be sharp, and Lachlan could admit he wasn't that.

Lachlan had anchored off the North Carolina coast. Far enough away from New Atlanta to give him some breathing room but not too far he couldn't get back to Hunter and the Stone Clan if they needed him. There were several marinas to choose from, and he didn't frequent one more than any other so he wouldn't become too familiar with the locals. Not that he was worried about the humans, but Lachlan wasn't in the mood to make acquaintances and be forced to make idle chat. He wasn't opposed to humans. He *was* opposed to putting on a smile when he had nothing to smile about. He knew it was his own fault, having worked for Alistair. He just never thought he would get caught in the crossfire between the Greek and the Stone Society. Lachlan had never bowed down to any one King, not since he left his home so long ago.

Traveling the world one body of water at a time, Lachlan never felt the need to commit to any one group of Goyles until he sailed to Greece and fell in love with a twin named Hector. When he met his mate, Lachlan was under the impression the twins were loyal to the Greek King, so he remained in the country to be close to Hector. What Lachlan didn't know at the time was the twins were working against Alistair. Their loyalties were with the Italian King, so when Lachlan fell in with Alistair, he unknowingly sealed his fate. The twins were on a mission, one that didn't include Lachlan. He and Hector became lovers. Hector admitted they were mates, but his focus had been single-minded, and Lachlan didn't play into the brothers' plans. For years, Lachlan took what little Hector gave him, hoping one day the brothers' plan would come to fruition, and then Hector would join Lachlan. But Hector – or Hunter as he was now known – chose his twin over Lachlan, and his hopes waned. When Hunter released Lachlan from their bond, his hopes died.

Now all he could do was finish this one last mission. Take out Eden, and Lachlan would call it a day.

Or a lifetime.

CHAPTER FOURTEEN

EDEN SPENT THE previous day going head-to-head with whomever was on the other side of the screen. She still had no idea who they were. Out of self-preservation, she didn't dare check them for fear the other hacker would track her movements and do the same thing to her they had her father. If nothing else, Eden would share her millions with her parents, if her father didn't kill her first.

The return call from Kallisto never came, so Eden decided to go have a look for herself. After studying an aerial map of the land around the prison, Eden bundled up and headed that way. She drove to an outdoors store and purchased a pair of high-powered binoculars before making the rest of the trip. After parking about half a mile away, Eden trudged through the woods on the southern side of the prison. With the dense trees as cover, she lifted the binoculars to her eyes. A tall fence topped with razor wire surrounded the property. There were several guards stationed outside and another in the tower. As a matter of fact, none of the guards carried weapons. If she didn't know what happened earlier on the inside, Eden would think this was any other day. That is until an ambulance traveled down the long road that wound around to the back of the building. Neither the lights nor the siren was on.

The vehicle backed up close to the door, and a young-looking attendant stepped out of the driver's side. The door to the prison opened, and a familiar red-headed man stepped out, pulling the attendant in for a swift kiss. The EMT opened the back of the ambulance and grabbed an armful of black bags before following the other man into the building. Eden searched her memories and snapped her fingers in the otherwise silence. "Jasper Jenkins, the detective."

Eden waited for what seemed like hours before they returned. Jenkins had one of the bags tossed over his shoulder while a Black man carried another. Two more guards exited also carrying bodies. The EMT followed behind and waited while four bodies were deposited into the back of the ambulance. After closing the back doors to the vehicle, the driver and Jenkins spoke as if they had all the time in the world. Since whoever they put in the bags were dead, she guessed there wasn't a need to rush. But who was in the bags? Were they prisoners? Was one of them Kallisto? Was that why she hadn't returned Eden's call?

Several people joined the couple outside. Eden focused the binoculars. She recognized most of them from tracking Rafael Stone and his family. One was Geoffrey Hartley, the owner of the gym and the man who'd delivered her shooter to the prison. Before Eden could get a good look at the others, the group disbursed, and the EMT kissed Jenkins again before getting into the ambulance and driving off.

Eden had to know if Kallisto was in the ambulance. There was no way she could catch it, not having to travel half a mile back to her car by foot, but she could go to the local hospital where the morgue was, and then what? How the hell was she going to get inside? Maybe she didn't have to. Maybe she could hack into the security feed at the hospital. If the morgue had cameras inside, she could see who was in the body bags. If one of them was Kallisto... No, Eden wouldn't borrow trouble – or heartache – just yet. And no way would she think herself responsible, even though she was the one who opened the cell doors. No, this was on Rafael Stone and his family. They were the ones who put Kallisto behind bars. No matter what Kallisto had done in the past, she shouldn't be held in the same prison as killers

171

and rapists. Eden retraced her steps to her car, then headed home. One way or another, she would find out if Kallisto was still alive.

By the time Eden got back to her house, she was vibrating. She couldn't stop thinking about the larger-than-life woman she met in Greece. About their time together. Kallisto had stepped out of a shop looking like sex on high heels, and Eden had been gone. The tall blonde was even taller in her stilettos, and she towered over Eden's short frame, but when they had been horizontal? That hadn't mattered. Their chemistry had been off the charts. Eden knew at a young age she preferred girls to boys, although she had her share of both over the years. She liked the soft edges, the curves, the smooth skin of a woman beneath her fingertips, and Kallisto was all that and more. Well, maybe not the soft edges. Kallisto Vargas had a bite to her tongue and an attitude for days.

It wasn't until their weekend was over that Eden knew she wanted Kallisto in her life for more than a few days. Kallisto hadn't promised Eden more than those three nights, but her gentle caresses and the way she tenderly cupped Eden's face before they parted implied she felt their connection. Eden had spent the last several years tracking down her lover. Spent more time on finding her blonde than doing work for Nexus. It was a good thing she could multitask with the best of them, or her father's business would have suffered long ago. But now, what if all that time had been for nothing? No. She wouldn't believe the worst. She hadn't come this far, gone to all this trouble, only to lose Kally now.

Sitting down at the computer, Eden ignored her father's completely drained bank account. She ignored the other hacker and tapped into the security feed at the hospital. When she found the cameras located in the morgue, Eden frowned. The EMT was not the one working on a body. Instead, it was a handsome man who looked to be in his late thirties, and the body appeared to be a middle-aged woman. Definitely not Kallisto. The guy driving the ambulance should be there by now. Eden checked New Atlanta for any other morgues and found one on the outskirts of the city. It was at a smaller hospital, but there were no cameras inside. Eden checked security footage for the parking areas, but there were no emergency vehicles in the lot.

"Where did you go?" Eden pondered aloud as she tapped into as many CCTV cameras as possible between the prison and the hospital. She caught sight of the ambulance on a couple, but she lost it when it drove out of the city. Why would he not take the bodies to the closest hospital? Granted, Eden didn't know anything about how inmates were handled if something happened to them on the inside, but something didn't add up. Wouldn't the deceased be taken to the morgue so next of kin could be notified? Just because the inmates had been behind bars didn't mean they didn't have family who would want to bury them or have them cremated. Maybe that was it. Eden searched for a local crematorium and found it was in the direction the ambulance was headed.

"Shit!" If Kallisto was in one of those bags, Eden couldn't let her lover be cremated. And what if she still had family back in Greece? Did those running the prison not care about doing the right thing? Of course they didn't. They had imprisoned Kallisto like she was nothing, so why wouldn't they toss her away? Or burn the evidence they had her in the first place? Making note of the address, Eden rushed out of the house and to her car. She plugged the address into her GPS and took off. She had to get there before those two bodies were disposed of. If she was too late, she'd never know the truth unless Kallisto happened to call her. Praying to any deity who would listen, Eden begged she not be too late.

Less than an hour later, Eden slammed her hands on the steering wheel. The crematorium was closed until

Monday. So where the hell had the ambulance gone? It was possible he'd driven to a different hospital, but she didn't think so. Eden pulled out of the parking lot and headed to New Atlanta Hospital. When she arrived, she drove around back to where the emergency vehicles were parked and compared tag numbers. The one she had been trying to locate was parked alongside the others. That didn't make any sense. Deciding to go home and attempt to retrace its path backwards, Eden made her way to the exit. Before she got on the street, her phone pinged. Eden looked in the rearview mirror to make sure she wasn't blocking the exit and checked to see which notification she'd received. "Well, well, well." She might not have found where the bodies were taken, but she now had something even better.

TREVOR PULLED THE bus onto the private road where Paxton was waiting. He didn't know the Goyle well, but Frey trusted the male to take care of the bodies, so Trevor helped transfer them all to the back of Pax's SUV. There were dead Unholy back at the Pen, but Trevor didn't have to worry about their disposal. The Gargoyles would handle that task.

"Thanks, Trevor. I'll take it from here." Paxton didn't hang around to chat, and Trevor didn't blame him. The sooner Kallisto, Sergei, and the two snipers were disposed of the better. Make that three snipers. Paxton had stopped off at Gregor's, and that body was also in the back of the SUV. Besides, Trevor needed to get back to the morgue. Dante's friend, Simon, was as capable as Dante, but Trevor still liked things a certain way. He liked to make notes of each body, testing blood samples. Notating any clones who came across a slab. His schoolwork was going well, but now that Simon had taken over, Trevor wasn't sure he wanted to continue training to be an ME. His interests lay more in studying clones. He wasn't sure what he would do with all the information he'd gathered over the last few years, but he knew he wanted to do something with it.

Just as he reached for the key in the ignition, his phone rang. Figuring it was Jasper checking on him, he started the engine and let the Bluetooth connect. Instead of it being his mate, a different male's voice sounded in the cab.

"Trevor, this is Lachlan."

"Oh. Uh, hey?" Trevor's spine tingled.

"I'm pretty sure Eden is trying to figure out where you are. I disabled your GPS so she can't track you. As soon as you're back at the hospital, I'll enable it."

"If you can track everything she's doing, why can't you stop her?"

"I'm trying. I promise I am. But she's good. I'm trying to get a lock on where she's working from. As soon as I do, I'll send the information to Frey."

"Yeah, okay." Trevor reached up to disconnect. Right before he did, he added, "Thanks, Lachlan."

Trevor drove back to the city, eyes scanning the area around him. He didn't know what kind of car Eden drove. Hell, he didn't know what the woman looked like. He imagined someone like Cruella de Vil, but that was illogical since Kallisto had a fling with the woman. And Trevor knew better than most that evil didn't equate to ugly. At least not on the outside. All those who had attempted to harm the Clan had been handsome, or in Kallisto's case, beautiful in appearance. The ugliness was below the surface.

If Eden was trying to find Trevor, that meant she had eyes on the Pen. Instead of calling Frey from his cell phone, Trevor waited until he arrived at the hospital. After backing the bus in its parking space, Trevor scanned the lot for anything out of the ordinary. There were no cars back there that shouldn't be, so he climbed down and rushed inside. He didn't breathe easier until he was inside the cold morgue.

Simon looked up from the body he was working on and frowned. "Are you okay?"

"No. No, I'm not." Dante had filled Simon in on the Clan's troubles before he left for New York, and Trevor had explained why he was taking a bus to the Pen when he stopped by to get one. "I got a phone call from Lachlan after I made my delivery. He said Eden was trying to find out where I went." Trevor paced the small room and shook out his hands. "I need to call Frey and tell him she was watching the Pen."

Simon put down the scalpel and stepped in front of Trevor, placing his hands on Trevor's shoulders. "Stop. Think for a second. If she was trying to find you, that meant she didn't follow you, right?"

"I guess, but still. This woman has caused so much trouble. What if she followed and I didn't see her? What if she's following, uh, someone else right now?" Trevor didn't want to say Paxton's name aloud in case Eden had somehow bugged the morgue. "Shit, do you think she got in here? She could be listening right now."

"Trevor, stop. No one has been in here. The morgue hasn't been unmanned since you were here yesterday." Simon removed his hands but didn't step back. Trevor had gone to the Pen and injected the four bodies with embalming fluid. It wasn't often the morgue performed embalming autopsies, but Trevor was glad to have the chemical on hand. Frey didn't want to move the bodies immediately in case Eden was watching.

Trevor was also tasked with transporting the corpses in a bus. Frey didn't want to load them in an SUV in case word somehow got out about the riot. Everything had to appear legitimate. Since he was the one driving the bus, Trevor needed someone to watch Cailín. Sabrina was busy at the hospital, and Lilly had her new twins to take care of. Since the other mates were out of town, that left Caroline who was over the moon having been asked to watch Cailín. With Jonas spending so much time downstairs in his lab with Lucy, Trevor imagined Caroline was thrilled to have someone to focus on. According to Dante, her relationship with Isabelle was still a work in progress, and Maria continued to fill the role of grandmother for Connor. Sophia was grown with a child of her own, and Trevor wasn't aware of any other grandkids Caroline had with all her children scattered across the globe. Since neither Trevor's nor Jasper's mothers were in the picture, Cailín didn't have a grandmother of her own, and if Trevor could give that to Caroline, he would.

"It's just…" Trevor ran his hands through his hair and looked up at his new boss. "When does it end? When do we stop looking over our shoulders waiting for the next bad thing to happen? I'm scared, Simon. I know the badass club can handle themselves against other Goyles, but when the attacks are coming from a computer? And the mates and kids. Shit." Trevor blinked back the tears threatening to fall. What if Eden went after Cailín?

"I can't answer that," Simon said, bringing Trevor back to the conversation. "As long as this world has been spinning, bad shit has happened to good people. It will always be that way, so we do the best we can to look after one another. I will tell you to trust our King, his family, and your mate. Now, do you want to go home, or would you rather stay here and help out a while?"

"Where's Clark?" Dante hired the new guy once Trevor started school.

"He's on his dinner break."

Trevor looked around. "I'll go home unless you really need me."

Simon walked back over to the body. "We can handle things here. You go love on that precious girl of yours and trust the Clan to handle everything else."

"Thanks, Simon." Trevor placed the bus keys on a hook

in the office, then headed outside to his car. Not knowing if Eden was watching, he took as many backroads as possible getting to Caroline's house. He wouldn't make it easy on the psycho bitch to follow him.

TAMIAN WASN'T CRAZY about his mate pretending to be Kallisto, but he would never hold her back from such an important task. He would be close by when she met with Eden. When they arrived at Jonas's house, Trevor was inside with Caroline and Cailín. Jasper's baby sister – now daughter, thanks to Julian forging documents – was adorable with her curly red locks and bright green eyes. No one would doubt she was Jasper's by looking at the child. Tamian prayed his own child took after her mother. Not that they knew they were having a girl. But Lucy had taken to calling their baby "her" so they didn't call it something silly like a bean. That was another reason he didn't want Lucy going up against Eden. Yes, Lucy was a Gryphon, but she wasn't impervious to bullets or poison. The only reason he wasn't protesting aloud was Lucy's ability to voice the human. There was still the chance Eden could get the upper hand before Lucy had the chance to use her gift, but Tamian wasn't going to think about that. If he did, he'd grab his mate, haul her back to New York, and tell her family what was going on. Warryck and his brothers would side with Tamian and lock Lucy safely away.

"What's wrong?" Tamian asked Trevor once he was closer to the human.

Trevor brushed a purple strand of hair out of his eyes. "Eden's what's wrong. She was trying to follow me when I made my delivery."

"You saw her?" Lucy asked.

"No. Lachlan called and told me. He wasn't sure, but he

178

thought she was trying to figure out where I was going." Trevor's voice wavered, and Cailín scrunched up her nose, whimpering. Trevor took a deep breath, then blew it out. "Shh. Papa's okay," he assured the baby. Looking up from where he sat on the floor, he said, "She's so in tune with our moods. Doesn't like it when we're upset." Jasper had decided he'd be called Da while Trevor would be her papa. What would Tamian's little bean – gah, his child – call him?

"Do you think she could have followed you here?" Lucy moved to the front window and looked out.

"Anything's possible, but I don't think so. I dropped the bus off at the hospital, then went inside and talked to Simon for a bit. When I left, I looked around and didn't see anyone out of the ordinary. I drove around for a while, taking a lot of backroads to get here."

Caroline, who was sitting on the sofa, bent down and stroked Cailín's cheek. "That woman won't get anywhere near you as long as you're here."

"No, she won't," Jonas said, entering the room. "What's the latest? Trevor told us about Kallisto and Sergei."

"I have a recording to use on the voice modulator, so we just need a prosthetic," Lucy said, letting the blinds fall back in place. Tamian had already called his uncle asking if he would make one.

"Who's going to don the mask?" Caroline asked.

"I am." Lucy crossed her arms over her chest, a move Tamian was familiar with. Coming from a family of alpha shifters, she often felt the need to prove herself. "It makes the most sense. I'm a Gryphon and can hold my own against one measly human." She glanced at Trevor. "No offense."

"None taken. I'm used to Tessa's brand of badassedness, and you have her beat, claws down. Just don't tell her I said that." Trevor blushed when he looked at Tamian.

Tamian grinned at the young man. "Don't worry. I love my sister beyond measure, but I agree with you." Turning to

179

Jonas, Tamian said, "Lucy is the best option, and I'll be close by when she confronts Eden."

"But what's the plan? Does she not realize Kallisto is dead?" Jonas asked, his brows dipping low.

"Not as far as we know. She called the prison right after we got all the inmates back in their cells, and Aldredge told her the place was on lockdown, and he'd have Kallisto call her back. The plan is for 'Kallisto' to tell Eden she's being released, but we don't want Lucy to make the call until the prosthetic is ready in case Eden decides to pick her up immediately instead of asking to meet up somewhere."

"All I need is a photo," Jonas said.

"I've already sent it to your email," Lucy told the scientist. "If you don't mind, I'd like to watch the process."

"Then let's get to the lab." Jonas led Lucy downstairs where the two had been holed up for months working on a formula that could possibly lengthen lifespans. Gryphons didn't live as many years as Gargoyles, and when they mated with a human, that mate didn't get the same benefit of having their lives prolonged the way Goyle mates did. It was a project Lucy's adoptive father had been working on secretly before his death. Ryker's mate, Rhiannon, had found one of Lucius's journals hidden in a closet, and as soon as Lucy figured out what was in it, she and Tamian traveled down to New Atlanta seeking Jonas's help. The serum had come together rather quickly, but they had to test it out on animals first.

Lucy had been hesitant. She had such a kind spirit, and she didn't want to harm any creature, but needs must, and none of the mice had experienced any traumatic side effects. The only problem was they could live up to a year if not longer, so the experiment wasn't going to be considered a success or failure for a while.

Caroline stood. "I'm going to check on supper. Trevor, why don't you call Jasper and have him meet you here?"

"Oh, I've already imposed enough."

"Nonsense. I miss having babies in the house. You can bring Cailín over anytime you like. Besides, with that crazy woman out there, I'd feel better if Jasper followed you home."

"Yes, ma'am." Trevor leaned over so he could get his phone out of his back pocket.

"Trevor, where's your burner phone?"

"Shit! It's in the car." Trevor bit his lip. "Do you think she's tracking me?" he whispered.

"Anything's possible. Go ahead and turn yours off, just in case." Tamian tapped out a message to Jasper requesting his presence along with why he was texting instead of Trevor. He wanted to shake the young man for being careless, but instead, Tamian vowed to watch over Trevor and Cailín until Jasper could do the job himself. Jasper's job was an important one in the city, but Dane would give him leave in a heartbeat if he knew Trevor was in danger. Hell, they all were in danger with Eden running around unchecked.

Dane had Marley staying at Stone, Incorporated with Willow and Mason during the day where the young Goyle could watch over them both. There were two other males standing guard in the building as well. Sabrina had a security detail attached to her at the hospital since her job wasn't one she could shirk. Not that Marley's job wasn't important to her, but there were plenty of waitresses available to cover her shifts for a few days. Tamian hoped this situation with Eden would be resolved sooner rather than later. The Clan needed to get on with their lives.

Tamian didn't have Dante's calming abilities, but he attempted to soothe Trevor all the same by sitting next to him on the floor and playing with the baby. "I can't wait until our own daughter is here," he said, hoping to get the man's mind on something other than being followed by Eden.

"And I can't imagine what she's going to be, you know?

181

Will she be a Goyle, a Gryphon, or a hybrid? Your daughter is going to be one of a kind."

Tamian chuckled. "That she is, and to be honest, we don't know. We won't know until she's older. Either when she hits puberty or finds her mate and transitions for the first time."

"Have you picked out a name yet?" Trevor held Cailín's hips as the baby bounced up and down on her feet, chattering in that nonsensical way babies do.

"No. We both have a list that we aren't showing the other. We've decided to give it about six months, both jotting down any name we like. Then, at the six-month mark, we'll compare notes. If we've chosen the same name or names, we'll narrow it down from there." If Tamian had been able to read Lucy's mind like he could most everyone else's, there would have been no way for her to keep her list to herself.

"Wow. I don't know of anyone that's done it that way. That's cool. Maybe Jas and I can do that for our next child."

"Well, that answers that question. I was wondering if you would be content with just one." Tamian wanted a houseful. His childhood with Tessa had been strange, something he didn't realize until he was older and saw how most kids lived. He was her clone, and as such had felt closer to her than was considered normal. She had been his one constant even though their lives weren't spent side-by-side as most siblings were. When Tessa was with Jonas, Tamian was with Elizabeth, and vice versa. Looking back, his mother might have noticed his obsession with his sister and kept them apart on purpose.

"No way. I love this little bugger to pieces, but I want a child with more of Jasper's DNA, plus I don't want her growing up alone. Yes, she'll have the other kids in the Clan to play with, but that's not the same as having a sibling constantly by your side. Learning how to share. How to love and protect the other no matter what."

"The way Travis loved and protected you?"

Trevor sighed. "Yeah. Until he left for college, life was as perfect as it could be for someone like me."

Tamian didn't have to ask what Trevor meant by someone like him. He could read it clearly in the man's mind. Besides, he didn't want to reopen Trevor's wounds. He knew all about Trevor being a clone and why he was brought into existence. "I get that. I want as many kids as Lucy's willing to give me."

"And that would be seventeen," Lucy said from the doorway.

Tamian barked out a laugh. "That's oddly specific."

Lucy grinned and crossed the room to sit on the floor across from them. The coffee table had been moved back, more than likely to give Cailín room to roll around. "Because that's how many names I have on my list so far. I figure the more kids I have, the more names I'll get to use."

Trevor tilted his head. "Do you have more boy or girl names?"

"Girls, definitely. Most of my family is male, so I hope we get to balance that out a bit."

"Sweetheart, that'll be more than tipping the scales," Tamian said.

"And your point is?" Lucy gave him a mock glare until he winked at his mate. Then her face morphed into her beautiful smile. For so long, Tamian lived his life in the shadows, following Tessa around the globe. When she mated with Gregor, Tamian's heart broke. Not because he wanted her for himself. That would have been wrong on so many levels, but in his mind, they were a part of each other, literally. He had been created from her DNA, so he felt like an extension of his sister. He never expected to find a mate of his own, then Lucy happened. Now it was hard to remember life before his pretty Gryphon.

"Besides that, our child will more than likely be different, possibly a hybrid. I don't want just one child

183

feeling like they're the only species of their kind in the world."

Trevor sighed again. "I get that. I mean, I knew I wasn't the only clone out there, but until I met others like me in high school, I felt alone. Imagine my shock meeting this guy." Trevor jabbed his thumb in the air in Tamian's direction. "I guess I should thank you. If you hadn't been created, I wouldn't be here either."

"I would say 'you're welcome,' but I had nothing to do with it. That was all on Jonas."

"I'll say it. You're welcome, Trevor." Jonas entered the room holding something in his hand. "Here you go, Lucy. I made three of them, just in case. Now all you have to do is find the right wig and clothes."

"Thanks, Jonas. Tessa sent me a link to the woman who made all her wigs. I've already sent a photo, and she assures me she can have one to me by tomorrow. The good thing about Kallisto not seeing Eden in a few years is her hairstyle could have changed in that time, so we don't have to get it exact. As for clothes, I asked Rory to raid my closet and ship me some of my things. I had to dress the part in my old job, so I have plenty of items that scream 'rich bitch.'"

"I thought you were rich," Trevor added. "Not that you're a bitch. I'll shut up now." His face flushed red. In that moment, Cailín grunted, and it didn't take a shifter's nose to know what she was up to. Trevor stood. "Saved by the bell. Or poop."

Caroline, who was standing in the doorway, said, "Perfect timing, if you ask me. Dinner's ready."

Chapter Fifteen

TREVOR STOOD AND picked Cailín up. Before he could leave the room, Lucy stood in front of him after Tamian helped her to her feet.

"You should know it's hard to offend me. I have three uncles who love to tease. Living among bikers has taught me to loosen up. Ryker and my dad aren't as brash, but it's a different world than I was used to growing up with my great-aunt and uncle. Besides, I've heard how you and Tessa tease each other. I've missed that with my uncles," she said wistfully.

"So you *want* me to call you a bitch?" he quipped. Tamian growled, and Trevor shrank back.

Lucy smacked her mate on the stomach. "I want you to feel free to joke around with me the way you do Tessa. I love your snarky playfulness."

"I'll remember that. Now let me get the princess here changed. She's starting to reek." Trevor took Cailín to the guest bedroom and laid her down on the changing pad. When he got a load of the mess in her diaper, he said, "No more green beans for you, Little Miss. Gods." It was a good thing he had a strong stomach because baby poop was rancid. He was snapping her onesie when his phone buzzed in his pocket.

Shit! He had forgotten to turn it off, even after Tamian reminded him. Figuring it was Jasper, he was prepared to be chastised when he saw it was a video notification. His heart dropped to his feet when he pushed play. In the video, his father was walking from his car to the front door of his house. A red dot was centered on his head. A text message popped up.

Unknown: *If you don't want the dot to turn into a hole, you'll be at his house in fifteen minutes. Come alone and tell no one. If you're followed, he dies.*

Trevor knew who the text was from. He also knew getting out of the house would be near to impossible, but if he didn't go, his dad would die. They hadn't always had the best relationship, but Jack was trying. *Shit, shit, shit.* Did he tell Tamian so he could call Jasper? Trevor picked Cailín up and cradled her against his chest. He breathed her baby scent into his nose. What if this was the last time he got to smell her?

"Trevor?" Caroline called from the doorway.

"Sorry. She had a blowout. Took me a minute to get it all cleaned up." Hugging the baby tight one last time, he handed her over. "If you'll take her, I'll put this in the garage," he said, motioning to the bag of dirty diaper and wipes. "Too many shifter noses to leave it in the house." Caroline took Cailín, and Trevor grabbed the bag. He knew he should trust the Clan, but he had less than fifteen minutes to get across town, and even if traffic were light, he barely had time to make it. He did his best to casually walk down the hallway and out the door leading to the garage. After tossing the bag in the garbage can, Trevor unlocked the side door and let himself outside. He jogged to his car and slid inside, making sure not to slam the door. The shifters would hear it start, but he would have a few minutes head start. He picked up the burner phone with one hand, his thumb hovering over the button that would connect him to his mate. The phone was supposed to be untraceable, but what if Eden had some way of knowing he made a call? He couldn't risk his father's life, so he put the phone in the cupholder and focused on getting to his father's rental house.

Trevor pulled into the driveway with no time to spare

and slammed on the brakes to keep from plowing into the garage door. The lights were off in the house, but he didn't expect the place to be lit up like a runway. Something hit the passenger window, and Trevor screamed. When he turned his head, a masked person was pointing a gun at him. All during the drive, Trevor thought about trying to overpower Eden. He wasn't a big guy, but he was a man. All thoughts of getting the upper hand went up in a puff of smoke. He might be stronger than a female, but he wasn't a Goyle like Jasper. Trevor wasn't impervious to bullets. "Fuck."

"WHAT'S WRONG?" LUCY asked Tamian when he abruptly shoved back from the table.

"Trevor's gone," Tamian said, pulling his burner phone from his pocket. "I felt his trepidation when he walked through the house. He was worried about his father, but I didn't think he'd leave. Sweetheart, is the voice modulator ready?"

"Yes." Lucy stood, ready to run downstairs where she'd left the transmitter while watching Jonas create the mask. "The disguise isn't, though. I don't have a wig."

"We don't have time for that. Can you triangulate a call from here? You need to pretend you're calling from the Pen."

"I should be able to."

"Then grab the modulator. We're running out of time. I need to call Jasper."

Lucy was ready to meet Eden head-on and let her Gryphon loose. She turned toward the door leading downstairs, but Jonas beat her to it. In less than fifteen seconds, the scientist was back with the small transmitter. Lucy was nervous. She didn't know about Kallisto's relationship with Eden, and she was afraid she would say

187

the wrong thing.

Tamian pinched the bridge of his nose as he explained to Jasper what happened. Even if they all weren't shifters, they would have heard the male's angry voice loud and clear. When Tamian could get a word in, he told Jasper Lucy was going to call Eden as Kallisto and hopefully redirect her attention.

"This had better work!" Jasper yelled before hanging up.

Tamian flinched as he stared at the phone, but he didn't blame Jasper for being upset.

"I hate to admit this, but the female is better than any of us, Lachlan included." Lucy shook out her hands. "Jonas, if you don't mind, I'm going to use your office." Jonas readily agreed, and Lucy turned to her mate once again. "Will you come with me?"

"Of course." Tamian brushed a strand of hair off Lucy's face. "You've got this, Sweetheart."

"Let's hope so." Lucy grabbed her mate by the hand and led him into Jonas's office. She didn't bother closing the door before sitting behind the large desk. "Here goes nothing."

EDEN WASN'T A fan of guns. She had assassins at her disposal for those. But growing up with a military father who then started a mercenary company, she knew how to use one. Still didn't like them, but desperate times and all that. She didn't plan on killing the ambulance driver. She only wanted information, and this seemed the quickest way to go about it. The fact that he was partners with a detective should have deterred her, but time was running out. Eden had to know if Kallisto had been in one of those black bags. If so...

Trevor pulled into his father's driveway, sliding to a stop right before he hit the garage door. Eden stepped out of the shadows and tapped on the passenger window with the muzzle of the pistol. Trevor jumped, placing a hand on his chest as if that would slow his heartbeat.

"Unlock the door, Trevor." With wide eyes, he did as she asked, and Eden slid into the warm interior. The lower part of her face was covered with a bandana, and she had a knit cap covering her dark hair. She aimed the gun at Trevor. "Hand over your phone."

Trevor gave her a cheap burner. "Now the other one." He dug into his pocket and handed over the device that had allowed her to find him. "Drive."

"Uh, where are we going?"

"Just head south for now." When Trevor didn't put the car in gear, she pulled back the hammer. "I said drive."

As Trevor backed out of the driveway, he asked, "Is my father okay?"

"He'll be fine. Maybe a little headache, but nothing a few pain pills won't cure." Eden rolled down the window and tossed both his phones as far as possible while still focusing on her captive. "Get on the freeway. We need to put a little distance between us and the city." If Eden could get to the house she'd rented almost a year ago, she could put her plan in motion and hopefully get Kallisto back. "Here's how this goes. You tell me what I want to know, and I'll let you live." Eden pulled the bandana down around her neck, then reached out to adjust the temperature on her side of the vehicle.

Trevor glanced over at her. His blue eyes were wide, yet he still managed to laugh. "Right. I've seen the movie, Eden. The psychopathic villain lies to the innocent victim, promising to let him go."

Eden bristled at the use of her name, but with the other hacker out there, it only made sense Rafael Stone and all those associated with him knew who she was. That and

Kallisto had said her name on the phone. "I'm no psychopath."

"Please. Your photo could be in the textbook next to the definition. We both know you don't care who you hurt as long as you get what you want. So tell me, are you really trying to take out a whole family for one deranged female? I mean, the two of you are perfect for each other. Kidnapping. Attempted murder. Blowing shit up. What's your plan if you manage to get Kallisto out of jail? Go on the run and continue your paths of destruction together? Bonnie and Clyde? Well, I guess it would be Bonnie and Bonnie. My only hope is you're more like Thelma and Louise."

"Thelma and...? What the fuck are you going on about? Never mind that. Are you telling me Kallisto is alive?"

"Well, yeah, but if she weren't? Whose fault would that be? Yours. You're the one who opened those cell doors, including hers. Did you ever stop to think what would happen when a pretty blonde was suddenly available to hundreds of men who'd been locked up for years? No, you didn't. You're lucky her boyfriend kept her safe until the guards were able to control the inmates. Hell, Eden. Even if Kallisto weren't model-gorgeous, those men would have ripped her apart. Literally."

"Shut up! I'm not the one who put her in that situation. She shouldn't be locked up with hundreds of men as you put it. She shouldn't be locked up at all."

"Oh, right. Kidnapping and murder should go unpunished because you love her. What the fuck ever." Trevor kept glancing in the rearview mirror. Eden turned and looked behind them, but they were alone in the slow lane. Trevor drove like a grandma.

"You're testing my patience, Trevor. You need to keep this car at the speed limit." Trevor gradually accelerated until they were going seventy. "You said boyfriend. Kallisto—"

"Was an equal opportunity lover. She took advantage

190

of whomever could give her what she wanted in the moment. What? Did you think you were special? I have news for you. That woman would use anyone to her advantage. Did you know she kidnapped a kid? Who the fuck does that?"

Eden's phone rang. She moved the gun to her left hand so she could get the phone from her back pocket. When she saw the call was from the prison, her heart raced.

"Hello?"

"Hey. Sorry I couldn't call you back before now, but the prison was on lockdown. Somehow the doors were opened and there was a riot," Kallisto said.

"Oh, god, Kally. Are you okay? Were you hurt?"

"I'm okay now. I thought I was going to die, or worse, but I'm good."

"I'm so glad. Listen, you sit tight. I have a plan, but I have to go. I'll see you soon." Eden disconnected the call, a grin spreading across her face.

As they hit the freeway, Trevor's words came back to her, and her smile fell. Had Kallisto only used Eden that weekend? No. What they had meant something, and Eden would prove it to her lover once she had her back in her arms. She would remind Kally how good they were together. Besides, once Kallisto was free, she would need Eden to keep her safe. Eden rolled down her window and tossed her phone.

THE HOUSE WAS dark when Jasper arrived. He had broken every speed limit getting to Trevor's father's rental. When Tamian called and said Trevor left abruptly, Jasper had to rein in his beast. He needed a level head. Jasper hurried to the front door and banged. "Jack? It's Jasper!" Jasper opened his senses. If he hadn't been a shifter, he wouldn't have heard the low moan coming from inside. Jasper tried the knob to find it unlocked. He eased the door open to find Jack McKenzie lying on the living room floor, cradling his head.

"Shit." Jasper retrieved his phone and dialed for an ambulance after announcing who and where he was.

"Tr-Trevor," Jack moaned.

"Trevor's not here. It's me, Jasper."

"Trevor," Jack muttered again. Shit. Jasper needed to call Travis. First, he dialed Tamian while he waited on the medics to arrive. "Jack's hurt, and Trevor's not here. Did Lucy call Eden?"

"Yes, but Eden told her she had a plan and she'd call her back. Julian and Henry are already scouring the cameras in the area for Trevor's car."

"I'm going to put out an APB. He couldn't have gone far." Jasper hung up and called dispatch, telling the female the make, model, and license plate of Trevor's vehicle. His phone buzzed during the call, and as soon as he hung up, he read the text.

Julian: *Trevor's phone is not far from his father's house. I'm sending you the coordinates.*

Jasper couldn't leave Jack alone, but he desperately wanted to search for his mate's phone. He already knew in his heart what he'd find, but he couldn't leave it to chance. Thirty minutes later, Jack was loaded in an ambulance, and Jasper raced to his car, following the directions to where Trevor's phone had last pinged. Jasper found not only Trevor's personal phone, but the burner as well. He crushed both devices in his hand and roared.

Tears burned his eyes. Jasper couldn't lose Trevor. Not now. They had a lifetime to look forward to. One with Cailín and any other children they might have together. Sucking in a deep breath, Jasper wiped his eyes and made the call to Travis. He and Brynna had returned to Norway after having spent Christmas in New Atlanta. It hurt

Jasper's heart to tell Travis his father was injured, and his brother was missing, but Travis promised he was on his way.

With no idea where to look for his mate, Jasper headed to the hospital. He needed to hold his daughter, but she was safe with Jonas and Caroline. Jack was alone, and since his sons couldn't be there with him, Jasper would look after him until he got a clue as to where Trevor was or Travis got to the hospital first. Jasper prayed it was the former.

LACHLAN RETURNED TO the boat with enough food to last a week. Fueled and ready, he put the groceries away before going to retrieve his phone from the charger. When he saw it lit up with several notifications, his heart sank. While he had been ashore, Eden had been busy. Fuck! Lachlan jogged to his computer and almost missed his chair in his hurry to sit down. He went over all the alerts and the phone calls that transpired while he was getting supplies. Why in the gods' names had Trevor not turned his phone off? All the Clan were using burner phones. Lachlan tapped into the emergency services line. A call had come in for Jack McKenzie, then Jasper phoned in an all-points bulletin for his mate's car. Lachlan got busy finding Trevor's VIN and the unique tracking signature assigned to it. He figured Henry and Julian were probably doing the same thing, but he didn't waste time switching over to their computers to check. Three sets of eyes were better than one.

When Lachlan located the car, it was headed south on I-85. He sent the information to Julian through his computer. He didn't have Jasper's number since the male was using a burner. Lachlan trusted Julian to forward the information on. The one thing that surprised Lachlan was the phone call placed from Kallisto to Eden. Kallisto was dead. The Clan must have used a voice transmitter to fool the female. And why was Eden keeping her phone on? When he tapped into her device, he understood. It was the only way for Kallisto to contact her. After she heard from who she thought was her former lover, Eden had tossed her phone along the road because its signal was steady halfway between New Atlanta and where Trevor's car showed on the screen.

Lachlan tracked the vehicle's progress as it turned off the interstate onto a smaller road. "Where are you taking him?" He was sure Julian was tracking the car as well, so Lachlan trusted the male to send Trevor's location to Jasper. He turned his attention to Eden's computers. If that were Lachlan, he would have a destination in mind. He would have bought or rented somewhere to take his lover once he had her free. He didn't think Eden would go too far. Not without Kallisto. If she were smart – and she was – the information wouldn't be stored on her server, so he began searching sales and rentals in South Georgia in the woman's name. While he let the search do its thing, he started scouring her computer for aliases. Eden would have already set up new identities for herself and Kallisto. Coming up short, Lachlan stroked his chin. Either she had another server he didn't know about, or she didn't have the information stored electronically.

Taking a chance, Lachlan hacked into the Nexus system. Doing so was a risk considering he had sent that information to the GIA, but he was careful. He had to be. Too many lives were at stake. The Nexus files were full of aliases, but the ones he found were attached to the assassins who carried the monikers. Even Eden's father had his own – Nexus. That made sense considering it was his company. Well, it had been. Lachlan imagined the man was in the wind at this point. He also imagined James was ready to throttle his one and only daughter. She had brought down the once thriving business all for one woman. A woman who was dead.

Lachlan had to wonder if Eden would stop threatening the Stone Clan if she knew her plan to get Kallisto free had failed, or if she would rain hell on them even more than she already had. In thinking her lover was still alive, Eden still had hope. Lachlan knew the feeling. Or he had. Now he knew Hunter would never forgive him. He shook those thoughts aside. Getting lost in the past was the reason Eden had gotten the jump on him. If he hadn't lingered in the store, he could have possibly caught her before she managed to take Trevor. Lachlan vowed not to move from the computer until he found the young man and helped return him to his mate.

Chapter Sixteen

JULIAN'S BRAIN HURT. His heart did as well with his mate in South America. He would prefer Kat be sitting beside him where he could at least feel her presence, but her safety was more important than anything. When his computer dinged, he returned his focus to the task at hand. "Holy shit." While Henry had been searching for Trevor's car, Lachlan had found it, and Julian told Henry as much. "If we didn't need his help, I'd be pissed at how easily he finds things before we do."

"Be pissed later," Henry said, looking over Julian's shoulder. "Where the hell is she taking him?"

The question was rhetorical, but Julian wondered the same thing. Lucy had called Eden pretending to be Kallisto, so why was she driving away from New Atlanta? Still, Julian answered, "If I had to guess, she has at least one, if not more, houses or apartments scattered across the country. If her plan to get Kallisto out of the Pen worked, they would need somewhere to hide out, far away from New Atlanta. They would also need new identities, and that is something Eden could easily provide. I need to let Jasper know we have Trevor's car in sight."

Julian called Jasper at the hospital and told him what they knew. With Banyan sitting with Jack, Julian got Jasper on the road headed south and said he would keep him updated with each turn as long as the indicator continued moving. As soon as they disconnected, Julian called Frey, patching Tamian into the call, to fill them in.

"Jasper doesn't need to go alone. We don't know what

196

he'll find when he gets to Trevor," Frey said.

"I'll — hang on a second." Tamian paused his thought as Lucy said something in the background about going with him.

"I don't have a blonde wig, but I do have the prosthetics. I can wear a hoodie to cover my hair, and hopefully Eden will be none the wiser," Lucy offered.

"And how will you convince her Kallisto was released from the Pen and just happened to be there?" Julian asked.

"We won't have to tell her anything. As soon as I get close enough, either Tamian or I will voice her. I just need her attention long enough to get her away from Trevor. But we need to get going. If Jasper gets to her before we do, he might scare her into hurting Trevor further, if she hasn't already done too much damage."

"I'll let Jasper know you're right behind him. For now, head south on I-85. They took Highway 14 toward New LaGrange. I'll update you when they make another turn."

"We're on it," Tamian said, then disconnected.

"Jules?" Frey was still on the line.

"I'm here, Brother."

"I know you might not feel this way, but you're doing a great job."

Julian laughed, but he found nothing funny about the situation. "No. Lachlan is doing a great job. I'm sitting here waiting on him to feed me fucking breadcrumbs."

"No, you're taking the information he's finding and doing something with it. At least you're doing something. Rafe left me in charge, and to do what? Push back a bunch of human inmates and fight a handful of Unholy? Then again, Tamian's the one who took care of the humans. All I did was put down a few monsters, and anyone in our Clan could do that."

"Frey, he left you in charge because you're the one with the level head. You're the one who has seen war, and you know how to lead. You give us the willpower to keep going

197

when all looks lost. Do not discount yourself. I love Rafael. He's a good King. But you, Brother, you are my hero. Always have been. You are the best of us all."

"Gods." Frey cleared his throat. "Thank you, Jules. I'm going to clear the line so you can direct the others to Trevor." With that, his brother disconnected. Julian wiped a stray tear off his cheek and got back to work.

THE FARTHER AWAY from New Atlanta they got, the more worried Trevor became. He didn't do well with silence, and other than giving him directions, Eden didn't say a word. The thrum of the tires over asphalt was loud in his ears. He almost asked if she'd turn on the radio several times, but he didn't want to alarm her while she pointed a gun at him. More than once, Trevor thought about wrecking on purpose, but what if he didn't do it right and she ended up shooting him on accident?

When Eden told him to take the next left, he took a chance to speak. "I really need to pee."

"You're an adult."

"And adults don't have to use the bathroom?"

"What? I just meant you could hold it," she scoffed.

"I have been holding it. Plus, I have a nervous bladder. Just the smallest thing can set it off. I really don't want to sit in wet pants and stink up the car."

"A nervous— You're insane. Fine. Pull over up there." Eden pointed to the next driveway. "But leave the door open, and pee right outside the car where I can see you."

"You want to watch? Gross." Trevor didn't really have to pee, but he'd try anything to give Jasper more time to find him. Did Eden not realize all cars had tracking systems?

"Did anyone ever tell you that you have a smart mouth?"

Trevor turned in and put the car in park. The headlights shone down a deserted-looking driveway. "Yes. Supposedly it's part of my charm." He reached for the handle, but Eden poked the gun into his shoulder.

"Don't try anything foolish."

"Yes, boss," he responded before he could think better of it. Trevor stepped just outside the car and looked around. They were in a rural area that reminded him of where he and Jasper lived. It was dark save the glow from the headlamps. There was a streetlight farther down the road, and the crescent moon didn't offer much illumination. Keeping his back to Eden, Trevor debated whether or not to unzip and try to pee. He didn't know what she had planned or if they were near their destination. Once they got wherever she was taking him, he might not get another chance. He had peed plenty of times in front of Jasper but never anyone else.

"Hurry up," Eden demanded. "I thought you had a nervous bladder."

"I also have a shy one. Never could use a urinal in the men's restroom if someone else was standing there. Who knows if someone's taking a peek, you know? Some people say size matters, but I was always in the camp of 'it's not how deep you fish but how you wiggle your worm.' I guess that doesn't apply to you seeing how you like tacos and not sausage." *Oh, gods. Shut up!* "Unless you're bi like Kallisto. Or maybe she's somewhere else on the spectrum. Which is fine. No judgment here. Love is love, and there's not enough of it in the world is my motto."

"Jesus H. Christ. Shut the hell up, and either take a piss or get back in the damn car."

"I'm trying. Really, I am. Just, maybe you can close your eyes so I know you aren't looking."

"You are getting on my last nerve. If you don't hurry the fuck up, I'm going to shoot you and leave you here for the coyotes. I'll get Kallisto another way."

Ah. Now they were getting somewhere. Trevor attempted to relieve his bladder. After what felt like an eternity, he managed to go a little. After tucking himself back in his jeans and zipping up, he leaned down and asked, "Can you open the glove box and hand me a wipe? Not that I dribbled, but my mother drilled it into me to wash my hands after using the bathroom."

"Get in the fucking car," Eden seethed, pistol pointed at Trevor's face.

"Fine. Jeez." He glanced at the clock and mentally patted himself on the back. Ten minutes wasted was ten minutes extra for Jasper. "How much farther?" he asked as he buckled up, then put the car in reverse and backed out onto the road.

"About twenty miles. Now shut up and drive."

"Okay, but can I at least turn on the radio?"

"If it'll keep you quiet, then by all means."

Trevor kept his favorite metal satellite station cued up, so when the sounds of Cyanide Sweetness came through the speakers, Trevor relaxed a bit. Desi's band was on tour, and if he didn't end up dead, Trevor planned to see at least one of the shows. Trevor forgot about the precarious situation he was in and sang along. Eden surprised him by tapping her free hand against her thigh. He didn't take the crazy woman for a metal fan.

About half an hour later, Eden turned the volume down and directed Trevor through a larger town. She had him drive to an upper level of a parking structure that was all but abandoned. A lone car sat on the far end, and she told him to park next to it. She reached over, turned his car off, and kept the keys. She then used a key fob to unlock the parked vehicle.

"Let's go," Eden demanded.

Trevor did as she said. While he walked around to the driver's door of the other car, she kept the pistol aimed his way. Once seated, she handed him a ball cap. "Put this on."

"I'm not really a hat-wearing kind of guy."

"You are now. Put the damn hat on, Trevor."

Sighing, Trevor took the cap. He pushed his bangs back before settling the hat over his hair. He figured she wanted him to be less noticeable, so that meant there were probably CCTV cameras in the area. He didn't pull the cap low on his forehead, and Eden must have felt him wearing it was enough. She handed over the keys to her car. He fumbled with them, dropping them onto the floorboard. "Hurry up," she groused. Yeah, he was stalling again, but at this point, he wasn't sure it would make a difference. When they had been in his car, Jasper could track it. Now, unless Julian could find a car in Eden's name, they would lose Trevor's trail. Fuck.

With nothing left to do but follow orders, Trevor slowly made his way down to the exit. "Which way?" he asked, looking left then right.

"Left, then make a right at the stop sign. Keep driving until I tell you otherwise."

Trevor looked over at the woman. "I thought you said twenty minutes."

"Twenty minutes to here. Now, get moving."

Trevor eased his way onto the street, slowly driving toward the stop sign. He wracked his brain for some way out of this mess. Not for the first time, Trevor wished he was a Gargoyle. But mating with Jasper hadn't changed Trevor into a shifter. His life had been prolonged, but that was only if he didn't meet up with, oh say, a bullet. If he were a Goyle, Trevor would have already let the claws come out. But no. He was human. A mere mortal with no defenses. Sighing heavily, Trevor turned right and headed farther away from his mate.

201

As LONG AS Julian had eyes on Trevor's location, Jasper was calm. Tamian and Lucy were on his tail as the three of them followed Julian's directions. When Julian shouted, "Wait!" it was all Jasper could do not to slam on the brakes.

"What is it?" Lucy asked over the Bluetooth. They were all on the line together.

"His car stopped. He's at..." The sound of Julian tapping on his keyboard was loud in Jasper's car. His beast growled with impatience waiting for the male to speak. "It's a parking garage. In ten miles, take the exit for Highway 15 and go west. The structure is less than two miles from the exit."

"If they parked, does that mean she's taking him on foot somewhere close by?" Lucy asked.

"I'm looking," Julian said. "There are no cameras on the garage. Hang on." More typing. More waiting. "Shit, there's only one CCTV camera in the area. If they go a different direction, I won't be able to see if they're on foot or in a different vehicle."

"Then we'll at least know which direction they didn't take. That's something," Tamian said, his voice calm. Jasper felt anything but calm. His mate wasn't sitting beside him, safe and sound. Jasper took a deep breath. It wouldn't do to get angry at Tamian. He and his mate were there to help. Lucy was willing to put herself in danger for Trevor. Sure, she was a Gryphon, but even she could be killed if Eden had a gun. Considering the woman and her father ran a company full of assassins, it would make sense Eden had been around firearms at some point. Maybe. Or maybe the woman sat behind a computer all day and let the hired help do all the wet work.

When they reached the parking garage, Jasper drove every level until he spotted Trevor's car. His empty car. He got out of his own vehicle and hit the fob that unlocked Trevor's car. When he opened the driver's door, Trevor's unique scent washed over Jasper, and tears filled his eyes.

According to Julian, they were less than twenty minutes behind Trevor and Eden. Even knowing that didn't ease Jasper's pain. Twenty minutes with no idea which direction they were headed.

Tamian stepped next to Jasper, phone in hand. Julian was still on the line. "Here's what we know. They didn't go back the way they came, so when you exit the parking garage, there is a stop sign. You have to turn either left or right. I'm tracking both directions, but I'd suggest you split up for now."

"What if they're on foot?" Lucy asked.

Tamian looked around and said, "Hang on." He took off jogging toward the only door on that level. He returned a few minutes later. "I didn't catch Trevor's scent in the stairwell, so we need to assume they switched cars."

Jasper removed his shirt. "I'm taking to the sky. I'll go left at the stop sign if you two will go right."

Lucy looked at her mate. "I think Jasper has the right idea. I'll shift to my Eagle and head west."

"What about your prosthetics?" Jasper asked. "If you find them, you'll need your disguise."

"Tamian can carry the pouch. I'm not going to approach Eden without backup."

Tamian pulled his shirt over his head, then motioned toward the car. "Grab your things." He then said to Jasper, "We didn't think to bring comms, so we'll have to use our phones."

"We'll keep the conference line open," Julian added. "That way if I find anything, I can relay it to you both at the same time."

Jasper nodded, then stepped over to the side of the structure to have a look. They weren't on the top floor, but taking off from that level wouldn't be a problem.

"Over here," Tamian called out. Jasper jogged over to the other side of the garage where Tamian stood holding a bag. "This side is darker. I think it's the better choice."

Jasper didn't argue. He climbed onto the ledge and jumped, unfurling his wings as soon as he was free from the concrete roof. He thanked the gods for the dark sky, then asked them to keep his mate safe until Jasper found him. He rose higher as he flew east, following the two-lane road. The air was brisk at the higher altitude, but Jasper relished the cooler temperature. Pushing his body to its limits, Jasper rode the wind, searching. Praying.

LUCY STRIPPED OUT of her clothes, then shoved them in the bag alongside the masks. Tamian pulled her close and kissed her hard. "Let's fly." Lucy gave her mate a salute before shifting to her Eagle. Together, they launched into the dark sky, turning to the west. Tamian was a sight to behold with his massive wings unfurled behind him. Being a Gryphon, Lucy had the ability to shift into a larger bird, and she easily kept up with her Goyle. When she first learned she was pregnant, Lucy wasn't sure about shifting. Gryphon females had no trouble changing forms while pregnant, but Lucy was possibly carrying a hybrid. She and Tamian talked it over and agreed she could shift in the early stages of her pregnancy. As the baby grew, Lucy would refrain, just in case. Her Eagle's eyes were sharper than a regular eagle, and she scanned the area below for any sight of movement, both vehicles as well as someone on foot, just in case.

She and Tamian were able to communicate in their minds, so when his sexy voice came through, she wasn't surprised.

"I'll continue following the road if you want to scan the trees for any side roads or driveways."

"Got it." Lucy veered off to the right, circling back then forward again after not seeing anything. She moved to the left, making the same winding arc. She continued her figure eights, knowing if Tamian found anything up ahead on the

road, he'd let her know. Jasper would alert Tamian on the cell phone if he spotted anything. Lucy's heart hurt for Jasper and how tormented he was. Trevor was human and didn't have any special abilities to keep Eden from hurting or even killing him.

As she scanned the area, Lucy thought back to her early days with Tamian. When she'd been forced into a bunker to continue the research her great-uncle started. Monk, one of the Hounds, had gone toe to toe, or wing to wing, with Tamian until Lucy intervened. Monk had been in love with Lucy, unbeknownst to her at the time, but Tamian was her mate. Hounds didn't have fated mates the way the Goyles did, but she had felt the connection to Tamian. He explained it was the mating bond, and she didn't doubt it. Now, she couldn't imagine a different life. A life without Tamian at her side. In short order, he would take over the Italian throne, and the pair would become King and Queen.

If Eagles could snort, Lucy would have. Her, a Queen? Life had a funny way of changing the course you thought was yours and taking you down a completely different road. Being Queen was her destiny, one she accepted without question. Tamian assured her their lives wouldn't change drastically once he took over for his father other than traveling to Italy a couple times a year. Lucy asked that she be able to continue working on the formula she found in Lucius's journal. She and Jonas had been perfecting the serum for months, and now they had to wait on their wee test subject before having an answer to whether it would work or not. When Gargoyles mated, their human's life was prolonged with the bite. Gryphons didn't have that ability. Gryphons also didn't live nearly as long as Goyles did. Three or four hundred years was an extensive lifespan for them, and their humans were lucky to see their nineties. With this serum, both could enjoy extended years together if they so chose.

But that was a worry for another day. Right then, she had to find Trevor, capture Eden, and ensure their American Clan found some peace. At least for a little while. According to her mate, the Stone Society had been fighting one battle after another for a few years. They were due some peaceful days.

"Sweetheart, I have a car in my sights."

Lucy angled toward the road and flew faster. When she reached Tamian, Lucy could see the red glow up ahead. With it being the middle of the night, it was probable they had found Trevor. If he was even in the car with Eden. The car turned right, the lights bouncing. Together, Lucy and Tamian veered that direction, then found a tree to perch on so they could watch the house.

A woman Lucy assumed was Eden exited the vehicle holding a gun, and seconds later, Trevor got out of the driver's side. Lucy and Tamian didn't have a plan further than finding the pair. She couldn't voice Eden in Eagle form, but Tamian didn't have that problem.

"What now?" Lucy asked silently.

"I'm texting Jasper with our coordinates, but I think we put an end to this now. Since I'm impervious to bullets, I'll get her attention, and you shift to your Gryphon and get Trevor out of there while her back's turned."

"Here, unlock the door," Eden said, holding out a set of keys.

"How cliché. A cabin in the woods," Trevor snarked, holding out his hand. If Lucy didn't know better, she would think the young man wasn't nervous, but from where she waited gripping the tree branch with her claws, she could see his hand shaking.

Tamian silently dropped the twenty or so feet to the ground behind the pair. Lucy launched from the tree, shifting in midair. She dove for Trevor, trusting Tamian to keep them both safe, but as plans often do, theirs went awry.

206

"What the hell?" Eden gasped, raising her weapon.

As Lucy flew toward Trevor, Tamian yelled, "Drop the gun, Eden," at the same time a shot rang out. Eden did as commanded, but she'd already gotten a shot off. Eden's finger had to have been on the trigger when she flung the gun to the ground. Lucy expected to feel pain. Trevor had been reaching out for Lucy and ended up between her and Eden. Trevor collided with Lucy, knocking them sideways. Lucy shifted into her human form, but she wasn't quick enough to keep Trevor from landing hard on the ground. Lucy scrambled the short distance to where Trevor lay on his side, unmoving.

The coppery scent of blood hit Lucy's nose before she noticed the scarlet fluid leaching into the dirt beneath Trevor's body. Carefully, she rolled him to his back, red blossoming across his chest where the bullet entered. "Shit, he's been shot!"

"Ka-Kallisto was right. You-you're not hu-human. Wh-what the hell are you?" Eden stammered.

"Shut the fuck up," Tamian voiced her, and Eden's teeth clacked together as she obeyed. He pushed her to the ground. "Do not move," he demanded as he knelt on Trevor's other side.

"Trevor!" Jasper's wings sent a current of air through Lucy's hair as he landed behind her. "Trev? Oh, gods. Trevor!" Jasper's body shook as he cradled his mate in his arms. If he hadn't been so focused on Trevor, Lucy would have scrambled for her clothes.

"Jasper, let me look," Lucy said, trying to gauge the severity of the wound.

"Don't touch him!" Tears marred Jasper's face as he clutched Trevor to his chest.

"Jasper, let us assess the damage," Tamian said firmly. It wasn't his commanding voice, but it was strong enough to get the male to let them look.

Squatting sideways so her bent knee covered her chest, Lucy inspected the wound. "Through-and-through. Jasper, it went through his upper chest, but I don't think it hit anything vital. We need to get him to the hospital."

Jasper shocked Lucy when he placed Trevor in her arms. Tamian crouched beside her as Jasper stalked over to where Eden was seated. Tamian took Trevor from Lucy. "Why don't you get dressed?" Lucy agreed and turned to get the pouch from where Tamian left it at the edge of the trees. When Jasper lifted Eden with a clawed hand, Lucy froze. She glanced at her mate, but Tamian shook his head. This was Jasper's decision. It was his mate who had been taken. Lucy braced for Jasper to punch the woman, but that didn't happen. Eden swung her legs and scraped at Jasper's arm with her nails, but the male wasn't deterred.

"That man you kidnapped is my mate. The father of my child. You fucked up when you took him. And for what? A woman you had a weekend fling with! You tried to ruin our family for a piece-of-shit female who didn't even remember your godsdamned name. You opened those cell doors, and two inmates got to Kallisto. Raped her before they tore her apart. That's on you, you evil bitch. Kallisto is dead." Eden's eyes were impossibly wide and filling with tears. Her bladder released, and urine coated the front of her jeans. Jasper continued in the same chilling voice as before. "And now, you can join her. Eden Wood, for your treachery against our Clan, for all the evil you rained on our family, I sentence you to death." In one swift move, Jasper placed his free hand on the back of Eden's head and snapped the woman's neck, letting her body drop to the ground. As if he hadn't just murdered a human, he strode to where Tamian was holding Trevor and gently took him in his arms. Jasper bent his knees, then launched into the sky without a word to either Lucy or Tamian.

CHAPTER SEVENTEEN

LUCY SHOOK HER head. "That was —"

"Nothing more than I would have done if it had been you she kidnapped," Tamian admitted, hugging her from behind. "But he's going to need help at the hospital. They're going to call the cops in if one of us doesn't get there and stop them."

"Uh, guys?" Julian's voice sounded from far away.

"Shit, the phone." Tamian picked it up from where he'd dropped it. "Jules, it's over, but Trevor's been shot."

"I heard. I'll do my best to intercept any call the hospital makes to the cops, but hopefully one of you will get there first. And maybe we keep how Eden died to ourselves."

"Agreed." Tamian said, because what was done was done, and Jasper needed them now.

Lucy placed a hand on Tamian's cheek. "You go. Jasper will need your strength. I'll stay here and wipe Trevor's prints from the car, then figure out how to make it look like she had an accident."

"I'll get help headed that direction to retrieve the vehicles," Julian said.

"Here." Tamian held the phone out. "You keep this. I'll be back as soon as possible."

"I'll be fine. Now go."

Tamian kissed her hard before unfurling his wings and launching into the sky. Lucy shook her head as she eyed the dead body of Eden. So much turmoil from one person. Letting out a deep sigh, she turned toward the house and scanned the area for the keys Trevor dropped. When she found them, Lucy unlocked the front door, then stepped inside, taking in the sparse furnishings. It definitely wasn't somewhere Eden frequented. She poked her head in the two bedrooms, only one of which had any furniture, and bypassed the bathroom to return to the kitchen. There was no food in the fridge. Before she could search the cabinets, Lucy felt as well as heard a soft humming below her feet.

The only door she hadn't opened led to a small pantry, which was stocked with canned goods and boxes of pasta. Not finding a door leading downstairs, Lucy went outside and walked the perimeter of the house. When she couldn't find any type of opening, Lucy returned inside. There were no rugs visible, so she retraced her steps throughout the small house and opened each closet door including the one in the bathroom. That's when she found it. The linen closet floor was different than the tiles in the bathroom. Kneeling, Lucy let her talons come forth and scraped along the edge of the flooring until she found the spot she needed to peel the fake tile back. A small trap door opened to a steep set of steps.

When Lucy reached the bottom, her mouth fell open. Hidden underneath the house was a hacker's wet dream. Rubbing her hands together, Lucy forgot about cleaning supplies and sat in the wide leather chair. She wondered how Eden managed to get everything downstairs through the small opening, then decided that didn't matter. Knowing Eden could have rigged the system to shut down if anyone other than her messed with it, Lucy took a chance. She was in luck. The computer came to life when she moved the mouse with her shirt-covered hand. Not wanting to press her luck, Lucy typed in a code using her talons so as not to leave fingerprints. It was slow going, but she managed to send Julian and Henry an encrypted message. As much as she wanted to dive into Eden's secrets, Lucy pushed back from the desk and returned upstairs.

The cabinet beneath the bathroom sink was where she found what she needed to remove Trevor's prints from Eden's car. As she cleaned, she considered ways to make it look as though Eden had an accident. Thinking about the steep stairs leading to her secret room, Lucy had her answer. She went over the car twice, making certain there were no prints, no stray hairs, nothing which could tie Trevor to being there.

Lucy placed the cleaning supplies on the hood and turned toward Eden's lifeless form. Staring at the woman, Lucy tried to imagine how someone so innocent-looking could hide such evil inside. She understood doing whatever it took to protect those you love, but Eden and Kallisto weren't in a relationship. Hadn't seen each other in years. Eden chose to willingly target not only adult males, but women and children too. That was beyond the pale. Something Lucy would never be able to comprehend.

Giving it no thought, Lucy picked Eden's body off the ground and hefted it over her shoulder. She cringed when Eden's head struck the doorframe of the bathroom. Lucy lowered the body so it was "standing" in front of her, then she unceremoniously gave it a push down the hole. It landed with a thud, and Lucy grimaced. She should feel bad, disrespecting the dead that way, but she didn't. In the end, Eden got what she deserved. Kallisto's end might have been more than was called for; then again, she, too, had kidnapped a child and helped poison Jasper. No, the world was better off without the likes of Eden and Kallisto.

Lucy left the hatch open but cleaned her own fingerprints off the handle and everything else she had touched in the house. By the time Tamian returned, Lucy was leaning against the tree the two of them had perched on to watch Eden and Trevor arrive at the house.

Tamian got out of their vehicle and held his arms out. Lucy walked into her mate's embrace. He held her as she told him what she did with the body.

"I would have done that for you."

"I know you would, but it's done. Unless someone else knows about this house, it'll be a long time before she's discovered. Any word on Trevor?"

"There wasn't when I left." Tamian kissed her temple. "If you're finished, we can head back there."

"I'd like that. Trevor saved my life, and I want to be there for him and Jasper."

Tamian gestured toward the car. "Your chariot awaits, M'lady."

"IT'S OVER," RAFAEL announced. He strode over to where Kaya was seated on one of the sofas and picked his mate up. Kaya laughed and batted at his chest as he nuzzled her neck. "We can go home now."

"Is everyone okay?" Kaya asked.

Rafael sobered. "Trevor was shot. We need to get back to New Atlanta so we can be there for him and Jasper."

"Who has Cailín?" Tessa asked.

"My mother," Isabelle answered. When Tessa frowned at her cousin, Isabelle shrugged one shoulder. "I do talk to her on occasion."

Gregor stood from where he and Tessa were lounging opposite the sofa Kaya had been resting on. "I'll get Santiago to ready the jet."

Rafael set Kaya on her feet, then cradled her face in his hands. Leaning down, he pressed his lips to hers. Breathing in her essence, Rafael relaxed for the first time in months.

Xavier and Elizabeth arrived while everyone was gathering their belongings. The Italian King held out his hand to Rafael, and they gripped wrists. "Thank you for allowing us to hide out in your home." The two males had butted heads on more than one occasion over the years, but Tessa had brought them to a truce.

"Our home is always open to family." X clapped Rafael on the shoulder. "I take it things have been straightened out if you're preparing to leave?"

"Yes. The hacker has been dispensed, but not before Trevor was shot."

"Can't you stay a few days?" Elizabeth was asking Tessa.

"No can do, Mom. Like Rafe said, Trevor was shot, and I need to go. I'm sure Caroline is doing a fine job of watching over Cailín, but I need to be there for them."

"I understand, but once Trevor is feeling better, maybe you and Gregor can come back? Your father is turning over the throne to your brother, and we're going to have a lot of free time on our hands. Maybe the four of us could take a trip somewhere? Go relax somewhere tropical."

"Sounds good. Plus, Desi's band will be playing a concert here later this year, so we'll definitely be back for that."

As much as Rafael loved Sebastian as a baby, he couldn't wait until his son was old enough that they could do things together like go on vacation as friends. Then again, Rafael was ready to cherish each moment of his son growing. One day, Rafael would turn his throne over to Sebastian, and Rafael had to wonder what the world would be like then. Thinking about the drawing of Bas and the wolf, would the world be full of shifters living harmoniously together?

"You ready to go, Brother?" Dante asked, interrupting Rafael's thoughts.

"Yes. Thank you again, Xavier. Elizabeth." Rafael fisted his heart and bowed his head to the female. Rafael was more than ready to get home and enjoy some peace and quiet with his mate and their son.

213

JASPER WAS GLAD Tamian caught up to him. In his desperation to get Trevor to a hospital, he hadn't been thinking clearly. With his mate cradled in his arms, Jasper had no idea which direction the hospital was in, and he didn't have a free hand to check his phone. Tamian was a balm to Jasper's soul. He calmly directed them to the hospital as well as came up with a plan for when they arrived. Tamian was able to use his abilities on the hospital staff. Tamian also convinced Jasper to stop long enough to put their shirts back on before walking into the emergency room.

Less than an hour after entering the building, Jonas and Caroline showed up with Cailín. Jasper hadn't realized how much he needed to see his baby girl until she was in his arms. With the older couple there to sit with Jasper, Tamian left to help his own mate get rid of any evidence of them being at Eden's house in the woods. Nobody mentioned how Jasper had killed the female. He figured he would be held accountable at some point, but he didn't have it in him to care. Not while his mate was in surgery.

"Can I get you anything?" Caroline asked. Jonas, wearing his Joseph Mooneyham prosthetic, had disappeared soon after arriving, saying something about overseeing the surgery. Jasper didn't know if that was allowed considering Jonas wasn't in New Atlanta. He wasn't sure if they were even in Georgia.

"I'm good, thanks." Jasper wasn't good. He wouldn't be until he knew Trevor was going to be okay.

The door to the waiting room opened, and Matthew strode in followed by Slade. Matthew made a beeline to Jasper and wrapped his arms around Jasper and Cailín. The young man was one of Jasper's favorite beings in the world, and his presence made waiting a little bit easier. It wasn't long after that when Deacon and Sabrina came in along with Paxton, Oakley, Dane, and Marley. Jasper didn't question why they were all there. It was what family did. What their Clan did. When one was hurting, the rest rallied. He knew as soon as Tessa could, she would be front and center. The feisty redhead was particularly close with Trevor.

By the time Jonas came back to give Jasper an update, Tessa had arrived along with Gregor, Dante, Isabelle, Connor, Rafael, Kaya, Priscilla, and Sebastian. The waiting room was crowded with so many of their Clan, and knowing they were there for him and Trevor, Jasper couldn't hold back the tears.

Jonas gripped Jasper's shoulder, and the male was smiling. "There was a small issue with the anesthesia, but the surgery was successful. Trevor's in recovery. He won't be able to use his left arm for a while, but with rehab, he'll be back to his old self before you know it and toting this sweet girl around."

Cheers went up from all their family, and Jasper choked back a sob. His mate was going to be okay.

Jonas patted Jasper on the arm. "If you want to let someone else hold her, I'll take you back to see him." Tessa made grabby hands, and Jasper handed the baby over. As they walked, Jonas said low enough so no one else would hear, "While you sit with him, I will make arrangements to have Trevor transferred to New Atlanta. I'll make sure he's in a room next to his father."

Shit. Jasper had forgotten all about Jack. "How is Jack? Do you know?"

"He's going to be okay. Eden hit him pretty hard, and he lost quite a bit of blood, but with a little rest, he'll recover quickly. Speaking of recovering, Trevor will also be fine, but if you bite him, it might help speed *his* recovery."

Jasper nodded. "Thank you. For everything."

"No thanks needed. You and Trevor are family." Jonas strode through the small hospital as if he worked there.

Jasper didn't ask how he'd managed, because to him, it didn't matter. All that mattered was Trevor was alive. With Eden dead, the Clan could breathe a little easier. Jasper would get Trevor home and wait on him hand and foot until his mate got sick of him.

Trevor was paler than usual, but his heartbeat was strong. Jasper picked up Trevor's right hand and kissed his palm. Jonas pushed a chair up next to the bed, and Jasper sat, not letting go. He pushed Trevor's purple-streaked bangs off his forehead as he stared at the face he couldn't live without. Jasper couldn't imagine a world without his snarky mate. If Trevor had died, if the bullet had punctured his heart, Jasper would have wanted to die with him. He had already made arrangements for Cailín to be taken care of should something happen to him and Trevor. Hopefully, Jasper and Trevor would be the ones to watch their daughter grow into a fierce Gargoyle. Jasper was looking forward to seeing this next generation of shifters rule the Clan and possibly the world.

After checking to make sure no one was lingering outside the door, Jasper lifted Trevor's arm and sank his fangs into the tender skin of his mate's wrist. The mating bite had cured Trevor's color-blindness. Jasper prayed this bite would help his shoulder heal quickly so Trevor could get back to taking care of Jasper and Cailín the way no one else could. The world was a brighter place with Trevor Jenkins O'Donnell in it.

BANYAN STOOD GUARD just inside the door of Jack McKenzie's room. He had wanted to go help look for Trevor, but Brynna begged Banyan to watch over Jack until she and Travis could get there. The couple had left Norway as soon as they heard about the situation, and flying direct would have them arriving in about four more hours.

Urijah was home with Levi and Nova. The kids were officially theirs as the adoption had been finalized the week before. Instead of uprooting them to Norway immediately, Uri and Banyan decided to stay in the States so the kids could finish out the school year. In the short time they'd had the siblings, they took them to visit with Connor and Amelia often. The more Levi and Nova were around the others of their Clan, the more they got used to most of the males in the family being large yet loving.

Banyan's phone buzzed with a text from Julian explaining what happened. The important parts were that Eden was dead, and Trevor was going to be okay after surgery. Banyan blew out a sigh of relief. Knowing the female hacker was dead and that Trevor would recover from the gunshot wound to the shoulder had Banyan breathing easier. Jack was resting, so Banyan didn't bother to wake the man and give him the news.

He and Uri texted several times during his wait. Nothing important, but they missed one another when they weren't together. When Brynna and Travis arrived, Banyan hugged his sister tightly. It hadn't been that long since they'd seen one another, but he missed her when they were apart. Travis thanked Banyan before stepping up to his father's bed. As he stood against the wall listening to Travis and Jack talk about missed opportunities and promising to be better about calling one another, Banyan made a silent vow to always show his children how much they meant to him. The siblings had a rough start in their lives, but with Banyan and Uri as their fathers, the two would want for nothing, including unconditional love, soft words, and softer hands.

Banyan held Brynna's hand as he took advantage of a lull in the father and son conversation. "The crisis is over.

Trevor was shot, but it wasn't life threatening. As soon as he's out of recovery, they're transferring him here."

Tears streamed down Jack's face as he grasped Travis's hand. "Why was that woman after Trevor?" Jack asked.

Brynna and Travis looked to Banyan to answer. Jack wasn't aware of Gargoyles, but then, neither had Eden been. Banyan kept his answer as close to the truth as possible. "She wanted to hurt Trevor's boss, and she thought she could get to Dante by kidnapping Trevor. It's over now, and everyone is safe."

"She's in jail? What if she gets out? Will she come after Trevor again?" Jack asked.

"She'll never get free. Eden Wood was killed by a cop," Banyan explained, leaving out crucial details.

Jack wiped the tears from his face. "Good. My boy has had enough grief for ten lifetimes. He deserves to live a peaceful life with Jasper and their sweet baby."

"That he does. Speaking of sweet kids, I'm going home to mine. If you need anything, just give us a call."

"Thank you, Banyan," Travis said, pulling Banyan into a hug. Brynna joined them, and the three of them held each other.

"Come on, B. I'll walk you out." Brynna kissed Travis softly, then said, "I'll be right back." Brynna looped her arm through her brother's as they walked down the corridor. Speaking quietly, she asked, "So it's really over?"

"Yes. I don't have all the details, but Eden's dead."

"Good. I hope it was painful." Banyan agreed. "We'll stay here to be with Jack and Trevor a few days, then I want to come by and see my niece and nephew."

"I'm looking forward to it. Nova especially needs some Brynna time."

"I'll do something with her, just the two of us. Girl time is important, especially when she's surrounded by so much testosterone."

"You aren't wrong." And with the threat contained, Amelia and Connor would hopefully be on their way home. When they got to the door, Banyan pulled his sister into his arms and held her close. Now that she was back in his life, he hated being away from her, so having her there in New Atlanta was nice, even if the reason she visited wasn't a good one.

"I'll see you soon." Brynna pressed a kiss to his cheek before strolling back the way they'd just come.

Banyan turned away with a smile. Happy to have his sister in his life. Happy to be headed home to his mate and their two children. Banyan knew as well as anyone life could change on a dime, but for the time being, he was going to enjoy what the four of them had together.

When Banyan entered the house, it was early morning, and Nova was sitting at the kitchen island with a cookie in one hand and a frosting-covered spoon in the other. She glanced up with wide eyes and froze.

Banyan grinned at his girl. "Are you decorating one of those for me?" He slowly walked to where she waited and leaned down, pressing a kiss to the top of her head. Levi had warmed up to his new fathers quickly, but Nova was still hesitant. Waiting for the next shoe to fall or fist to fly. Banyan ran his finger through the frosting on the spoon and popped it in his mouth. "Mmm, tasty."

"You're silly," Nova whispered.

"I know I am, but what are you?" he joked. The little girl gave him a tentative smile, and that was all he could ask for. Banyan would show his daughter every bit of love he had to give until she realized she was safe.

"Dad?" Levi called out from the living room. Banyan turned toward Urijah whose eyes were wide. Since Levi had yet to call them anything other than their names, they didn't know who he was referring to.

"In here, Bud," Banyan responded.

When Levi appeared in the doorway, he gave a little

wave. "Uh, I was talking to Uri, but I'm glad you're home."

"I'm glad to be home. Everything okay?" Levi bit his bottom lip as he stared at the floor. He was still hesitant to ask for things he wanted. "Levi?"

"I was wondering if we could have pancakes for breakfast."

Banyan and Uri did their best to provide nutritious meals for the kids, but if they wanted pancakes, they could have pancakes. "Banana with extra whipped cream?"

Levi's face lit up. "Yes, please." He turned and went back to whatever he was doing in the living room. Probably watching some sports show. The kid lived and breathed what the Americans called soccer. Banyan turned to Nova. "And what about you, Princess? You want banana too?" Banyan already knew Nova only liked blueberries on hers, but he hoped she would feel safe enough to answer.

When she remained silent, Levi piped up from the other room. "She likes blueberries."

"Got it. Thanks, Levi."

Banyan walked across the room until he was in Urijah's space. Their sex life had become creative since the kids came along. No more tossing each other into walls. No more shouting the house down. Now they had to clamp a hand on the other one's mouth to keep them quiet when they came. The only time they got to let loose was when the kids were in school. They spent a lot of their daytime fucking. Banyan ran his hand through Uri's hair and kissed him tenderly on the lips. "And what about you, Dad? What kind of pancakes do you want?"

They didn't hold back their affection for one another in front of the kids. They wanted the siblings to grow up in a loving environment. To know that it didn't matter who you loved as long as it was a healthy, happy relationship.

"I'm easy," Uri whispered, and Banyan couldn't hold back the laugh that escaped. Nova was staring at them, but her cute mouth was turned up on one corner. Her smiles were few and far between, especially in front of him and Urijah. "How's Jack?"

"He's going to be fine." Banyan relayed silently what he knew about Trevor and Eden. The kids had been through enough trauma in their short lives; they didn't need to hear about someone else's. "Not to jinx anything, but it looks like things will be better for everyone going forward."

"It's about time."

"That it is, *Min Eneste Kjærlighet.*"

CHAPTER EIGHTEEN

LORENZO AND JORDANA were enjoying coffee in the garden the next morning when Frey called to say Eden was dead and it was safe for them to return home. They put their small wedding on hold, but instead of heading back right away, Lor and Nik took the females sightseeing, visiting different places in Brazil the mates might not have a chance to see for a while otherwise. Francisca and Eliana once again watched the babies. Lor had forgotten how stunning his former home was, so he enjoyed their trip as much as the others. Jordana was the perfect tour guide, and Amelia was entranced with Lor's mate as she doted on the little girl.

When it came time to fly home, Jordana and the others gathered their things while Lor sought out his mother. He knocked on the door to the bedroom she was using.

"Come in," she said in English. When she saw it was Lorenzo, her face lit up.

"It is safe for us to return to the States, and I wanted to ask you to come with us."

Francisca's smile faltered. "I appreciate the offer, but for now, I wish to remain here for Diego. With Jordana going away, the boy won't have any family if I go too."

"I thought Diego was going to travel for a bit?"

"He is, but still, I do not want to be too far away if he returns home. Plus, I have offered to help Fallon get his feet underneath him. Without a Queen by his side, he needs my assistance. You understand, don't you?"

"I do. But you and Diego both are welcome in my home whenever you wish to visit. Or if you decided you like it in

New Atlanta, you have a home for as long as you want."

"Thank you, my son. I promise to visit soon. Now, if your friends are packing up, I would like to go say goodbye to them and get one more kiss from those precious children."

Diego had taken off after catching Lor and his mother in bed, so Lorenzo didn't have the chance to say goodbye, but Jordana said they could talk to him on the phone later. Francisca snuggled with the babies while Lor and Nik got all the luggage loaded in the vehicles. Gannon chose to remain in Brazil for a while, so Lor thanked the male for accompanying his mate on the flight to Texas.

After a long round of goodbyes, Lor was headed home, and unlike the last two times he left Brazil, his heart was completely stitched back together.

LACHLAN BREATHED A momentary sigh of relief when the call went through that Eden was dead. It was over. The Stone Clan could handle things from that point forward. His assistance was no longer needed. Well, there was one last thing he could do, and he had nothing but time to see it through. Lachlan sat in front of his computer and began digging through Eden's accounts. He was sure the female had a server he hadn't come across, but with her dead, it wouldn't cause anyone harm. He set up a private, offshore account, then transferred all her money to it. Lachlan then sent an encrypted message to Henry and Julian. They could do with the money as they saw fit.

Lachlan erased every trace of Eden Wood he could find. There was nothing he could do about any physical papers her father had, but Lachlan figured the man wouldn't look too hard for his daughter. He would figure she took her money and disappeared after putting her parents in such dire straits. Nexus would be too busy trying to stay out of the hands of the GIA.

He was just about to head upstairs for a drink when his computer pinged. It didn't take but a few seconds to read the encrypted message. Lachlan's heart raced as he dove headfirst into Eden's secondary system. Everything he needed to prove his innocence to the Stones was there in ones and zeros. After ensuring Julian had access to the same information, he dismantled her server from the inside in case anyone should ever come across the computers. Lachlan scrubbed his hands down his face. It was well and truly over.

With nothing left to do, Lachlan maneuvered his boat out onto the open waters and set course for the North Atlantic. He would travel until he ran out of fuel, and after that? After that, it wouldn't matter.

HUNTER WAS TORN between letting Lachlan sail off into the sunset alone or going after him. When Frey called to let him know Julian had the proof they needed of Lachlan's innocence, Hunter offered to go get the male and bring him back to the Pen.

"Rafael and I discussed it, and we feel he's paid his penance. If it weren't for him guiding Julian and Henry, we might not have caught up to Eden when she took Trevor. Whether or not you forgive him is up to you." Rafael had forgiven Lachlan, but Hunter didn't think he could.

If you don't, then we might as well cross over. What's a life without our mate?

Hunter bristled at his beast's angry voice in his mind. Ever since he walked away from Lachlan over a year ago, his Goyle had been silent, leaving Hunter more bereft than ever.

"That was X. He's got a job for us."

Hunter jumped at Carter's voice. He'd been so lost in thought he didn't hear his twin come into the room.

"Are you okay?" Carter sat down on the sofa, angling his body toward Hunter.

"I'm fine. What's the job?" Hunter swirled the ice in the tumbler that had moments before been filled with whiskey.

Carter reached over and plucked the glass from his hand. "You can lie to yourself all you want, but you can't lie to me."

Hunter ran his hands through his too long hair and blew out a breath. "My beast is pissed."

"I'm not surprised." Hunter swiveled his head to glare at his brother. Carter set the glass on the coffee table, then met Hunter's gaze. "Look, I get Lachlan's a tool, but he's *your* tool. We only get one mate. Some of us don't even get that."

"You're saying you'd take a manipulative liar over being alone?" Hunter huffed.

"Maybe? Hell, I don't know. What I do know is he didn't have to help after he escaped from the Pen. He could have disappeared, but he didn't. He went the one place he knew you'd easily find him."

"What's the job?" Hunter wanted to think about something other than Lachlan Rokesby for a few minutes.

"Something I can do on my own."

"Carter—"

"No, seriously. Now that Tamian is taking over the throne, X has decided to build Elizabeth a new home as a surprise. He's asked me to oversee it."

"I thought you said he had a job for both of us."

"Eh. If you decide to forget all about your mate, you can help. If not, no big deal."

Hunter stood, grabbed the glass off the coffee table, then walked to the kitchen and dumped the melting ice in the sink. Carter followed and placed his hands on Hunter's shoulders, massaging the tense muscles.

"I love you, Brother. You are the better part of me, but I won't fault you for forgiving Lachlan. And who knows? Without you joined at my hip, maybe I'll attract my own mate."

Hunter ducked away from his brother's hands and turned to face him. "What the hell's that supposed to mean?"

"We both know you're the more handsome twin," Carter joked.

"Whatever." Hunter took the empty glass to the counter and refilled it, forgoing ice.

"Seriously, though. I'm going to pack and head to New York to visit X. He wants to go over the plans for the new house. Why don't you take some time to think about what you want to do? If you decide to go after Lachlan, great. If not, you can meet up with me when I get back."

"Where's the new house going to be?"

"Here in New Atlanta. Tessa spends most of her time here, and Tamian splits his time between here and New York. Elizabeth misses her kids, and now that Lucy's pregnant, Elizabeth will want to be wherever her grandchild is."

Hunter tossed back the contents of the glass. "I'll just go with you now."

"Brother, why don't you give it a little more thought?"

"Why is this so important to you? You were the one who wanted to take Lachlan's head when he broke my neck."

"I was pissed."

"And now you're not?" Hunter brushed past his twin and stalked to the back window.

"No. I had time to think about why he was so desperate to get away. To clear his name. And he's done that."

"Yes, he cleared his name for the plane incident, but that doesn't excuse him lying about working for Alistair."

"We can go round and round about this until the end of time. Yes, he lied. Yes, he fucked up. Yes, he did everything you've mentioned every time we talk about this. But he also made it right in the end. Either you forgive him, or you don't. But like I said before, we only get one mate. I don't think the fates would give you Lachlan if he were unredeemable. Just think about it. I'll go visit X, and when I get back, if you still don't want Lachlan, I'll drop it."

Hunter didn't respond, and Carter finally walked away to pack. When he returned to the living room, he said, "Call me if you need me. I love you, Brother."

"I love you too." And he did. Hunter loved his twin more than life itself. It had been the two of them together ever since their birth. They rarely spent more than a week apart, and Hunter didn't know who he was without Carter. It was that thought that scared him most. If he did forgive Lachlan, that meant moving on with his life without his twin.

But what happened when Carter found his mate? Twins or not, Carter would want alone time with whoever she happened to be. He wouldn't want Hunter in the next bedroom listening in as they made love every night. *"Without you joined at my hip, maybe I'll attract my own mate."* Fuck. Did Carter really feel that way? Hunter thought his brother had been joking. What if he wasn't? Gods, Hunter was a selfish prick. Not only had he abandoned his mate for his brother, he'd manipulated his brother's time just so he wouldn't be alone.

He needed to do better. Hunter would give Carter space. Let him do the job for X without Hunter hovering. Maybe he and Lachlan could start over. Slowly. Spend some time together until Hunter learned to trust him again because Carter was right – they only got one mate. And after having spent time in Lachlan's bed? Hunter knew no other male would fill *that* particular void. Now that he'd decided to go, Hunter grabbed his keys. If he stayed in their

227

rental house one minute longer, he would talk himself out of going.

Hunter made good time getting to North Carolina, but when he searched the area where he'd found Lachlan before, the boat was gone. Hunter scoured the marinas close to where Lachlan had been anchored, but it wasn't to be found. Again, he lied. Lachlan said he'd be waiting for Hunter to come back.

You waited too fucking long.

Was that it? Had Lachlan waited, then finally given up? It had been close to a week since Eden had been killed. That long since Lucy found the computers which proved Lachlan's innocence.

He's fading.

What do you mean?

I mean I can barely feel him.

Oh no. Hunter might not be certain he wanted Lachlan in his life, but he didn't want the male to cross over.

You did this. You released him from the bond, and now he has no hope left. Fix this!

Lachlan isn't without blame. If he were an honorable male—

You still would have chosen Castor over him, and you know it.

Hunter sighed, grabbing his hair with both hands and pulling. His beast was right; he had chosen his twin. Scanning his gaze over the water, Hunter thought about which direction Lachlan would have gone.

Northeast. I can guide you, but you need to hurry the fuck up.

There was too much light for Hunter to take to the sky. Staring at the inky depths of the Atlantic, he knew he only had one choice. Hunter took off at a sprint away from the marinas. When he reached the beach, he walked until he was away from any buildings. With it being daytime, he still could be seen, but if he wanted to go for a swim, that was his prerogative, even in the chilly waters of March.

228

Removing his shirt, Hunter tied it around his waist before wading into the surf. After kicking off his boots and socks, he walked past the waves until his feet no longer touched sand, then dove beneath the surface.

Hunter had swum in oceans before but never with such purpose. Nor had he encountered great beasts such as killer whales or sharks. When he was far enough away from land, Hunter released his wings, using them to propel him forward. He powered past schools of fish, darting out of his way. Hunter was joined by several dolphins at one point, but he didn't slow to enjoy them. His beast kept him on course, and after what felt like hours, Hunter angled for the surface. He couldn't die from lack of oxygen, but after so long without it, he was getting lightheaded.

He gasped in a lungful of air as he treaded water. Hunter turned in all directions, scanning the ocean for any signs of life. When he saw none, he propelled himself into the sky, flying high enough he would appear to be a large bird should human eyes see him. His beast was frantic in his mind, begging him to hurry. When a lone boat came into view, Hunter shifted course, angling his trajectory downward, praying he wasn't too late. Hunter didn't breathe until his feet touched down on the pristine wooden deck, his wings retreating into his back.

"Lachlan?" Hunter shouted as he slid open the glass door, which led into the galley. "Lachlan? It's Hunter," he yelled again. If his mate were close to crossing over, his hearing might not be at its peak. Before he could head to the bedroom, his beast urged him to the deck at the stern where he found Lachlan. If Hunter didn't know better, he would think the male was enjoying some sunshine, reclined on one of the plush, cushioned lounge chairs. They had spent many a night wrapped around each other on one of them as they gazed at stars while the water lulled them with its small ripples.

Hunter dropped to his knees and brushed Lachlan's

hair off his face. "Lachlan? Can you hear me?"

"Fuck you," Lachlan mumbled.

"I get it. You're pissed, but I'm here now. I'm sorry."

"You couldn't let me pass over in peace? Have I not paid for my sins?"

"Yes, you have."

"I came out here to forget him."

Forget him? Him who? "Lachlan, who are you trying to forget?"

"Hector. My love. He freed me, but I'll never be free. Not until it's done. Please let me die in peace."

"No, it's me. Hector. I'm here."

"No more, I'm begging you."

You have to bite him. It's the only way.

Not without his permission.

It's the only way to bring him back. He's almost gone!

Fuck! Hunter knew his beast was right, and if he did this, they would be bonded for the rest of their lives. But wasn't that why he'd come to find his mate? To forgive him? To be with him?

"Forgive me," Hunter said, then released his fangs. He straddled Lachlan's body, tilted his head to the side, and sank his sharp canines into the meat between his mate's neck and shoulder. Too many emotions hit Hunter at once. Despair. Regret. Resignation. Those were Lachlan's, not Hunter's, so he pushed his own feelings into the bite. Hope. Forgiveness. Love.

Hunter removed his fangs, then licked over the two punctures. Lachlan's skin tasted of salt and sunshine. He sat back on Lachlan's thighs and took his face between his palms. "Lachlan, come back to me," Hunter begged. Lachlan's eyes were unseeing as he stared off into the distance. "Please, Lachlan. I'm here. I'm sorry I made you wait so long, but I'm here now. Please come back to me." Hunter leaned down and pressed their lips together. Using his thumb, Hunter pulled Lachlan's lower jaw down and breathed his essence into Lachlan's mouth, silently begging the gods to release his male from their grips. After kissing him once more, Hunter angled his body so he was lying next to Lachlan, then pulled his mate into his arms. He had done everything he could; now it was up to his mate to make the choice.

Hunter held Lachlan tight, muttering promises and apologies. He stroked Lachlan's hair over and over because it was something his mate enjoyed in the past. Hunter pressed kisses to his temple, then offered more promises of a future together if Lachlan would come back to him.

"You bit me," Lachlan whispered.

Hunter bit back a sob at his mate's voice. "You left me no choice," Hunter whispered in return.

"Did you mean it?" Lachlan remained still in Hunter's arms.

"Every last word. I'm so sorry. I'm sorry for releasing you when I was angry. Sorry for putting my brother first. Sorry for making you wait. Sorry for letting you—"

Lachlan pressed his lips to Hunter's, the last apology cut off. Lachlan turned in Hunter's arms, wrapping him in his own embrace. When Lachlan teased Hunter's lips with his tongue, Hunter opened for him. As though no time had passed since they were last together in a lover's embrace, their mouths and tongues came together, melding, moving, dancing, tasting. Loving. Lachlan angled his body so he was lying more on Hunter than beside him without breaking the kiss. As the sun bore down on their skin, the waves danced beneath them, gently rocking the large boat.

Lachlan pulled away only to press his forehead against Hunter's. "Did you mean it? Not your apology, but the bite? Because if you did it only to keep me from crossing over, I'll understand."

"I meant it. I didn't realize how selfish I've been all these years. If it's something you no longer want, I'll understand."

231

"You're all I've ever wanted. From that first moment I saw you coming out of the bar in Greece, laughing at something Castor said, I wanted you more than anything. You're my mate, Hector – Hunter – and without you, well, you see what I become without you."

"You can call me Hector. It is my name, after all." Hunter would give his male anything to make him happy.

"I'll call you whatever you wish, but in my mind, my heart, you will always be Hector, the male who stole my breath as well as my heart."

Hunter brushed a strand of hair off Lachlan's face. "Will you do something for me?"

"Anything, My Love." Lachlan's dark eyes glittered with promise.

"Make love to me, and right before you come, I'd like a return bite. But first, I probably need to shower. I smell like everything that swims in the ocean."

Lachlan nuzzled Hunter's neck, inhaling deeply. "No. You smell like my mate. My Hector."

Lachlan did let Hunter shower, but he joined him. Instead of consummating their bond on the bed, Lachlan took Hunter against the shower wall. He managed to fuck him slowly, using his Goyle strength to hold Hunter aloft while making love underneath the warm spray. As Hunter requested, Lachlan sank his fangs into Hunter's neck as he spilled his release deep inside Hunter's body. Once sated, they took turns bathing each other. Washing the other's hair. Tenderly drying one another before retreating to the bedroom to get dirty all over again. Hours later, they returned to the deck where they snuggled on the same chaise lounge where Hunter had found Lachlan.

Looking out over the endless expanse of water, Hunter asked, "Where do we go from here?"

"Nowhere fast. We're out of fuel."

Hunter laughed and nuzzled Lachlan's neck. He was good with going nowhere anytime soon. They had the rest of their lives to figure out a destination.

CHAPTER NINETEEN

LOR'S HEART THUMPED wildly as he stood next to Victoria Holt. He and Jordana were already mated, but he wanted this day to be special for her. He couldn't help but think of a different wedding. One that changed both their lives. With springtime weather in Georgia being a crap shoot, Rafael and Kaya offered to host the wedding inside the manor. Those who normally attended Family Day were gathered around, along with Dominic, Lilly, and their twins. The couple had quickly become part of the New Atlanta family, and Lor was glad to see them.

Instead of having the wedding right away, Lorenzo and Jordana got settled in his house while the others took time to relax now that Eden was dead. Jordana insisted his house would make a fine home once he told her to go crazy decorating however she saw fit. Since they spent most of their time in bed the first week, it was a slow work in progress. When they finally left the bedroom and Jordana saw Lor's Harley in the garage, she insisted they ride every afternoon. His mate loved the wind in her face. Now, here they were, almost a month later.

Lor blinked back tears with all the love being sent his way. Julian had set up a video camera and was live-streaming the wedding so those who weren't there could watch if they wished. Malakai and Josie were in Samoa. Remy, Isla, and Rain were in California where they were gathered with several of the West Coast Clan. Sin, Rocky,

Sixx, and Rae were watching from Sin's home. The males who had traveled to São Paulo with Lor were also watching as were his mother and Diego from Brazil.

When the music started, a hush fell over the group. Even the babies were quiet. Amelia expertly tossed rose petals on the carpeted floor as she made her way down the makeshift aisle toward him. Lor's favorite girl in the world, donning the pretty new dress Jordana bought her, smiled at him when her basket was empty. "I love you, Lor Lor," she whispered before taking a seat with her mom and Connor. Gods, he loved her too.

When the song changed, Lor turned his attention to the doorway. As Jordana made her way down the aisle, Lorenzo couldn't stop the tears. He didn't try. His mate was the most beautiful female in the world. Her smile didn't falter when she noticed his wet cheeks. When she reached him, Jordy handed off her bouquet to Kaya who was standing in as Matron of Honor. Even though all the mates had welcomed Jordana into the fold, the two Queens had formed the strongest bond over the last few weeks. Lor had asked Frey to stand with him. While all the Goyles were family, Frey was the one Lorenzo looked up to the most.

Jordana cradled Lor's face in her hands and used her thumbs to brush the tears away before clasping his hands in hers. They turned their attention to Victoria, and several minutes later, she announced them married. There was no need to recite vows. In Jordana's suite at the São Paulo estate, the two had shared their hopes and dreams. Their promises of the future. Then they shared their story with the Clan upon their arrival in the States. Everyone had heard how Jordana was forced to marry Leo. Lorenzo had spoken of leaving Brazil to find his own path. This wedding was to overshadow the other one so long ago as well as to let Amelia be a flower girl once again.

As soon as their kiss ended, cheers erupted, then Rafael announced Family Day was officially underway. Priscilla, with Maria's help, outdid herself with a feast unlike any Lor had seen. He and Jordana spent their wedding day eating delicious food, laughing with family, dancing with one another and Amelia, and passing around babies. The day couldn't have been any more perfect; at least that's what Lorenzo thought.

Priscilla rolled out a three-tier cake she'd hidden somewhere, and Rafael and Kaya passed out champagne. Jordana tugged Lorenzo to the front of the room, and everyone quieted, giving her the floor.

"I have a gift for you," Jordana said, smiling up at him.

"What? We agreed no presents," Lor huffed.

"Well, this one is for both of us." Jordana held out her hand, and Kaya placed something in it. Lor was worried when Jordana's eyes filled with tears, but her smile as well as the joy from their beasts let him know she was happy. Jordana handed over one of Connor's drawings, and when he looked at it, he couldn't believe his eyes.

"You're—?"

"Yes, we're having a baby."

More cheers went up as Lor grabbed Jordy around the waist, lifted her off her feet, and spun her in circles while kissing the shit out of her. When they came up for air, he turned to the room and called out, "We're having a baby!"

Lorenzo had feared they wouldn't have a biological child, not after Jordana hadn't been able to give Leo an heir. But Jordana hadn't been Leo's mate. She was Lor's, and he thanked the gods for this blessing, especially so soon after they mated. The drawing depicted Jordana several months along, but even so, he couldn't believe it. Lorenzo dropped to his knees and pressed his ear to her belly. There was no heartbeat, and when Lor looked up, Jordana cradled his face.

"You won't be able to hear it for a few more weeks."

Lor should know that. He should know everything about her pregnancy. As soon as possible, Lor was going to study so he would be the best mate to his Jordy. The best father to their baby.

Their child would grow up with the other offspring. Theirs would be part of the next generation of shifters who would lead the Clan in future days. Maybe they would have a girl, and Cailín and Lydia wouldn't be the only full-blooded females. Lor believed this was the beginning of something great for the Gargoyles. For their family. Their Clan.

TREVOR PEEKED IN on Cailín who was napping with Sebastian and Jonathan on a pallet in Sebastian's room. When the babies were all together, it was as if they were in sync with one another, all fussing at the same time no matter their age differences. When he returned to the gathering, he sidled up next to Lucy where she and Tamian were talking to Lorenzo and Jordana. "So, have you two compared names yet?"

Lucy glanced at Tamian, and he nodded at her. "Actually, we thought we'd let you name our daughter."

Trevor laughed until he realized Lucy was serious. "Me? Why?"

"Because you risked your life for my mate," Tamian said, pulling Lucy against his chest. "We would be honored if you chose a name."

"I think it was more dumb luck," he admitted. He had been reaching out for Lucy's Eagle talons. Even though he'd never seen her Gryphon, he had known it was her.

"Whether inadvertently or not, that fact remains you took the bullet. Please do this for us," Lucy said.

"Oh. Wow." Trevor thought for a moment. "Your daughter is going to be special. Likely a hybrid of her parents, so how about a hybrid of Lucy and Tamian? Maybe

Cymian." Trevor gauged their reaction, and when they didn't absolutely love it, he tried something else. "Let's see." Trevor tapped his chin. "She needs a warrior's name. And there's this badass chick in one of my video games. What about Harlow?"

Lucy clasped her hand over her mouth, and Trevor took a step back. "I'm sorry. Did I say something wrong?"

Tamian kissed Lucy's temple, but he didn't look like he was going to take Trevor's head for offending his mate. "Not wrong. Harlow was Lucy's mother's name. She died protecting Lucy. I happen to love it." Tamian turned Lucy so she was facing him. "What do you think?"

"It's perfect," Lucy whispered as Tamian thumbed the tears off her cheeks.

"Harlow St. Claire does have a nice ring to it," Jasper said.

"Actually, she'll be a Montagnon. With Tamian taking over the Italian throne, he'll be using his birth name."

"Princess Harlow Montagnon. Sounds regal," Jordana added.

Lucy grinned. "It does. Thank you, Trevor. Not only for choosing the perfect name but for everything else. I would ask you to be her godfather, but I have four uncles who've already called dibs, plus my dad said being grandfather trumps being uncle. Then again, maybe they'll stop fighting over who gets to claim that title if I chose someone else."

"Oh, no. No, no, no." Trevor held his hands in front of him. "No way am I going up against five Gryphons. I'll be honorary uncle and offer my services as babysitter whenever you and Tamian come visit."

"Deal." Lucy rubbed her belly. "Miss Harlow is demanding another piece of cake." Lucy grabbed Tamian's hand, and together they walked away.

"So that just happened," Trevor muttered.

"It did, because you are amazing." Jasper wrapped his arms around Trevor from behind, careful not to jostle

Trevor's shoulder. It still ached from time to time, but with Jasper's bite, the wound healed in record time. For that, Trevor was grateful, because he had a mate to love on and a daughter to care for.

"Baba," a little voice called out from where the babies were resting.

"That's our cue," Rafael said. If Sebastian was awake, Cailín and Jonathan would be too.

"I'll get her," Jasper offered, and Trevor let him because Trevor had a different redhead to pester.

GREGOR SMIRKED AS Trevor strode with purpose toward Tessa. If someone asked him when he first met Dante's assistant, he would have laughed at the young human being such an integral part of their lives. Trevor O'Donnell was still the snarky, heavy metal music-loving man he'd always been, but now? He was not only Tessa's biggest champion but also one of her best friends. Gregor enjoyed their banter. Couldn't help but laugh at the silly names they called one another.

"Yo, Morgue Man. How's it hanging?"

"A little to the left, as always. Well, not always. Sometimes it's pointed—" Trevor snapped his mouth shut with a blush and downward cast eyes. "Anyway. What's up with you now that we have some breathing room?"

"We're headed to Atokos for a little sun and relaxation on our own private island," Tessa said. Gregor called Sixx and requested the use of the Greek island the Stone Clan owned. Something was different with his mate, and he wanted to get her alone to find out what. After the shit with Eden Wood, they all deserved some downtime.

"Wow. That sounds exciting."

"What about you? Are you looking to get back to

school?"

"Not really. I..." Trevor brushed his purple bangs off his forehead. "I still want to be an ME, but now that Simon is here to fill in for Dante, it's not that pressing. I would like to focus on DNA and cloning. Don't get me wrong," Trevor added. "Simon hasn't said anything to me about it, but he would rather I work one autopsy, then get on with another. I think I might be better off changing my course of study and maybe start my own lab?"

"If you're interested, I could talk to Jonas. Who better to teach you about cloning than the male who started it all?" Tessa offered.

"What? No. That's... I couldn't."

"Why not? Jonas loves passing his knowledge on, especially to those who are eager to learn. This way you could get the information you need without having to pay for college courses and study under professors who aren't as knowledgeable. If you decide it isn't something you want to pursue, no harm no foul."

"Do you really think he'd be willing to teach me?" Trevor's voice was so hopeful it hurt Gregor's heart. The young man didn't realize how treasured he was.

"I know so. Come on. Let's give him a call."

"Now?" Trevor's voice cracked.

Tessa reached over and ruffled Trevor's hair. "Why not now? It's a time for new beginnings." Tessa grabbed Trevor's wrist and led him out the patio door where they would have some privacy.

Jasper followed the couple with his eyes as he made his way to Gregor. When Gregor held out his hands, Jasper handed his precious daughter over.

"What was that about?"

"Tessa suggested Trevor let Jonas teach him about cloning."

"Oh, wow. That would be amazing. I don't know anyone more excited about the topic than Trevor. And who better to learn from than the one who created the first clone?"

"That's exactly what Tessa said." Gregor bounced Cailín on his hip, a wistful longing hitting his chest as she babbled. "That way he could take Cailín with him. I have no doubt Caroline would love to watch the baby while the two are sequestered down in the lab."

"That is perfect. Trevor deserves every happiness he can get." Jasper's eyes were wet, and Gregor pretended not to notice.

"I know what it's like, Jas. To feel like you let your mate down. When she was in that wreck after being chased by the redhead killer, I didn't think she deserved me as a mate. I felt so guilty that I hadn't been there to stop the car from rolling over. It took some wise males to convince me it wasn't my fault but that of Gordon Flanagan. Like Eden, he was obsessed, and gods help anyone who stood in his way. Do you blame Trevor for not stopping Theron from poisoning you?"

"You know I don't, but Trevor's human. He couldn't have stopped a Goyle."

"And Eden was a brilliant, if deranged, hacker who manipulated Trevor by threatening his father. She gave him fifteen minutes, Jas. Even if Trevor had called you, that wasn't enough time for you to get to Jack's house. You have to let this go, Brother. Trevor doesn't blame you. And if what Tamian said is true, you flew like the wind to get to Trevor once they located him."

"I did. I've never pushed my beast that hard before, but I had to get to him before something happened." Jasper's frown morphed into a handsome smile as Trevor and Tessa returned. "Good news?" he asked his mate.

Trevor stepped into Jasper's space, wrapping his arms around his mate's waist. "The best. Jonas has agreed to teach me about cloning, and Caroline asked if she could watch Cailín. It's a win-win all around."

Jasper mouthed *thank you* to Tessa over Trevor's head, then pressed a kiss to his temple. "I'm happy for you."

Trevor tipped his head back, smiling brightly. "I'm happy for all of us. Not to jinx anything, but I have a feeling we're all going to have good days ahead."

When Cailín grabbed for Gregor's nose, he grinned down at the baby. He had to agree.

WHEN JULIAN'S PHONE buzzed in his pocket, he kissed Katherine on her temple. "I need to take this," he said, grinning.

"What are you up to?"

"You'll see." Julian retrieved his phone and stepped outside for privacy. "Julian here."

"Hey man. Are you ready?"

"If you are. Just give me about two minutes to get everything set up."

"Take all the time you need."

Julian rushed back inside and got the computer set up so it hooked to the large screen television. "If I could have everyone's attention?" All eyes turned his way. "I have a surprise for Trevor. Well, I'm sure more of you will enjoy it, but Tamian and Lucy wanted to show their appreciation to Trevor for what he did with Eden." Julian hit a few keys, and Desi Rothchild's face filled the screen.

"Hey, Trevor and everyone else."

"Oh, my god," Trevor whispered. "Uh, hi there."

"Dad told me what happened, and I have the perfect song. It talks about troubles and hope. It's from one of my favorite bands, 7's Mistress. The lead singer, Taggart Lee, wrote it for his man. It's called 'Deliver Me'."

Every eye in the room focused on Desi as his melodic voice crooned a message each one of them felt to their core,

Julian especially. His heart wasn't quite as heavy as it had been chasing down Eden Wood, but he was still off kilter knowing it wasn't him who was able to track her every movement. For the longest time it had been Julian who kept his Clan safe from behind his keyboards. Knowing he wasn't the smartest or the best hit him hard. Yes, he was grateful to Achilles for doing what neither Julian nor Henry could do, but if Julian couldn't keep his family safe, he didn't deserve to be in charge.

Like Gregor handing the Pen over to Deacon, Julian was turning the lab over to Henry and taking his mate and daughter on vacation. He had already rented a tricked-out motorhome, and the two of them were going to go wherever the road took them for the next month. Carleigh wasn't due until the end of April, and Julian planned on using the time to reboot his own system.

Standing behind Katherine with his hands cradling their daughter in her stomach, the words to the song resonated in Julian's heart.

The other side of paradise
Looks better every day
The other side of the coin
Help me find my way

The other side of paradise
Is wherever you are
The other side of the coin
You already have my heart

Julian knew with time away and the birth of his daughter, he would find his way back. With nothing *but* time on his hands, Julian was looking forward to a future where he wasn't depended on twenty-four seven to sit behind a computer.

WHEN THE SONG ended, Dante cheered along with his Clan. He wasn't necessarily a fan of Desi's harder songs, but the one he chose to perform for Trevor was perfect. The meaning behind the lyrics could have been written for any one of them in the room. Isabelle was the other side of Dante's coin. She was the best parts of him. Her and Connor both. His mate was a brilliant doctor, and he couldn't be prouder of her. Knowing Connor would do amazing things when he was older? What more could a male ask for? Dante had another son growing in his mate's belly, and their lives were close to perfect. The only thing Dante could frown on was his son's visions. If Dante could take the gift from Connor, he would.

Dante believed Connor when he said little Alyssa was his mate, and he would move heaven and earth to find the child. He had already started Henry on the search. Without knowing her last name, it would be close to impossible to find the girl, but Dante wouldn't stop until his son was reunited with the lizard girl as Tessa called her.

With Simon running the morgue, Dante had nothing but free time on his hands. The Reborn serum, thanks to Isabelle, had been a success. The few Unholy left in the city were being rounded up on nightly patrols, but for all intents and purposes, New Atlanta was safe from the monsters. Isabelle had approached Dante about finding a new tutor for Connor. Marigold was a lovely young woman, but Connor was already growing bored. They would have to speak with Frey and Abbi to break the news to Amelia. The girl was used to having Connor with her daily, but as parents, he and Isabelle had to do what was best for their son.

One of those things was to give Connor every opportunity to grow into the well-rounded young man

Dante knew he would be, and that included furthering Connor's love for art. The three of them were leaving the following day on a trip to Europe where they were visiting all the famous galleries and museums. Whether his son chose to be a doctor like his parents, a scientist like his grandfather, or an artist like his pretty blonde aunt, the world was wide open, and Dante would do everything in his power to make sure no matter what Connor chose to do, he would be happy doing it.

NIKOLAS SNUGGLED HIS mate and daughter on one of the large sofas as he breathed in both their scents.

"Gorgeous, did you just sniff me?" Sophia asked, scrunching her cute bunny nose.

"You know it." Nik nipped her ear, and Sophia laughed. "How would you like to go visit your sister?" Sophia spoke to Xenia on the phone at least once a week. Even with their age difference, the two were like peas in a pod. Sophia had since forgiven her parents for keeping her sister's true identity from her.

Sophia's nose scrunched again. "Really?"

"Why not? There's no reason we can't take an extended vacation now that things have calmed down. Besides, I have a bone to pick with a certain camel."

Sophia barked out a laugh. "Nikolas Stone, if you go anywhere near those animals, let's just say I want it on video this time."

Nikolas grinned. "Seriously, I would love to go back and visit Egypt and see the sights with a competent tour guide or two."

"Then let's do it. When do you think we can leave?"

"Tomorrow morning soon enough? I have it on good authority a jet is fueled-up and ready to head east. Gregor is taking Tessa to Atokos, and Dante and Isabelle are taking Connor to Europe, so we can all fly together."

"Yes! I've missed hanging out with my cousins, so even if it's just a short flight, I'd love to spend some time with them."

"I thought you might like that. Now, what do you say we go mingle with the others since we'll be gone a while."

"How long's a while?"

"Until your heart's content." Nikolas would give his mate anything.

"Oh, Gorgeous. My heart is already content. You have filled it to overflowing."

"Likewise, my little Bunny. Likewise."

FREY STOOD OUTSIDE enjoying a cigar and beer while Matthew chased his sister around the yard. Slade sat on the far side of the patio feeding Jonathan a bottle. Jon loved his Uncle Slade. The March weather couldn't have been more cooperative for Family Day, and his kids were taking full advantage of the sunshine. Matthew was still coming off the high of Desi singing them a song, and running around after Amelia was helping get rid of some adrenaline.

Their Clan was enjoying peace after many months of chaos. Things were getting back to normal. Or maybe he should say their new normal, what with so many babies being born. If he were honest, Frey was looking forward to going back to running the gym and spending his time worrying about nothing more than dirty diapers, tutus, and getting some alone time with Abbi. He was also looking forward to being the one to look after his little whirlwind of a daughter.

Lorenzo had been amazing, taking care of Amelia as though she were his own, but now he had a mate to focus on. Frey had been honored to stand next to the male. Lorenzo was as integral to Frey's family as his own brothers, and he'd told the male as much. With tears in his eyes, Lorenzo grasped Frey tightly, then promised to babysit anytime Frey wanted so he and Abbi could be alone. It was an offer Frey would gladly take him up on.

"Daddy, daddy, daddy! Save me!" Amelia raced onto the patio and hid behind his legs.

Matthew's skin was flushed as he skidded to a stop in front of Frey. In a move he hadn't made since becoming Slade's mate, Matthew leaned into Frey's chest and hugged him. Being in college meant Matthew was hardly ever home. Frey cradled the back of Matthew's head and kissed his hair. "I'm glad you're here, Son."

Matthew nodded against Frey's chest, clinging to him tightly. "Me too."

"You okay?"

Matthew's head popped up, and a smile so like Abbi's adorned his face. "Perfect. I've just missed you and Abs."

"Uh, what about me?" Amelia fussed as she wiggled her way between the two.

Matthew released Frey and picked his sister up. "Of course I missed you too. Duh."

"Duh," she mimicked.

"What's going on out here?" Abbi asked, stepping up to the trio.

"Group hug," Matthew said, wrapping his free arm around his sister, and Frey didn't hesitate to join in.

"What about Slade and Jon?" Abbi asked, looking over Matthew's shoulder.

Slade set the empty bottle down and patted Jon's back as he walked over to get in on the action. Amelia snaked her small arm around Slade's neck just as Jonathan let out a wet burp.

Amelia jerked back and pinched her nose. "Ooh. Babies are so gross."

Frey kissed his daughter on the forehead before taking her from Matthew. "You don't think Lydia's gross."

"Cause she's a girl."

Matthew tweaked his sister's nose. "But she burps too."

"Not like that. Jon stinks."

"Uh, I think that's his diaper." Slade held the baby out in front of him. "You need a clean diaper, Little Man?"

Abbi reached for her son, but Slade cradled Jon against his chest. "I got him. Come on, big brother. You can help." Matthew followed his mate inside. They were experts at taking care of feedings and dirty diapers, both enjoying babysitting duty whenever they came to visit.

"I can help too!" Amelia took off after the males, leaving Frey with a rare moment alone with his mate. For all Amelia's fussing about her baby brother, she never hesitated to spend time with the little guy.

"Alone at last," Abbi whispered against Frey's chest.

"For at least two minutes." Frey tipped Abbi's chin up and kissed her pretty mouth. "Have I told you lately how wonderful you are?" he muttered against her lips.

"Not in the last half hour." Abbi slid her fingers into his hair and pulled him down for another kiss. Frey placed his hands on her slender hips and rocked them side to side to a song playing inside the manor. He loved dancing with his ballerina almost as much as he loved watching her dance solo. His mate was a thing of beauty when she donned her slippers and let the music wash over her. He enjoyed watching as she taught the next generation of children the art of ballet. Abbi Hartley was an amazing creature, and he thanked the gods several times a day for bringing not only her but Amelia and Matthew into his life. Theirs hadn't been an easy road, but they were a solid unit. One filled with love and a bright future.

RAFAEL'S HEART WAS full to bursting as he took in the family laughing and mingling. The same heart that had splintered a few months back when his mate had almost been taken from him. Most days, he didn't feel worthy to lead his Clan, but the duty was his, and now that the latest threat was over, Rafe looked forward to a peaceful existence with his mate and child, however long it lasted.

He was grateful to his blood family as well as those who were family of the heart, and he wanted to tell them so. Rafael stepped over to his mate and pressed a chaste kiss to her lips.

"May I have your attention please?" Rafael wrapped an arm around Kaya's shoulder as she cradled their son to her chest. He waited until everyone moved from wherever they were in the manor to the large family room. Sensing he was going to make a speech, Julian grabbed the camera and aimed it Rafe's way. They were still live-streaming with those who couldn't be there for Family Day and Lorenzo's wedding to Jordana.

Once everyone was gathered, Rafe continued. "I apologize to Lorenzo and Jordana for interrupting their celebration, but I need to say a few words while we are all gathered. Two years ago, I was a male without a mate. A King without his Queen. Our Clan was vast but not great. Not until we met the other halves of our souls. We have endured pain, loss, and suffering at the hands of others, but more than that, we have experienced joy, love, and most of all, new life." Rafael bent and kissed Sebastian on his fuzzy head.

"Baba," Sebastian prattled as he reached for Rafe's nose.

"Two years is but a blink in the scope of our lives, but in those few months, we have gained so much more than I ever dreamed was possible. Our family, our Clan, has grown and will continue to do so with each new addition we bring to life. Sebastian and the other children are our future. I make this solemn vow to each and every one of you

249

to be the best King and leader our children will have until one day they take over the mantle. That future is uncertain. I have no doubt we'll endure more hardship along the way, but we'll handle those tough times as we have these past months – together. They will need all of us teaching them how to love, how to fight, how to trust in one another when their days aren't easy, the way I trust in all of you. They say it takes a village, but I say it takes a Clan. A Clan of Goyles, and Gryphons, and whatever type of shifter we encounter along the road.

"I thank the gods every day for bringing each of you into my life, and I thank each of you for propping me up when I fall short. For standing by me when I feel like walking away. For reminding me it isn't a King's job to rule from his throne in solitude but with his Clan by his side and at his back. In short, I raise my glass to you, my family, my Clan, my world. *Salute.*"

ON THE WEST Coast, Sin closed the laptop after he, Rocky, Sixx, and Rae said their goodnights to the Clan gathered at Rafael's manor. The wedding had been beautiful if quick, and Rae was still gushing over seeing her son even if it had been on a screen.

"I still can't believe that's my son," she said. "And the song he chose? How perfect was that?"

Sixx kissed his mate on her temple. Rae was sitting on his lap, and Sixx rested his hands on Rae's belly where Mikayla Desirae Gentry was growing every day. "Absolutely perfect, just like Rafe's speech. If anyone deserves a bit of happiness, it's our King."

"Truer words have never been spoken," Sin said, his voice low.

"You miss him," Rocky whispered against Sin's neck.

"I do. I miss them all, but Rafe especially."

"We should go see them then."

"I second that," Sixx said. "With Kai and Josie taking ownership of my old place, there's another house I've got my eye on. We should all go and check it out."

Sin had no reason not to agree. Things in California were calm, and Remy had the new prison well in hand. "Maybe Rocky and I could look for our own house while we're there. Nothing fancy, just somewhere we could use as a getaway." Sin never let on how badly he missed his older brother. He and Rafael had been inseparable growing up, and these last years spent on opposite sides of the country had nearly killed Sin. Especially with Rafe going through so much. Sin hated not being there for him. For not taking some of the responsibilities from him. Frey was damned good at leading the Clan in Rafe's absence, but he wasn't Rafe's brother.

And now that Sebastian was in the picture? Sin wanted to spend some time with the future King. Rocky had come a long way in accepting she'd never give Sin a biological child, but they planned to adopt, and that was enough for him.

"I'll call the pilot and have him ready the jet for tomorrow morning," Sixx offered. He helped Rae to her feet, then stood with her.

"I'd appreciate that. We'll meet you at the airport around nine?"

"And I appreciate *that*," Rae said, causing the others to chuckle. It was no secret Sixx's tatted surfer liked to sleep in.

Sin and Rocky walked their best friends out, and once they were safely in their car, Sin closed the door and locked it. When he turned, his mate began a slow striptease.

"Raquel," he warned, but she continued removing every stitch of clothing she wore. "It's like that, is it?" Rocky bit her bottom lip, knowing what it did to Sin. He scooped her into his arms and carried her through to their bedroom.

Ingrid had stopped living with them and only came by a few times a week, so they didn't need to worry about getting naked whenever or wherever they wanted.

"It's exactly like that." Rocky nibbled on Sin's neck, a move that drove him crazy. Instead of tossing her on the bed, he gently lay her down. As he removed his own clothes, he admired her bare body. His pretty female still struggled with her memory, but to Sin, she was perfect. He spent every day doting on her so she would never forget what she meant to him. Sin settled between her slender, dancer's legs and made slow, gentle love to her.

Hours later, as Rocky slept curled up in his arms, Sin laid awake as he did most nights. His life was close to perfect, but knowing he would see Rafael the next day settled something in Sin he hadn't realized he'd needed. Tomorrow he would have both his mate and his brother by his side. Tomorrow, he would be whole.

EPILOGUE

Utah, 2065

CONNOR, HIDING UNDER the shade of an umbrella with a very pregnant Willow, smiled when Cailín pushed an unsuspecting Anthony in the pool. His cousin broke the water's surface, sputtering before he quietly cursed the female. Connor glanced over to gauge Jasper's reaction. He and Trevor were in the shallow end playing with Cailín's little sister, Haylee. Before Jasper could say anything, a fierce feminine voice rent the air.

"Anthony Andrew Stone!" Anthony ducked back under the water at his mother's chastisement. Connor didn't blame his cousin; Tessa was scary. At least she hadn't used the Italian version of his name. That's when she was really pissed.

Anthony's twin, Tabitha, plopped down on the patio chair next to Connor, her fruit tea sloshing over the side of her glass. Tabby was a younger replica of her mother with a long, red braid resting over one shoulder. Both females wore skimpy bikinis, much to Gregor's dismay. The male spent most of his time trying to cover Tabitha with a long T-shirt or a towel. It was a losing battle.

"Gah, that is the cutest kid ever," Tabitha told Willow as Mason plucked their three-year-old off Willow's lap and set the little girl on his shoulders before jogging across the lawn. Gianna – or Gigi as everyone called the girl – giggled loudly. Tabitha wasn't wrong. Gigi was adorable as was her daddy. For a badass bodyguard, Mason was a cream puff

253

when it came to his daughter.

Most of their extended family was on vacation together to celebrate Connor getting his master's degree. They used any excuse to gather together, and this time, they had rented a Goyle-owned hotel – yes, the whole thing – at the base of Mount Emmons in Utah. Their family was large, and they could afford it.

During the school year, everyone stayed close to home, but during any and all breaks, their families would pack up and spend weeks in a different city. Rafael said it was so all the kids could experience new places and cultures. Over the years, they had traveled across the US as well as abroad. One of Connor's favorite trips was when they stayed at the Di Pietro Italian villa. It had brought him closer to his mate, Alyssa. At fifteen, he had been too young to go in search of her, but being on the same continent where they met all those years ago had his heart beating a little faster. It was also where he transitioned into a Goyle. Connor barely carried the Gargoyle gene since his biological father had been human and Isabelle was a half-blood. But the Montagnon bloodline was strong, resulting in Connor shifting when he was younger.

His ability to see glimpses of events yet to happen never included himself. Not once had he envisioned even a snippet of his future life. His mother asked how, then, he knew Alyssa was his mate, but Connor couldn't explain it properly to her. He just felt it within his soul. He often drew pictures of the little girl she had been all those years ago, but he could only imagine how she appeared as an adult. He couldn't wait to find out.

"How's it feel?" Tabby asked, breaking him from his pondering.

"How does what feel?"

"Graduating again. Being an adult. Getting ready to head off and do more great things in the world."

"Scary," Connor admitted. "But you know I'm headed back to school in the fall, so not that scary." Connor loved school. Loved learning when he encountered professors who could actually teach him something new. Having Jonas Montague as a grandfather, Connor had spent many hours at the male's feet, by his side, learning from his many years of experience. Jonas's approach was scientific. Having two parents who were doctors meant he learned even more from them and in different ways.

Connor had been accepted to every med school he applied for, but he chose Stanford in California so he would have family close by. Since Deklan and Christina were still in high school, he couldn't ask his parents to pull up stakes and go with him. With his high grade-point average, Connor could have graduated high school two years early, but he was awkward enough socially that doing so would have meant being singled out in college. Instead, he used his spare time studying things which interested him like art.

Connor's paintings were being sold in galleries around the globe under an assumed name. He never attended showings, and that mystique added to the value of his work. When he wasn't reading, Connor was happiest painting or drawing alongside Lilly. The pretty witch's talent rivaled Connor's, even though she didn't believe it. Her artwork was for family and friends, whereas his added to his bank account. He had been able to pay for college and still have plenty left for med school. If ever the time came that he figured out where Alyssa was, Connor had enough saved to offer her a grand life together.

If he only knew where to find her. His parents had taken him on a family vacation to Greece a couple years ago. They retraced their steps from back when Connor had been kidnapped and his mom had come after him. They requested Lachlan Rokesby's help when neither Julian nor Henry could find any trace of Alyssa in Greece or any of the surrounding countries. It was as though his mate had disappeared, thus Connor's perpetual state of melancholy.

"I don't see why you're going to med school. You've already found the cure for cancer. You could probably teach all the courses you're going to take," Tabitha said.

"I didn't exactly cure cancer. I found a cure for one specific type. The disease is still evading the sharpest minds, and the more I learn, the better equipped I'll be to further my research."

"Yeah, I guess." Tabby, like Tessa, was more interested in her next adventure than studying. Anytime she could do something exciting like bungie jumping or skydiving, she was the first one in line. When her twin splashed water on her, she yelled, "Hey! Watch it, you big oaf." With no warning, Tabitha lunged from the chair, a good six feet from the edge of the water, and dove toward Anthony's head. He jerked back at the last second, another near miss. Connor often wondered how those two stayed alive. Then again, they were Goyles. Even though Tessa was a half-blood, the siblings had both transitioned once they hit puberty. They weren't the only ones either. Several of his cousins and friends as well as his younger brother, Deklan, had all come into their shifter. And Harlow? That female was crazy scary being a hybrid. She was with her parents and Liam and Tamlyn, her twin siblings, in Italy since Tamian had a World Counsel meeting to attend. Where he went, Lucy and offspring did as well.

Connor was torn. He wanted to go on to med school in the fall, but he also wanted to revisit Greece and travel around searching for his mate. When he told his da as much, Dante persuaded Connor to let the computer geniuses continue searching. Connor didn't trust they would find Alyssa since they hadn't already. With all the cruise ships that came in and out of Greece, she could be anywhere in the world. In his heart, he felt he would only locate the female by putting boots to ground. Or in his case, loafers.

While his cousins dressed in the latest trends, Connor preferred khakis and bow ties. His mother told him to embrace his own style, so he did.

Willow angled out of her chair. "Excuse me. Again." It was the third time the female had to go pee since they had sat down. Zuri, Lorenzo's daughter, climbed out of the pool and took the vacated seat. Z, as everyone called her, was the spitting image of Jordana. For a full-blood, she was the most serious of all the teens. Connor enjoyed being around the quiet female. She had a sharp mind, a quick wit, and could wield a sword with the best of them. Lor and Jordana had left that morning with Frey, Abbi, Amelia, Rain, and Jonathan to visit Rain's parents and sister, Summer.

"Why didn't you go to California?" Connor asked.

Zuri turned her dark blue eyes his way. "I don't like being a third wheel. Besides, they're coming back in two days." Connor knew what that felt like. He and Amelia were as close as siblings, having spent so much of their early years together, but now that she and Rain had mated, it was like the rest of the world disappeared. Then there was Jonathan and Summer's relationship. The teens swore they were just friends, but everyone doubted them since Jon already transitioned. Remy and Isla had moved back to New Atlanta several years after Remy took over the new prison in California, but they kept their house there for vacations.

Kaya frantically yelling for Rafael had everyone turning their attention toward the hotel. Rafael, who was sitting at another table with Seven, launched out of the chair so fast it toppled over backwards. As though they were one unit, everyone abandoned their activities and headed that direction, Connor included. Being Queen, Kaya was the essence of calm, so when she panicked, something was wrong. As he neared the entrance, Kaya's words hit Connor hard.

"Something attacked him. Please, we need to get him to the hospital." The him in question was Sebastian.

Rafael pulled Kaya into his arms. "Let Dante take a look."

Connor's parents knelt next to Sebastian's bloody form. His chest was torn open from what looked like claw marks.

"It was a wolf," Lydia said. "We were jogging along the pathway, and Bas froze. When I asked what was wrong, he said he smelled something and took off through the trees. Before I could stop him, a large, gray wolf attacked. Then a smaller wolf struck the larger one, and while they were battling it out, I grabbed Bas and brought him back here."

"Thank you, Lydia," Rafael said at the same time Sophia shouted, "Are you crazy?"

"What was I supposed to do, Mom? Leave him there?"

"No, of course not, but... Sorry. You did the right thing."

"Damn right I did," Lydia muttered. When Sophia arched an eyebrow, Lydia just shrugged. As a full-blooded Goyle, Lydia was strong. She was Frey's star student in martial arts. The female was fearless.

"I've called for an ambulance," Nik said, moving to stand next to Sophia.

"Someone find my mom," Luna yelled. She and Solara pushed their way past Dante. The twins knelt beside Sebastian, their fingers spread above the gashes as they both began speaking low.

"I'm here," Lilly said as she dropped to her knees beside her daughters. The three of them closed their eyes, hands hovering inches above Sebastian's skin.

"Muh... muh...," Sebastian mumbled as he tried to curl into the fetal position. Rafael pushed Bas's shoulders down, keeping him flat.

"I'm right here, Bas." Kaya squatted next to her son's head, pushing his hair off his face.

Connor had witnessed Luna and Solara practicing magic with their mom, but never had he seen them try to heal someone. Within a couple minutes, the torn skin on Bas's chest knitted back together.

"Muh… mate," Sebastian muttered as his body shook.

Kaya looked up at Rafael who lifted Sebastian into his arms when the three Dubois females moved aside. "I don't think an ambulance will do any good. If he met his mate, he's going to transition," Rafael said.

Kaya turned to Lilly and the twins. "Thank you." She placed a hand on each twin's cheek before squeezing Lilly's forearm, then she followed after Rafael and her son.

Dominic pulled Lilly and their daughters into his chest. "Well done, Lasses."

Bypassing the elevator, Rafe ran up the steps. With most of the adults following, they disappeared out of sight. Connor wanted to help, but Bas had more attention than he would probably like as his body changed for the first time.

"We need to find that wolf and kill it," Anthony declared.

"Don't be an idiot," Tabby argued. "You'd probably kill the wrong wolf, and then what would Bas do without his mate?"

"I wouldn't kill the smaller one," Anthony replied.

Tabitha grabbed her twin's hands. "But what if there's only one, and you don't know if it's the one who attacked? For once, I say we do nothing."

"I won't go out to the woods, but I can't do *nothing*. Bas is going to be starving once he transitions. Want to help me scrounge up some food?" Tabitha nodded, and the twins stalked off toward the kitchen, arm in arm.

"Well, that's one way to find your mate," Connor said to no one in particular. He prayed when he found Alyssa, their meeting would be much less eventful.

259

SEBASTIAN WAS DYING. He had found his mate, and now he'd never get the chance to know her. But why had she attacked him? He only wanted to talk. Well, he wanted more than that, but his momma raised him right. Bas would be a gentleman and date her properly until—

"Ungh, fuck!"

"Sebastian!"

Before he could apologize to his mom, his papa said, "I think he's allowed a few curse words. Why don't you go back downstairs? This is going to be painful for Bas, and it'll be equally painful for you to watch."

"But he's hurting."

Yes. Yes, he was. Sebastian was on fire. His chest no longer throbbed where his little she-wolf had ripped him open, but he was burning with fever. "I-ice." If he could bathe in a tub of ice, maybe it would slow the dying. "L-love y-you, Mom. S-sorry."

"You have nothing to be sorry for. But your papa's right. I can't watch this." His mom kissed his fevered forehead. Wait! She was leaving him to die?

"I'll turn down the thermostat. I remember burning up when I transitioned," Isabelle said.

Transitioned? So that's what was happening. Sebastian let out a giggle. He wasn't dying!

"Is he giggling?" Dante asked.

"He's probably delirious. We need to clean the blood off his chest. Tessa, please grab some wet towels," Isabelle requested.

"On it."

How many adults needed to watch this? "Papa." Bas started to ask him to clear the room, but his father was a mind reader.

"I appreciate everyone's concern, but I also remember my first shift as I'm sure you all do. How about you go assure the kids he's going to be fine?"

"But is he?" Sophia asked. "We didn't transition after being sliced open by a wolf."

"Come on, Soph. Let's let nature do its thing," Uncle Nik urged his mate.

The next few hours were nothing short of excruciating. Bas had listened each time his cousins recounted their transitions in every single painful detail. They hadn't been exaggerating. His fangs were first, and his lip was a bloody mess before he got the hang of talking around them. Bas ripped the bedding when his claws extended. But it was the appearance of his wings that had Bas yelling down the hotel. Tessa could sympathize to an extent, but his papa knew what he was going through. Tessa stayed long enough to clean his chest, but his father didn't leave his side.

"I'm proud of you, Bas," his papa said, wiping his brow with a cool washcloth.

"Thanks." Bas held his hands in front of his face as he got used to calling forth his claws. "I guess wolves don't sense their mates the same way Goyles do."

"Why do you say that?"

"Why else would mine attack me?" Sebastian blinked several times. He refused to cry in front of his father.

"Your mate didn't attack you, Son. At least we don't think she did. Lydia said a large wolf attacked, then a smaller one went after the larger one. If I had to guess, I'd say the smaller one was your mate and defending you."

"Really?" Sebastian couldn't help the hope in his voice.

"Yes, really. Once you're healed properly, we'll take a large group and search the area for her."

And that's exactly what they did. Two days later, Sebastian and his papa along with Nikolas, Dante, Jasper, and Gregor, went back to the site of the attack. They found Sebastian's dried blood on the ground, but there was no sign of the wolves. Using their shifter senses, they followed their noses, but when they came upon a road, the only smells were that of rubber, oil, and gasoline. His mate had either gotten in a car willingly or had been taken. Either way, she was gone. Now Sebastian knew how Connor felt.

Sebastian was graduating high school the next month, and once he did? He would return to Utah. He wouldn't stop searching until he found his little she-wolf.

A Note from the Author

Starting a series is a daunting task, but ending one? That's even harder because you need to end on a high note, make it exciting, give everyone their HEA, and tie up all loose ends. This series means the world to me. All these characters have become my family over the last seven years. It all started with Rafael when I was a new author with very little idea how to properly write a book. I've studied my craft, something I continue to do. I research marketing. I join writer's groups, and I listen to more experienced authors. I feel like I have improved with each book, and I hope to continue learning, growing, and bringing more fun stories to you. The Hounds of Zeus will continue in the same universe, but the new series, Rebel Moon Shifters, will feature kids from both series. Sebastian and Clan will be adults, finding their mates in all types of shifters. Their future world will look a little different, and I hope you come along for the ride. Thank you for staying with the Stone Society until the end (although it isn't truly the end, as I hope to have novellas and short stories about the adults and their lives during those in-between years).

Acknowledgements

The past few months have been hard, but these ladies helped keep my head above water in one way or another. Candy, Jennifer, Katie, Kerstin, and Nikki – I couldn't do this without you.

To Kelli and Kerstin – Thank you for being an extra set of eyes.

Jay Aheer of Simply Defined Art, another stellar cover.

To my reader group, thank you as always.

And to the man, I love you.

About the Author

Multi-genre author Faith Gibson began writing in high school, and through the years, penned many stories and poems. As her dreams continued getting crazier than the one before, she decided to keep a dream journal. Many of these nighttime escapades have led to a line, a chapter, or even a complete story.

"Love is love, and there's not enough love in the world." This belief she holds strongly, and it's the prevailing theme in her works, all of which come with a happy ending.

Faith believes her purpose in life is to entertain the masses, even if it's one person at a time. Living just outside of Nashville, Tennessee, with the love of her life and her American staffordshire pup, when she's not hard at work writing her next adventure, Faith can often be found reading, cooking up something in the kitchen, listening to live music, or off on an adventure of her own.